For the wife and kids,
with love and gratitude

chapter 1

Fucking Mick Jagger.

He's skinnier now than when he was a teenager. What's he doing that I don't?

Stee Walsh wrestled himself into his washed-out plaid swim trunks, letting the string tie out at the waist with a defeated grunt.

Maybe I should have done more heroin.

He padded through the sliding door from his bedroom down to the patio, nabbed a towel from the shelf behind the bar and tossed it onto the chaise lounge. The sky was a typical shade of café au lait and the Windex-colored pool water rippled, a little steam coming off it in the 7 a.m. chill. Another perfect spring day in Malibu.

Stee pulled on his goggles, raised his arms in a vee overhead, sucked in a lungful of air and dove in. The water was warm and velvety, just like he liked it, and drowned out the drone of the planes on the approach to LAX. He dolphin-kicked to the opposite end of the pool without breaking the surface, flipped, took his first measured breath and set off for the other side. He settled into a moderate freestyle rhythm—four strokes head down, head to the right on the pickup, just like the opening drumbeat under "Shoot Me Now": *Dum, dum, dum, dum—SLAM! Dum, dum, dum, dum—SLAM!*

One lap turned into three, then ten, leaving him gasping but pleased. He held on to the side with his left hand and gazed out over the ocean, water dripping off his beard. He counted about a dozen surfers, tiny shiny bullets shooting for shore. The sky was warming and would probably be white with sunshine in a couple of hours, at which time he would be on his way to confer with Silicon Valley's best. The BetaComp boys wanted to show off a major marketing promotion for the release of the River Runners' next album on their Squeezebox MP3 player. While there, his manager wanted to go over ringtone revenue and whether it made more sense for that album to be sold as a unit on Busker or broken into singles.

Blah, blah, blah.

Lately, the music business had been *all* business and not much playing. Yeah, they'd put out the live CD in '08. He and the band appeared on the New Orleans tribute album after Katrina and he'd taken a few charity gigs in the meantime to do right for some old friends and keep in front of an audience until he could cough up new material ... whenever the hell that was going to happen.

Five years and counting ...

That's why the water, that's why the quiet and the light schedule and the empty bed. That stillness inspired him. Or at least it used to.

Back at it.

He pushed off and soon fell into a steady 4/4 rhythm, back and forth through the water.

What's the first thing that comes in your head, Stee?

Stroke, stroke ... "I'm having a stroke ..."

Not what really sells these days.

Don't judge—just free associate. Stroke, glide, glass ...

"I stroke your face through a pane of glass" ... that could work.

It's about Tamara, isn't it? Again ... still.

Shit.

He halted and shook his head to get the water out of his right ear and the image of his ex-wife (*first* ex-wife) out of his mind. When the balance was restored, he went back under.

Back to work, Stee.

Stroke.

Stroke of genius.

Stroke of luck.

Stroke your joke and toke till yer broke ...

I give up.

He pulled himself out of the pool, scuffing his belly against the side on the way. Wincing, he struggled to his feet, located the towel and wrapped it around his waist. At least *it* still fit; then again, it was a beach towel.

Think about that later ... write it down, Stee.

Stee shuffled into the bedroom, nabbed his current notebook from the bedside table and scribbled the phrase that came to him in the pool:

I stroke your face through a pane of glass

Perched on the edge of the bed, he stared at the letters cobbled together in blue ink, willing more words to come. On a day when the muse paid a welcome visit, he could crank out an entire song, chords and all, in one sitting. If today wasn't that day, he had to write what he had in case it led to something later. The minutes wore on.

Whose face do you see through that glass, Stee?

Is it Tamara again, or could it be Kayla?

The day he cut Kayla loose five years ago, Stee had filled up an entire notebook with bitter, filthy language directed at himself. He had seen the disaster coming but married her anyway because, being over fifty at the time, he had been foolishly proud that a girl half his age thought he was hot. She was tasty, too—all limbs and hair and a voice like a margarita that sweet-talked him into drinking her up when he knew it would just make him dangerously stupid.

Kayla hadn't half of Tamara's smarts or class. He knew that when he met her but assumed he could put that aside for the rest of his life. He quickly reconsidered when her charm evaporated on their month-long Bali honeymoon. Once home, she was barging into clubs by dropping his name; shopping for a yoga studio and a dog breeder; cold-calling his engineer to get the number of a coke dealer; getting busted with said coke dealer. When her mug shot hit the internet, Stee filed for divorce. He needed to get out from under her before she dragged him down with her.

2004 was the last time he had recorded new material. Of course, "Cocaine Kitten" wasn't his most subtle work, but he needed a fresh single for the greatest hits album. And he had never done a reggae number. And Kayla couldn't very well call it libel, since she spent her first night in lockup looking like she had inhaled a bag of Hostess Donettes.

Maybe it's one of the other girls behind the glass ... if I could remember any of them.

The legions of young ladies he'd made time with—before, between and after his marriages—had swirled together over the years into an unholy army of boobs, mascara, thighs and underwear. It all made him ashamed of himself if he thought too long about it. Maybe a couple had meant something to him at some point, but now he couldn't pull up one name or face.

Maybe it's the girl I'm supposed to meet ... I need to meet ... if only ... I wasn't me.

Stee stared at the phrase again, losing hope. He rolled the pen in his fingers. He hummed insistently, trying to locate a melody to spur a rhyming line, but his brain was downshifting, then it braked to a complete stop. He looked at the clock; he didn't have time for this now. Better to throw in the towel—literally—and head for the shower.

As much as he tried to avoid it, Stee caught a glimpse of himself in the reflection off the sliding doors. His hair was slicked back, his gray hair transparent and his red hair darkened with the water. He could barely see his eyes, sunken as they were behind lax skin. Thank God for the beard; it was all that stitched his face to his skull anymore. The barrel chest was the result of thirty-five years of smokes; he quit cigarettes when he quit Kayla, but he was still hauling around the damage. Somewhere, somehow, his ass had dropped clean off his body.

At least you got nice legs, Stee. I'd date you for those legs.

Just wish my knee worked.

He heard Serafina upstairs in the kitchen making coffee and cutting up a mango for breakfast. She usually brought Salvadorian pastries for herself at the beginning of her shift and didn't mind if he snitched one. He'd better hurry since the driver would be here soon enough.

Stee went into the bathroom and sighed.

Art would have to wait. Again.

––––––––––

Stee chewed on a coffee stirrer and leaned back in an ergonomic chair. He stared blankly out of the window of the BetaComp conference room overlooking a strip of 280 and the Palo Alto hills, the occasional clump of oak trees looking like sheep gnawing the scrubby green grass. The glass and gleam of the interior reminded him of his lawyer's office and made him restless.

BetaComp's marketing director for the entertainment division, Jayesh whateverhisnamewas, was fussing over the patented gray USB cables connecting his computer to the projector in an attempt to restart his presentation. As the minutes ticked on, he rapidly muttered directions to a kid in front of the computer, who typed furiously in response. Jayesh whateverhisnamewas smiled nervously.

"Our apologies, Mr. Walsh."

Stee swiveled back toward the front of the conference room like a teenager caught daydreaming in English class. He heard a muffled snort from Daniel, his manager, seated to his left.

"*Mr. Walsh?* Shit, they might as well call you Grandpa."

"What did you say, Methuselah?" Stee muttered.

Daniel grinned for a moment, then said under his breath, "So, how's the songwriting coming?"

"Rolling along," Stee replied steadily as the commotion died down. Jayesh was smiling broadly.

"We're ready, gentlemen."

Jayesh waved a small clicker at the projector, and the presentation advanced to a photo of band from their 1978 tour, capturing the glory of their youthful potential. A fragment of "My Love, My Dear" thrummed through the impressive speaker system in the conference room. Stee heard himself sing,

I've been around long enough
To know that when the times are rough
The sweetest vict'ry is the hardest won

And that's what keeps me going.

"Stee Walsh and the River Runners is one of the most diversely talented, durable and prolific bands in rock and roll history," Jayesh asserted with a smile. "With over thirty-five years in the business, Stee Walsh is now considered the seventh most successful American rock musician still performing today."

Stee caught the ear of his manager. "We dropped to seventh?"

"Journey got bumped up because of *The Sopranos,*" Daniel whispered in reply.

Rolling his eyes, Stee returned his attention to the presentation, which was still mired in Jayesh's sticky praise. "Guitarist Chad Haines, Larry Mulholland on keyboards, bassist Caldwell Miller and drummer Bobby Brewer—and you, of course, Mr. Walsh, as lead singer, rhythm guitarist and songwriter—are among the most respected musicians playing today, enjoying strong male-female appeal and an enviably loyal fan base. Now it's time to bridge to the next generation."

A gleaming Squeezebox came into focus, the MP3 player sleek and monolithic. It melted into the background as a photograph from Stee's early career came to the fore. Stee's silhouette came into view, embossed onto the Squeezebox, its stainless steel case a vibrant shade of ruddy gold.

"We believe the Stee Walsh image, with such strong brand equity in the classic rock arena, is naturally suited for the next limited-edition Squeezebox," Jayesh announced. "Our research shows that millennial listeners are diving into the music of their parents' generation and so are eager to obtain your best-known material. Long-time listeners can fill in the gaps in their music libraries in an indestructible medium, and avid fans will have another prize to add to their Stee Walsh collections."

While he spoke, Stee's album covers whizzed by on the screen, each hovering front and center for a moment before being shunted to one side. Stee watched his image get older and saggier with each flip of the page. He clamped down on the coffee stirrer with his molars and sullenly tuned back in to the presentation.

"... a Squeezebox, preloaded with your entire catalogue—singles, albums, videos, even *Garden Graveyard* in wide-screen format— would be ready for the holiday rush. The exterior would be etched with your silhouette and autograph, and each piece will be individu- ally numbered. We expect a retail price at 15 percent above our high- end model and a limited sales window of six weeks—scarcity by design. You would receive a sizable percentage of all sales, domestic and international, with an additional amount to be earmarked for the One Campaign if you wish."

Daniel folded his hands and put them on the table in front of him. "What's our commitment then?"

"The TV and print campaigns, of course. We'd also require deliv- ery and exclusive distribution rights for the new Stee Walsh and the River Runners album premiering on the custom Squeezebox. The typical split applies for the sales but we'd want it to be a completely digital offering: no physical CDs for sale, and the only outlet would be Busker."

Stee felt a little ill. He had a storeroom of LPs, 45s, even some great blues 78s, and now CDs would join them there, preserved and catalogued and unplayed. With MP3s, it was if they were selling air instead of music, with cover artwork reduced to a postage stamp. Soon there wouldn't be any tangible evidence that he had ever pro- duced a thing.

"Mr. Walsh, is there a problem with the proposal?" Jayesh asked earnestly.

"No—no problem; I was just thinking about something else. Sorry."

Daniel assessed his client for a moment. "I'm not sure we could commit to a Busker-only release. A lot of our traditional fans would rather buy a physical CD and we'd get more of a cut than you're of- fering. This is a brand-new Stee Walsh album, the first new music in five years. That's valuable; we need to be able to present to as broad a base of fans as we can."

Jayesh smiled with a touch of indulging his elders. "I believe you are trying to skew to a younger demographic, yes? Our data shows that the majority of those under 25 listen to nothing but digital music, albums included. If you're worried about volume of album sales, we can restrict the sale of singles so that some are offered as 'album-only' selections; we'll force the consumer's hand to buy the entire album or nothing."

Stee took the coffee stirrer out of his mouth. "That just doesn't sit right. Look, I'm the idiot who went to the Supreme Court to protect bootleggers from being sued by my record company for taping my shows. Now, I'd be forcing fans to buy an album even if they only want one song? That's not who I am, folks."

Jayesh sat on the corner of the boardroom table. "We track and trend the buying patterns of our Busker customers with considerable precision. The timing is right to make the move to all digital, Mr. Walsh. It's the way music exists now. Buying tracks on Busker is convenient and it's environmentally friendlier than CDs since it's a much easier supply chain to manage. Busker won't close down if there's an earthquake in China."

He pressed on. "Mr. Walsh, I expect your fans will want to buy your new album in its entirety anyway. You're one of only a handful of performers of your era whose new work still sells well. You never went out of style. You're like a fine wine."

Stee heard a discreet cough. He stared dead ahead.

Don't look at Daniel. You do, and you'll both be laughing your asses off.

"We will certainly take that under advisement," Daniel stated, rising out of his chair. "All in all, this is an intriguing proposal and I'd like to hash out the details with you without boring the talent, if you know what I mean. Shall we go to your office?" He extended his arm toward the door and ushered Jayesh and the other BetaComp execs out of the conference room, using a move Stee always admired: acting as if he owned the place so he could dictate the terms. That's how Daniel earned his percentage; that's why he could afford to fly Stee out to his place in Tuscany for Christmas each year.

Before the door closed, Stee tossed a final question to his host.

"Hey, Jayesh, what is your favorite Stee Walsh song?"

Jayesh smiled broadly. "There are so many ..."

"Just pick one, for the sake of argument."

Jayesh's eyes flickered. "I'd have to say 'Shoot Me Girl.'"

"'Shoot Me *Now*'," Stee asked with an edge in his voice, "or '*No Way* Girl'?"

"Of course, 'Shoot Me Now'—I misspoke."

Daniel shot Stee a murderous look as he guided Jayesh out of earshot, then popped back in the doorway.

"Cut the crap, Stee," he hissed. "Too much is at stake here for you to go off embarrassing these people."

"Dan, have they even *heard* my stuff before? Can't this guy even keep my two biggest hits straight?"

"They're marketers, not fanboys, for Christ's sake. They know what they're doing, Stee. Don't worry; we'll do right by your fans and you. I'll get them to see sense." Then Daniel flashed a sharkish smile. "It won't take long, buddy; have another bagel."

As the door closed with an airtight whisper, Stee tossed his coffee stirrer into the trash and went to the window. The hills were still green from the winter rains and the sky, unlike the brown goo at home, was unadulterated blue.

I wonder why I never got a place in San Francisco. I'd be close to Fantasy Studios ... see Neil more often ... buy a place with a view of the bay ...

Stee then noticed the kid at the laptop staring at him. When Stee caught his eye, he rapidly looked back at his screen, the images reflected on his glasses. Stee decided to break the ice.

"Whatcha working on, sport?"

The kid froze, unable to look up through his oversized glasses. "Uh, nothing, Mr. Walsh."

"No, please call me Stee." The kid nodded slowly, still noticeably overwhelmed. Stee ambled over to see what was on the screen. "So what is all this?"

"Consumer traffic data collection. I'm watching how your material is selling right now on Busker. Each time someone makes a purchase, it's reflected real time in the graph." Stee watched the lines on the charts pulse up and down.

"Is this sales worldwide?"

"Yes, sir, and I can slice it up by country, state, city, even zip code."

"Those are *my* sales?"

"Yes, sir."

"Not bad for a fine wine, huh?" The kid still was not meeting his eyes, trying to hide beneath his flurry of grease-tipped frizzy hair. Stee figured he was a few years out of college yet still a virgin, what with the boy boobs and the grime under his nails and his bottom-of-the-hamper funk.

"What's your name?"

"Leonard." At last, he looked away from the computer and up at Stee.

"Did you write this program, Leonard?"

"Yes I did, sir."

Stee sat down next to him. "Leonard, are you at all familiar with my music or are you just a guy from marketing moving product off the shelves?"

"I'm a big fan. I love your work."

Stee had heard that before. "Well then, what's *your* favorite Stee Walsh song?"

His answer was immediate. "'White Pines.'"

That was unexpected and actually sort of sweet. For anyone under forty, the answer to that question was always "Shoot Me Now" or maybe "No Way Girl," which had been licensed to Major League Baseball and the WNBA a few years back. They were played to death in commercials, effectively searing Stee Walsh into the brainpans of the next generation.

"White Pines," though—that song was an acoustic lullaby from his third album, *Bait and Switch,* and received zero airplay due to his fight with the label over the bootlegging case.

"Let me guess: your mom used to sing it to you when you were little, right?"

Leonard blushed a bit. "My dad, actually, before he left."

"It was meant for a man to sing. I wrote it for Candace when she was born."

"I know," Leonard nodded. "You wrote the lyrics while you were in the delivery room on a paper towel from the hospital john."

Stee's eyebrows arched. "You *are* a big fan."

"I'm a HUGE fan, sir!" Leonard blurted apologetically. "I begged to be in on this presentation so I could meet you. I know every word you ever wrote. It's scrambling my brain that I'm even in the same room with you right now."

Long ago, Stee had made peace with the fact that his music connected him with total strangers in deeply emotional ways. He had been an unwitting participant in the biggest moments in the lives of millions: proms and road trips and bad dates and good sex. For Stee to actually appear in the flesh could be a mind-blower for some fans. The best way to handle this was to be gracious and shift the spotlight onto them.

"Leonard, relax, *you're* the big dog here. Look at this ... *thing* you created, man. I mean, if it weren't for you, no one would have any clue how I was selling. I owe you a lot. Without you, I'd be selling shoes at Payless back in Richmond."

Leonard beamed gratefully and Stee felt good. A happy fan was a satisfying thing to behold.

With that, though, Stee was running out of topics of pleasant conversation. He looked out the frosted glass wall of the conference room, hoping that Daniel was somewhere nearby. When no one appeared and he realized he would have to babysit Leonard a while longer, Stee reluctantly rolled behind his chair.

"What else can you do with that program of yours?"

"I can do sales projections, demographic analysis, comparisons of sales against radio airplay ... pretty much anything."

"That's amazing shit, Leonard. Truly amazing. You're ... a whiz."

Leonard checked for shadows crossing on the other side of the frosted glass then took a deep breath. "Can I trust you?"

Caught off guard, Stee replied, "Why?"

"Because I've been working on an off-label use of this application that is *truly* amazing shit, sir."

"Is that so?" Stee could see that the kid was bursting with a secret. "Wanna tell me about it?"

Emboldened, Leonard clicked a few keys, then pointed at the screen. "I created an algorithm to extract even more specific consumer data, down to the individual purchaser's entire online library."

"Uh, wow," Stee said, feigning as much awe as he could feign.

"Unless you're in customer support, you're not supposed to know any details about the buyers," Leonard continued, gaining steam. "But you can learn so much from a person's music library—Busker purchases, CDs from their personal collection or from friends, pirated copies, legal downloads. It's a shame not to peek."

Stee considered this carefully. "So you're telling me you can tap into someone's computer and see any song they've ever downloaded?"

Leonard nodded excitedly. "When someone purchases a song through Busker, a bot I've embedded into the song file burrows into the hard drive and reads what's saved in the music folder. A couple of clicks, and I can see it all and analyze it."

Stee's eyebrows furrowed. "Leonard, BetaComp will fire you for this. It's invasion of privacy. You could even go to jail."

"I've got it hidden where those idiots in legal will never find it," he replied dismissively. "Look, I'm not doing this to steal someone's identity. I have a bigger mission: to prove you can know a person purely through their musical taste. Music makes us who we are. You gotta understand that, right?"

"Uh ..."

"You've been on a date and gone through the girl's music collection while she's out of the room, right? You see Black Keys and figure she's worth the cost of dinner and a movie; you see Nickelback, and you suddenly remember you have to go home."

Stee saw his point. *In my day, I'd stay if I saw a Johnny Cash LP and take off if there was even a whiff of disco.*

"With people's libraries at my fingertips, I can figure out who they are and how they tick," Leonard said. "Just think how this could help you connect to new fans and continue to inspire your loyal listeners." He paused. "Do you want to see it in action ... Stee?"

Stee mulled this over for a moment.

I've tried everything else to get my writing back on track ... why not this?

Stee rolled closer to the computer. "Sure. Show me what you got."

"Awesome!" Leonard clicked happily, exiting out of the company firewall and into his own carefully controlled corner of cyberspace. Waiting for the program to load, he gave Stee a conspiratorial smile.

"Do you know what I call the program?"

"Tell me."

"ISPeye: capital isp, then 'eye' like an eyeball. Get it?"

Stee chuckled warily, knowing there was a joke in there somewhere that he couldn't identify.

"Now, take a look."

Where there had once been graphs and trend lines, innumerable customer records tiled across the screen, each resembling a manila card from the back of a library book. Leonard leaned back in his chair, immensely proud. "Here we are: the music collections stored on just some of the millions of Squeezeboxes in existence today. I can aggregate the data or I can home in on one device, do searches—the works. Give me a zip code."

Stee shrugged. "23229."

"Ah, the zip code of your childhood home," Leonard said appreciatively. The screen adjusted to show a few hundred records. "First, let's sort according to who's bought your music in the last 30 days." The screen readjusted. "We can expand any one of these individual records. Any preferences—man, woman?"

"I'm pretending I know nothing about this, Leonard. I don't want to be incarcerated. You pick."

The kid double-clicked on a name. The library card expanded. In the top right corner was a tiny color photograph of an overweight bald man in a faded green t-shirt. Stee frowned.

"Jesus, Leonard, is that a *driver's license* photo? How'd you get that?"

"Trade secret," he replied craftily. "How about this one?"

Stee shook his head. Leonard closed the file and opened another, featuring a white guy with a big neck and a gray fringe of hair.

"No."

Another file, another photo of a middle-aged white dude needing Rogaine and a few more salads for lunch.

"These are my fans?"

"They're buying your music in quantity, so I guess so."

Stee sighed. "Any women in there, maybe below retirement age?"

Leonard complied. "Here we go. Stee Walsh, meet Ms. Connie Rafferty."

She looked to be mid-forties, dark-haired and -eyed, and in need of some sleep. Stee shrugged.

"She'll do."

Leonard began to plunk through the facts on the screen. "Let's see what can learn about Ms. Rafferty to start." He frowned at the screen. "We can't use this one, Stee."

"Why not?"

Leonard pointed to the library. "Her sample size is too small. She only has 187 songs in her library."

"That's all?"

Leonard examined the screen more closely. "And they're all your songs." He moved back in his chair. "That's weird."

"Weird that she only has a couple hundred songs or weird that they're all mine?"

"Both," Leonard nodded. "It looks like she downloaded your entire catalogue by buying one song a day and now listens to nothing else. She started with "Come On Up," then bought the rest of your eponymous debut, then she purchased each track of *Double Down* and on and on."

Stee mulled on this. "Why not just buy the albums? It's cheaper."

Leonard tapped away. "I dunno. She hasn't bought any other artist's music during this time and hasn't added any from other sources, either. It's just wall-to-wall Stee Walsh and the River Runners."

"What's up with that?"

The door swung open, with Daniel in the lead and Jayesh nodding and laughing. Stee rose as his manager came to his side. Leonard hit a combination of keys that eradicated any evidence of ISPeye; the graphs returned, pulsating red and green.

"Well, *Mr. Walsh*, I believe we've got a good deal for all involved," Daniel said with a smile that could launch a thousand used cars. "I'll brief you on the way to the airport, but I can safely say that your career has entered its next great phase—as soon as you deliver that album, of course."

Stee smiled distractedly as the BetaComp gang laughed it up. Daniel gathered Stee's leather jacket and handed it to his client. Jayesh then stuck his hand out for the perfunctory handshakes all around.

"It's been a true pleasure."

Daniel held the door, expecting Stee to stalk straight out. Instead, Stee turned around and leaned into Leonard, speaking under his breath.

"How about you see what else the data tells you about her and send me a note through my website? I'd like to learn more about what you find out. I'm intrigued."

Leonard nodded vigorously. "Anything you want, Stee."

His leather jacket on, his shades in place, Stee Walsh left the building.

———————

As Stee settled into the back of the Town Car, Daniel pulled a file from his briefcase. "God, these BetaComp people, they've got us right where they want us since they're still the currency of cool. I can take you through this before lunch. There's a lot here and we'll need to brief the boys, so I want you to be fluent in all this."

Stee stared out the window, rubbing his thumb across his bottom lip. He was trying to put Ms. Connie Rafferty and her one-a-day Stee

Walsh habit out of his mind, but it nagged him nonetheless.

Daniel barreled ahead. "There's other one thing we need to talk about. Your hair."

That snapped Stee to attention. "My hair?"

"They want to mix a color for the skins of the Squeezeboxes to match your hair. Problem is, your hair these days is a little ... faded."

Stee's lip curled in disbelief. "It's going gray; you're allowed to say it."

"You'll have to do the beard, too ... probably the eyebrows while they're at it."

"At least I *have* hair, unlike some guys I know."

Daniel refused to take the bait. "Hey, hey, hey—you know I love you just the way you are, but they are insisting on this as a condition of the contract. Your hair was your most distinctive feature back in the day. This collector Squeezebox is meant to celebrate how you're still as exciting and fresh today as when you were just starting out. The hair holds that image together for a lot of people."

Stee whipped back around. "BetaComp thinks my *hair* is the most significant part of my career?"

"Well, you made the world safe for redheaded rock stars. Axl Rose owes you a thank-you card."

Stee was not amused. "Fuck this. I'll just self-release and be done with it."

"Stee, don't be a baby," Daniel stormed back. "You don't want to blow a deal this good over something so minuscule. It's just a little dye and some time in a salon chair. If you're that shy about it, I'll have someone do it at the house."

Stee rolled his eyes and turned to look out the window. Daniel was losing his patience.

"Stee, this hair thing is the least of your problems and you know it. This album's set to drop October 1 and you haven't written any songs yet, have you?"

Stee craned his neck to get a better view of the landscape rolling by the Town Car. Daniel laid his head back on the leather headrest and let out a guttural groan.

"Christ, Stee, what is the issue?"

"It'll come," Stee said evenly. "It'll come."

"How much more time could you possibly need? The only reason I allowed Chad to tour all these months was to keep him blissfully unaware of your writer's block, and he'll be back in California in three weeks to start charting these nonexistent songs."

"Chad knows how I operate," Stee said, watching a turkey buzzard draw slow circles in the air miles away. "He won't be worried if I'm running a little behind."

"A *little* behind?" Daniel retorted. "It's been five long years of waiting for new material, Stee. You used to be the most diligent songwriter on the planet. You'd clock into the studio like a factory worker, and when you'd clock out you'd have another amazing piece of work rolling off the line."

Daniel paused. "Stee, don't get angry when I ask this; I have to ask you as your friend. Are you drinking again?"

Stee sighed, appreciating the intent of the question but pissed by its necessity. "No, I'm not drinking."

"You still doing the steps? Getting out to meetings?"

"Yes, and yes. My sponsor will tell you the same when you call him later today to check up on me without me knowing."

"Any other addictions entering the picture?"

"No. My coke days are long done, and you know it."

"Something from Tamara?"

"The last time I heard from her was when she told me she was marrying her divorce lawyer."

"Is Kayla still challenging the pre-nup?"

"No, man, she's safely back in her cage."

"The girls okay? Candace's new baby doing all right?"

"Yeah, they're all beautiful. Just had them over to the house last week."

Daniel folded his arms. "Stee, you have to level with me. What's going on?"

"You're not gonna like what I have to say."

"Probably not. I need to hear it anyway."

Stee stared at his boots. "Once this Squeezebox deal is done, that's it. No more new music. I'm retiring."

Daniel smirked. "You can't retire. You don't know how."

"I might as well. My sales have been falling off for years."

"You haven't had any new material. What did you expect?"

"The new fans aren't coming anymore. I look out in the first few rows at the gigs and the crowd just keeps getting older and fatter and balder. No new faces."

"No hot girls, you mean."

"That's not what I'm talking about."

His manager sized him up. "How long since you've had a date, Stee?"

"That's changing the subject."

"I'm not so sure. You can level with me. I'm not here to judge. You getting any lately?"

Stee watched a convertible zoom past. "Not for a while."

"Since Kayla?"

"Yes—jeez, that was five years ago. I'm not a monk. Why are you suddenly interested in all this?"

"I'm just checking to see if you have any vices left. You may need them."

Stee's eyebrows arched. "Really?"

"Vice is what built rock and roll ... and your music was better back when you were drinking and having a snort once in a while. There, I've said it."

Stee's jaw dropped. "You've got to be kidding."

Daniel shrugged. "Coke made you impossible toward the end but at first you were full of energy and up for anything. And you were never a mean drunk, you were a *fun* drunk. The music back then was delicious. Lately, not so much."

Stee's voice hardened. "As my manager, you're telling me to throw out seventeen years of sobriety to save my career?"

Daniel frowned. "Christ, no, Stee—I want you alive. I don't want to be managing your estate. What I'm saying is, when you were young and boozy you had an invincibility about you. There were no wrong answers back then. There was no cynicism and you and the guys were clearly having a great time. That energy infused your songs. That's been missing."

"*Santa Monica Pier* wasn't exactly unicorns and rainbows and it was my best work."

"*Santa Monica Pier* was a very good, very adult album dealing with very mature subjects but it wasn't a downer. It was a pretty ferocious piece of work but I think all the critical praise did something to you: you got convinced you had to top it. You cared too much about making it all perfect before you laid down a track. Now here we are, fifteen years later, waiting for you to put out perfection when all we really need is something fun."

Stee sighed in resignation. "I'm no fun these days, Dan."

"No, you are not. That's why I was thinking of sending a couple of girls over, just to give you a moment of inspiration."

"I'm not that desperate, Dan."

"Shit, *I* am. I need your album written in the next few weeks, you idiot. By any means necessary."

It took Stee a moment to figure out he wasn't serious about the girls. He hissed in mock disgust. Daniel smiled in triumph.

"You don't want to retire, Stee. You'd miss me too much." He leaned in closer. "And you'd miss the gig too much, too. You're one of those poor bastards who can't draw a breath without an audience. You'd go out of your mind if you stopped making music."

Stee shifted to face his manager. "This album is my comeback, Dan. I don't want be doing a sorry imitation of myself from thirty years ago. I want it to be relevant to who I am at this point in my life but shit, I'm fifty-nine years old and that'll be a hard sell. 'Boy-meets-girl, boy-loses-girl, boy-moves-on-to-next-girl' is pathetic at my age. I can't write about Tamara; I've overfished that sea and truthfully, I don't want to relive that part of my life any longer. The less said about Wife Number Two, the better. So, what's left to sing about—my cat?"

"Well, you'd appeal to that coveted over-75 listener demographic then."

Stee chuckled. Daniel settled back in his seat, ready to spitball a few ideas.

"Why don't we treat this as your 'last album' and see what you still want to say about life and the world and all that. Want to do a life on the road piece?"

Stee considered this. "Who really cares about the pain a rock singer suffers to get from gig to gig? That sounds like heaven to anyone who isn't humping around doing it."

"Maybe some sort of ode to the common man?"

"Shit, I haven't had a straight job in my life. I only know people in the business. How many 'common men' do I know, Dan? My last phone call was from Bob Dylan asking me for a word to rhyme with 'incorrigible.' Besides, Springsteen has that base well covered."

"Your kids—your new grandson. Something sweet about them?"

"Off limits."

"Your life growing up in Virginia, maybe something about your parents?"

"Not ready to talk about that yet."

Daniel looked squarely at his client. "Not ready yet? How old *are* you? Stee, your mom's been gone for decades."

Stee's mouth went dry. Daniel persisted.

"You haven't been back to Virginia in almost thirty years and you never had a good answer for why. I know you've got some unfinished business there that's probably been eating at you for a while." He poked Stee's shoulder. "Some of your best songs came out of what you didn't want to discuss. Going home to sort things out with your family could be your ticket."

Stee remained silent. Daniel knew he had the advantage, so he decided to press it.

"Your brother still looks after your grandparents' farm, doesn't he? Out in Devon?"

"Yes," Stee said tersely.

"I say go out there for a visit. Maybe that would give you something new to say. Hey, maybe you'd even meet a common man in Virginia and talk to him about what you should write to get him to buy your new album." Daniel snorted, then added, "Or maybe a common *woman*."

Stee suddenly felt like he had smacked into an electric cattle fence.

Like Ms. Connie Rafferty.

After a few silent seconds, Daniel shook Stee's shoulder. "Dude, you in there? Flashing back to Tokyo again?"

For the first time in weeks, Stee grinned.

"Daniel, I think you just earned your percentage."

chapter 2

"STEEEEEEE!"

Stee pulled the phone away from his ear until his brother had run out of air.

"Yep, it's me, Duane. Don't sound so surprised."

"What can I say? I haven't had a call or an email in a coon's age."

Sprawled across his bed, Stee stared at the ceiling, actively ignoring that the fact his brother only used that phrase because it sounded like a slur. "I'm sorry, Duane. I've been an asshole. Let's just say I fell into a ditch and am trying to crawl back out."

"Gertie has been talking about you. She wants to know if she's old enough to listen to *Come, Come, Come* yet. I told her not until she's eight."

"I don't think I'll listen to it again until I'm eighty. That whole album was a piece of shit."

Duane chuckled. "She misses you. We all do."

"Stop busting my chops, brother. I flew you all out last fall."

"Yeah, you were a lot of fun. We had to go to the beach by ourselves ..."

"Duane, I'm sorry ..."

"And Disneyland ..."

"Jeez, Duane—"

"The Santa Monica Pier ... you know, that place you sang about."

"I GET IT!" Stee was sitting bolt upright on the edge of the bed, gripping the side of the mattress. "I'm a bad brother. I'm not a great-uncle, I'm a pathetic-uncle. I've neglected you far too long, and I have nothing to show for all that neglect because I still don't have a single song written for the album that's coming out in five months."

There was a pause on the other end of the line. "Christ, Stee, take a breath, okay? I was just joking with you."

Stee's voice involuntarily shrank. "It's hard to tell sometimes."

After another irritated pause, Duane ventured back into the conversation. "Stee, hey, it's good to hear your voice."

Stee lay back down. "Actually, I wanted to talk about paying you and Gina and Gertie a visit, maybe stay out at Granddaddy's farm."

"Huh." Duane sounded reluctant to continue. "I'm not sure how I feel about that."

"Why?"

"Well, you've made it pretty clear all those years ago you never wanted to set foot in Virginia again, and by God, you kept your word. What changed?"

"It's Daniel's idea. I need to get out of LA and get in touch with people living normal, run-of-the-mill lives, and you and Gina are the only people I know who fit that description."

"Did you just insult me?" Duane asked, with no humor in his voice.

Stee felt his jaw tighten. "Uh, I didn't mean to if I did."

"You want to visit me here for the first time since Momma died, but not because you want to get back in touch with your blood. You want to *watch* me be *run-of-the-mill* so you can write a *song* about it?"

"That came out way wrong."

"No shit."

Stee hated that phone calls with Duane could spiral downward so quickly. He began again.

"Duane, 'run-of-the-mill' is a compliment. I envy you and Gina, being married for forty years. I barely made fourteen."

"Years or months?" Duane joked.

"Years for the first marriage, minutes for the second," Stee replied, relieved that calm had been restored.

"Well, shit, you and Chad have played together for forty years.

Even when you go out solo, he's your side man. That's married in my book."

Forty years. I hadn't done the math.

Duane coughed, rattling his ribs to clear a hole in the cigarette muck in his lungs. "Stee, I never believed that bootleg lawsuit was why you left Virginia. I always knew once Momma was gone, you wouldn't come back. I'm glad you changed your mind." He paused. "So if you're coming all this way, are you gonna finally visit—"

"Duane, don't waste your breath."

When the silence was almost unbearable, Duane asked, "When are you coming out?"

Thank God.

"Let me check with my assistant. Maybe in a week or two. I'm warning you, I may be playing at all hours in the farmhouse, waking the rooster up in the morning myself."

"We'll just be there for a night anyway because of school. Gertie will be thrilled, Stee. She loves your hair." He snickered. "She said it's just like Ariel's from *The Little Mermaid.*"

Great. Just great.

"Stee, you there? It was just a joke!"

chapter 3

Stee pulled his red Mustang convertible into the garage. His next four *Vinyl Idols* shows were in the can, so he wouldn't have to report back for his talk show gig for the next month in case he needed more time at the farm. He'd also caught a meeting in North Hollywood to prepare himself for flying out to visit the home country in a few days.

He walked into the kitchen and shouted down the hall. "Serafina?"

The vacuum cleaner stopped. "Yes, Mr. Walsh?"

"Just letting you know I'm home. Anyone call?"

"No, Mr. Walsh. Angela is coming at 2."

"Right. Thanks, Serafina."

The vacuum restarted and moved far down the hall. Stee sat down at the kitchen desk, woke up his laptop and checked his email. Larry sent him a link to an article on freak folk music. Chad was doing his daily check-in from the road. Caldwell was silent as he usually was when he was producing someone else's material. No news from Bobby, but that was typical, too; often his internet connection got dropped when he was between royalty checks. With nothing urgent, Stee closed out the mailbox and logged into a second one tied to his website.

He prided himself on maintaining direct contact with his fans in this way. Lately, most people sounded an awful lot like his manager and bandmates ("Dude, when are you coming out with new material?"). A few were searching for obscure bootlegs or long-forgotten TV performances. There was a steady stream of unsolicited songs, and the occasional marriage proposal (from women and men) or paternity suit (also from women and men).

Sometimes he got messages intended for *Joe* Walsh. As soon as he saw a screaming Subject line ("BEND OVER—YOU'RE GLENN FREY'S PUNK-ASS BITCH!"), Stee forwarded it to Joe with a note (*"But at least you got a pretty mouth. XO Stee"*).

This morning, with the BetaComp meeting only 48 hours in the past, he saw there were already a handful of messages from Leonard, who was clearly reveling in his new job as info pimp. Figuring this could take a while, Stee grabbed an apple and a bottle of sparkling water out of the fridge. He opened the first in the series.

> To: stee@swatrr.com
> From: whitepines@hotmail.com
> Subject: SO G33KED TO HAVE MET U

Hoo boy.

> Stee,
> In those brief minutes we had together, you validated the purpose of my work. ISPeye is so not a toy for my own amusement. It is a way for you to know what your fans really want by knowing who they really are.
> I'll send you more research as I get it. Anything you need, just tell me. I am at your command from this day forward.
> Your faithful fan,
> L

Stee took a long drink of water and moved on.

> To: stee@swatrr.com
> From: whitepines@hotmail.com
> Subject: Double super-secret background
> Real quick, here are the highlights of Connie R's

SWATRR or SW purchases:

1. Starting about a year ago, she purchased all of your regularly released material: all fourteen albums, plus the bonus songs off of your greatest hits discs

2. She also got your collaborations and single songs off of tribute and benefit CDs

3. She bought her Squeezebox the day she downloaded that first song of yours. I'm still trying to—

Shit—boss is coming. TTYL

L

Then, number three:

To: stee@swatrr.com

From: whitepines@hotmail.com

Subject: WHO ARE YOU? WHO WHO? WHO WHO?

The following is what I've been able to pull up on our guinea pig thus far using openly available sources, since her Busker library is woefully underfed:

Here's her LinkedIn profile verifying her graduation dates (putting her age to be 43-45). Work history is pretty depressing if you ask me, wasting a life in SF by working for some monster financial company. Now she's in the VA suburbs doing who knows what.

My initial hypothesis? She needs your music just to get through the day, cuz her life right now is pretty pathetic.

Stee clicked on the link. Up popped a blue-bordered write-up of what this woman had done with her professional career, along with a corporate headshot considerably more flattering than the one from her driver's license: smiling wide, with a dimple on one side.

Kinda sweet.

He skimmed the information. She had been something called a "change officer," whatever the hell that was, for some place called Tripton Reid in San Francisco. He wasn't certain how "increased compliance through incorporating video into training and support materials" could be called an "accomplishment," either. Bored, he skipped to her academic history and homed in on a very interesting bit of information:

> University Art Academy
> MA, Film & Video Arts, 1993

This is what she's using her degree for—increasing compliance or some shit?

Leonard's right: that is depressing.

On to the next missive:

> To: stee@swatrr.com
> From: whitepines@hotmail.com
> Subject: More to consider
> I was right about her needing to feel better:
> When I Googled her, I found this:
> www.sfchronicle.com/obit/matherc032108
> Let me know what else you wanna know—L.

Stee sat back and folded his arms.

There were many felonious consequences that could result from what Leonard was doing on his behalf, which ought to be reason enough to tell the guy to cool it (and to figure out how to block all his email in the future). But the last thing he wanted was to cause this woman any pain with this little parlor game by meddling in matters he had no business being a part of.

He eyed the link to the obituary. He didn't feel quite right about reading it; it was like rifling through her bureau drawer to look at her love letters. It sat there, glowing blue in the middle of his screen.

And yet ...

Click.

> MATHER, Chris Allen. (b. June 30, 1963). Died after a valiant fight with pancreatic cancer on March 23. A resident of San Francisco, he is survived by wife Connie (Rafferty) and their fifteen-year-old daughter Amanda; his parents, two brothers and a sister. Visitation 9:30 a.m.—2 p.m. March 25 at Holy Rood Funeral Home. In lieu of flowers, donations can be made to the American Cancer Society.

He felt bad. It's not like he knew the guy personally, but a widow with a young daughter was melancholy by default.

There was a small photo. Chris Allen Mather wore glasses. He had dark hair. He looked smart. He was smiling as if someone had just told him a bad pun and he couldn't believe he was finding it funny.

He looks like a great guy.

At that moment, Stee understood why Connie had made him a regular part of her life. He was tied to her in the most intimate way possible:

I'm helping her get through her grief.

His publicist had hunted down a few human interest stories like this one before in an attempt to, in her words, "show the world that your music fucking *matters* and you're not just some rich asshole with a couple of hit records a million years ago." A soldier in Iraq told CNN that he played "Chained No More" every morning before reporting for duty to "stay focused on the freedom we protect, not the battle ahead." A young mom was quoted in *Women's Day* as saying that she sang "My Love, My Dear" to her preemie every day in intensive care, and "now the boy dances any time he hears a Stee

Walsh song."

"Fucking heart-warming, tear-jerking *gold* mines, Stee!" his publicist crowed. "One of these is worth a year of charity concerts!"

Stee sent each of these people a personal note along with an autographed copy of his rarities boxed set. He would have done that even if his publicist hadn't been breathing down his neck. It was the least he could do for fans like these. It made the intangible relationship with millions of faceless listeners more concrete. It attached a name and a life story to those who felt most connected to him; it made them real people.

It helped him feel a little more real, too.

Maybe I can reach out to Connie—tell her I hope she's doing okay.

There was, of course, a problem. Connie didn't know he knew she existed, much less that he had access to her computer's music library and her husband's obituary. There was no rational, or legal, reason he should have her contact information either.

Wait—I bet she's a SWATRR!

The Stee Walsh and the River Runners' (SWATRR) Official Fan Club had been in existence since the days of mimeographed newsletters and reel-to-reel bootlegs. With online registration, links throughout the social media space, and a live chat every other month, the SWATRR Fan Club was now managed by one of Daniel's web geniuses and had mushroomed to include hundreds of thousands of members from over the globe, all willing to spend hours parsing lyrics or dissecting concerts. By paying a $40 annual fee, SWATRRs could be first in line for concert tickets. Scalpers scooped up the good seats in bulk no matter how much Stee's team worked with the promoters to lock them out, and SWATRR was the only reliable way to ensure that dedicated fans got a shot at decently priced seats. Daniel gleefully rubbed his hands together every time he read the revenue report; Stee always railed about the ridiculous unfairness of the system, but didn't return the money.

It stood to reason that Connie might have plunked down two twenties so she could catch his next show and get discounted band merchandise while she was at it. If so, the person who could find her address was ...

"Hey, Angela!"

Stee's assistant hauled into the kitchen, dropping assorted mail and periodicals onto the counter. She plopped her oversized purse into a corner next to Stee's desk and took a deep draught of her coffee before tossing the cup into the trash.

"Hey, yourself." Angela pushed her frosted hair off her brow until the product once again held it in place, then ran a finger over her lips to even out the gloss. She wasn't a young woman—well preserved and 50ish was all she'd admit to—and she still poured herself into the acid-washed jeans she had showed up wearing when she started working for him sixteen years ago.

As Stee Walsh's personal assistant, Angela Kinney had survived one wedding, two divorces, three moves, four cats, and a brief spate of veganism. She drove him to AA meetings; she slipped his sobriety chip in his pocket where he couldn't miss it. She had made Keith Richards tea when she found him sitting in Stee's kitchen, cooling his heels while his host was in the shower. She knew where guitar strings could be purchased at 3 a.m. in Bangkok. She might know who to call for great dope in Salt Lake City, but she would deny it to the authorities. She knew the right thing to say to an ex-Beatle when she knew her boss was asleep underneath a blonde (who had obviously enjoyed the previous night's show very, *very* much): "He's got his hands full right now; may I take a message, Mr. McCartney?" She knew to the second how long it took to get her boss from his Malibu bedroom, in boxers, to backstage of the Kodak Theater in a custom midnight-blue tux and bolo tie with his Gibson on his hip, ready to perform at the Oscars, factoring in traffic, photo ops on the red carpet, and a stop at the In-N-Out Burger in Santa Monica. (By the way, he'll have a number three, no sauce, raw onion and a chocolate shake—with a lot of ketchup.)

Angela was on call 24/7 with her cell phone charged and her car gassed up at all times. She had the endurance of a marathoner and the patience of a second-grade violin teacher. She kept him in line and always got him through, and for that he was eternally in her debt. Stee loved her more than any other woman in his life.

"Angela, I need a favor. Do you know the guy who runs the fan club?"

"Yeah, some guy in Daniel's shop—Nick something."

"Call him, would you please? I need him to find out if this lady is in the database." Stee found a sticky note and on it wrote Connie's name in block letters.

Angela pursed her lips. "Why do you need to find this lady, Stee? Do I *want* to know or should I stay ignorant in case the cops come by?"

Stee flushed slightly, then smiled a little too quickly. "Jeez, Angie, who do you take me for?"

She looked him straight in the eye. "Someone who once asked me to get the number of that escort service Steve Tyler couldn't stop blabbing about."

"That was a low point a long time ago," Stee huffed. "Give me credit. I never called the number you gave me."

"You should have. It was the number for Church of the Blessed Sacrament."

"I don't doubt it."

Angela looked at the note. "Seriously, can you tell me why you need to find this woman?"

"She's going through a bad time," he said, casually closing out of his email before she could see its contents. "I'd like to send her a boxed set and a card ... which I'd appreciate you getting for me, too."

"Ah." She stuck the note on the counter, took out her phone and texted Nick whatshisname before she forgot. Then she took an envelope from her pile of papers.

"Here's your walking-around money, Stee," she said, dropping the envelope on the keyboard. "Call me if you need an infusion. You have your credit card?"

"Yes, Mother," Stee retorted, fanning out the twenties and hundreds as he silently counted to two thousand, lining them up and putting them back in the envelope.

Angela collected the mail and her purse and headed across the kitchen. "I'll be in the office. I need to confirm the pilot and plane for your flight to DC and line up the driver to get you to Devon, and Daniel wants to post a press release to explain the trip."

"Oh, wait up on that." Stee stood as Angela did an about face in the doorway. "Can you call him off? I'm trying to keep this low-key. I need a change of scene to goose my creativity, and the last thing I need is a bunch of reporters breaking my concentration. I need to be left alone for a few weeks to bang this out."

Angela cocked her head. "I thought maybe you wanted some 'proof' that you're hard at work so the label will get off your back."

Stee smiled, admiring her for focusing on the bigger opportunity. "If anyone asks, just tell them I haven't seen my grand-niece in ages and it's high time I went back to the home country. None of that is a lie."

"People are going to wonder why you're back in Virginia after 30 years."

"Let 'em wonder."

"Got it." Angela turned again but spun around when Stee called her back.

"I have another favor to ask—"

"The Third Baptist Church in Gordonsville has meetings every Tuesday at 4 p.m."

Stee almost blushed. "Thanks, I had meant to ask you about that, too," he said, admiring her even more. "Could you check up on Bobby, see if he's ... uh, doing okay?"

"Want me to let you know what I find out?"

"Only if he's in the hospital."

"Not if he's in jail?"

"Then, too."

"Will do." Angela quickly returned, a shrink-wrapped boxed set under her arm and an embossed card with the sticky note in her hand, updated with an address. "Here you go. Just give them to me when you're done."

Stee took the items from his assistant. "I'll bring these to Virginia with me. She's from Richmond. If you give me her address, I can take care of it once I get there."

"Will you now?" Angela asked incredulously. "When was the last time you went to a post office?"

"Maybe I'll deliver it personally, Miss Know-it-all."

"So much for keeping the trip low-key. What do you think will happen if you just show up at her front door?"

Stee sighed in exaggerated exasperation. "Fine, you win. You send it. Now get out of here and assist someone." With a superior air, Angela walked out once more.

Stee looked at the address; after so many years, the street didn't ring a bell. He turned the note card over so his autograph in blue ink was at the front. He patted his shirt pockets and located a pen. He tested it on another sticky note and then sat down at the desk and stared at the card.

And stared.

Shit, this is worse than writing lyrics.

> Dear Connie,
> Thanks for supporting my band and my music.
> Here's a token of appreciation for being a fan. I
> hope you enjoy this addition to your River Runners
> collection.

There was still space for another sentence. He considered a few options:

> I noticed you have only a couple hundred songs
> on your Squeezebox, and they're all mine. Trust me,
> there are far better musicians out there. Let me know
> if I can suggest a few.

And

> Why just one a day? Is that all you can afford?
> Need a few bucks?

Also,

> Hey, I'm coming out to Virginia for a couple of
> weeks in a last-ditch effort to write my next and
> maybe final album after a long dry spell. It should be
> painful. Want to watch?

Thinking the better of it, he simply wrote

> Best,

He signed and sealed it, and taped the note to the boxed set before
he could think twice.

Have a good life, Connie ... whoever you are.

Death by interview. That's what this is.

Connie Rafferty hadn't worn a business suit in over a year, and
now her blazer stuck to her like a wetsuit in the airless conference
room. No longer glowing or perspiring, she was flat-out sweating,
facing the window as the sun hit her at eye level, forcing her to
squint. She was there to meet the executive recruiter highly recommended by her former boss, and while Connie trusted his judgment,
she wasn't much enjoying her first encounter with ...

Crap, what is her name?

The recruiter was blonde, tailored down to the stitching in her
slingback shoes, and unimpressed with Connie's resume, which she
held before her like a spoiled piece of meat.

"Take me through this from the bottom up, okay?" She spoke with a Southern lilt that Connie was not about to take as a sign of friendliness or sisterhood or stupidity.

Connie smiled brightly and followed orders. She began by glossing over her childhood—"born and bred in Richmond"—and had barely said the letters "BA" when the recruiter shot her a look.

"Went up north to college?"

"Is that a problem?"

"There's still a bunch of boys out here who make cracks about Yankees. Just be prepared. Go on."

As she spoke the letters "MFA" the recruiter halted her again.

"What did you intend to do with your master of fine arts in film?"

"I wanted to be a documentarian." Connie began one of her glib excuses for why she didn't become a documentarian when the recruiter—*damn it, her name rhymes with another name*—shut her down.

"Huh." She scanned the paper for a moment or two. Connie idly wondered what the woman had done before landing the headhunting gig.

Meter maid ...

IRS auditor ...

Slaughterhouse floor manager ...

"So instead of being a 'documentarian' you worked at Tripton Reid for eighteen years. How old are you, anyway?"

Connie laughed incredulously. "Isn't it illegal for you to ask that?"

"I'm not trying to *hire* you. I have to *represent* you—and my firm— so I can ask you whatever I want. Besides, the people who might want to hire you can look at your graduation date and do the math."

Connie hadn't been overly concerned about her age until that very moment. "I'm forty-four. Should I leave off my graduation date?"

The woman shrugged. "No, you look forty-four; no one's going to be fooled. So, one company your whole career: explain that."

"Tripton Reid gave me my first corporate job after art school, and once they found out I could use a video camera, they kept me busy. I didn't feel the need to look elsewhere."

The recruiter clicked her tongue doubtfully. "Stability's good up to a point. You really should have changed jobs somewhere along the line."

"I have that opportunity now," Connie replied curtly. The recruiter seemed pleased that she had finally gotten a rise out of her.

"You left Tripton Reid a year ago to move here. Why?"

Recouping her professional tone, Connie said, "I decided to take a break from corporate life to pursue other interests."

Carrie? Mary? What the hell is her name?—leaned in with a glossy smile. "I don't need the business-speak bullshit; I need the truth. Were you fired? Laid off? Came in drunk once too often? What?"

When Connie hesitated, the headhunter jumped in again. "If I'm going to represent you I have to know all your secrets. I can't be knocked on my ass by an HR assistant who's done a Facebook search."

Terri—that's it—that's her name.

Scary Terri.

"I got laid off."

"Why? Not valuable enough to keep?"

"You'd have to ask my former employer."

"I will." Scary Terri folded her arms. "So, why come back to Virginia before your unemployment ran out?"

"My husband died of cancer right before the layoff."

Scary Terri sat back. "My condolences. Got kids?"

"A daughter. She was fifteen when this happened."

"Ah. So let me fill in the rest of the tale: you moved back to your hometown to leave the pain behind for a fresh start in a familiar place?"

Connie nodded. "I figured I could do some video work on my own until I could land a full-time job again."

"That's what this 'Key Light Video' listing is," Terri added, holding up Connie's resume, now practically dripping with red ink from her notes. Her eyebrows arched. "So, how's the freelance video business?"

"Let's just say, after a couple of bridezillas and one too many months without a paycheck, I'm ready to return to corporate life."

Scary Terri chuckled. "So I'd expect. But here's the deal. You've got a solid background, and the peek I took at your online portfolio tells me you know how to do the video thing, but if you thought the economy was bad on the West Coast, it's even worse in our little section of the Mid-Atlantic. It could be months before I can land you an interview, much less get you a job."

"I know."

"So while I'm doing my magic, if I were you I'd cozy up to a few more bridezillas to make ends meet, and call anyone you know in the Commonwealth to see if they need a freelancer." She stood and handed her a business card. "I'll be in touch if something comes up."

Connie watched Scary Terri traipse out of the conference room, confident and employed, and shuddered.

Definitely slaughterhouse floor manager.

To: Rafferty, Connie
From: Barsamian, Kenneth J.
Subject: Guatemala video
Connie,
I have to tell you again, that fundraising video you did a couple of months ago is just amazing. Watching our donors cry makes me the happiest man on the planet. Such a thrill to watch the money pour in.
Looking forward to the next project; glad you're on our team.
Kenneth J. Barsamian
COO
Tripton Reid
P.S. Love the Stee Walsh song as the soundtrack. Big fan? Me, too.

Connie had been reviewing each of the items in her online portfolio, including emails from her former employer that glowed with praise. Ostensibly this was to make sure they were appropriate for the headhunter to pass along to prospective interviewers. Really, Connie was in a self-pitying mood and was determined to make herself completely miserable by contemplating what she had lost: a nice, orderly, stable job with health insurance and a 401(k) and vacation accrual—her Promised Land. Access to top-of-the-line cameras and editing software, plus a crew on retainer, was no longer possible unless she paid for them herself. She was down to her light kit, a lavaliere microphone, a couple of handheld cameras and a laptop that was making a worrisome whirring noise.

Officially bitter, Connie cursed loudly into the bottom of her wine glass. Immediately a small box popped up in the bottom right of her screen.

> dandymandy: you owe another quarter to the Swear Jar, Mom
> criffraff: Sorry—just going through some old emails from Tripton Reid
> dandymandy: stop torturing yourself
> criffraff: All done. Putting the rack and the iron maiden back in the closet
> dandymandy: thank god—you're ruining an otherwise excellent homework experience

Of course, they could have had this conversation in person, or Amanda could have yelled through the wall their bedrooms shared. That would have struck Amanda as ridiculous, and Connie was not going to squelch any form of communication her teenager would deign to have with her, considering how little they spoke these days.

Closing out of her email, she picked up her Squeezebox and selected a song as the soundtrack of her current misery: "Someday," track eight on the Stee Walsh 1994 solo release, *Santa Monica Pier*. Slipping onto her bed, she fitted her headphones over her ears and clicked Play.

An acoustic guitar crept into the silence, and after eight bars, Stee Walsh began to croon:

Your arms surround me
And pull me in deep
My pulse is still pounding
As you drift off to sleep.
My ardent protector
My citadel wall
But who will protect you?
Because I will fall.

Stee's clear, brave tenor was smooth as glass. He wasn't pushing the vocal—no crackling bravado in this song. It was simply a man pleading in the dark:

I ask your forgiveness
I beg you to stay
Still you should leave me
If not now, someday.

The band was in full force now: Chad's electric lead guitar, Larry's lush keyboards, Caldwell's steady bass, Bobby's thrumming percussion. Stee's harmonica line arched over the eight-bar turnaround, and the second verse started:

You wanted a partner
A lover and friend
Instead, you caught me
In trouble again.
Who then can blame me
For making you go
Before I consume you?
I love you so.

The chorus repeated in full harmony. Then the bridge began:

I can never atone
For the damage I've done.
My end is coming.
You have to be gone.

The song hung there, suspended in the air, unfinished, choked off. Within seconds, the band came in, wrapping back to the unsung chorus. As it wound down, Stee moaned:

Go—just go
I'm sorry, darlin'
Now go

Stee's harmonica mournfully played the song off into black silence once more, and Connie burst into tears ... just as the doorbell rang.

Knowing full well her teenager would never willingly leave her room except for the arrival of either friends or food, Connie quickly wiped her face with her palms and shook off her misery to deal with the FedEx guy on her doorstep.

The return address on the box puzzled her.

Who do I know in Malibu?

She broke open the package to find a note card, which she read. And reread.

This can't be real.

Connie turned the note over and over by the corners as if she didn't want to smudge any telltale fingerprints. The words on the card left indentations in the card stock. It was written by hand:

Dear Connie,
Thanks for supporting my band and my music. Here's a token of appreciation for being a fan. I hope you enjoy this addition to your River Runners collection.
Best,
Stee

But written by whose hand?

She thought through every possibility for why she could have received a rare and relatively expensive four-CD boxed set, out of the blue, from the singer who had occupied her every waking moment the last few months.

Was this because of SWATRR? Was there an announcement of some random giveaway?

She scoured the fan site for any hint of a contest. She went to Google, searched on "Stee Walsh," "River Runner Rarities" and "free," but came up with nothing relevant. It was a stumper.

A tiny pebble of hope splashed at the bottom of her stomach.

What if Stee Walsh really did write this?

She quickly put the idea out of her mind.

Why would he?

Mystified, she picked up the boxed set and ran her fingernail in the crack to cut a hole in the plastic wrap. The box itself was handsome, the outer cover textured like a leather-bound photo album with a cutout showing the band in their earliest days, lanky and scruffy. Stee peered out from under a fringe of red hair. The picture was too tiny to make out the navy blue of his eyes, but they were dark and sly, daring the camera to get closer.

She slipped the cover off and found each of the four CDs in its own sleeve, labeled to look like a 45. There was also a booklet, led off by a glowing introduction from Bonnie Raitt. Connie plopped on the couch in the living room, put her feet up and absorbed every word.

She inserted the first CD into her laptop and, once its material had been ingested into the Busker library, hit Play. The system cued up an early recording from Stee's days as part of Bobby Brewer and the Insiders: a cover of "Ready Teddy," which, thanks to the liner notes, she discovered was a Buddy Holly hit that Little Richard had originated and Elvis and even John Lennon had covered as well.

The recording was a bit of a mess. It sounded as if Stee hadn't figured out how to harness his voice yet. Yet his delivery was fierce and the band's playing didn't sound amateur in the least. Through it all Stee seemed a split second away from laughing his head off. It was simply joy—pure joy.

She flipped through the book to the photo of Stee, Bobby, and the Insiders bassist who dropped out of the band after a couple of years, probably to his eternal regret. Teenage Stee had an underfed homeliness, the sort of look that used to bring on an unexplainable crush when she was fifteen.

Kinda cute.

Even then.

Chapter 4

To: stee@swatrr.com
From: whitepines@hotmail.com
Subject: Radical change in CR buying habits

Sir Stee,
The guinea pig has stopped her daily purchases of your singles. She procured River Runner Rarities recently and she's put that into heavy rotation instead.
My theory? She's trying to bolster her street cred by getting to know your lesser-known catalogue. At least she knows quality now; of course, some of us always did. Reply when you can ...

Well, look at that.
Stee was tickled. Connie clearly appreciated his gift. It was as if he had heard a radio signal from deep space: faint and remote, but contact nonetheless.
There was more from Leonard that was even more intriguing:

To: stee@swatrr.com
From: whitepines@hotmail.com
Subject: Her roots are showing

Stee-san,
New behavior for the guinea pig: she just

uploaded a Buddy Holly song: his version of "Ready
Teddy." Makes sense since that was the B-side of
your first 45, the ones you used to send out to get
college gigs while you were in high school.

I was able to nab a copy of that 45 for my
personal collection a few years ago. Wanna chat
about it? Just text me ... my number is at the bottom
here in case you lost it.

*Well, ain't that great: I've turned her into a Buddy Holly fan. The
world needs more of us.*

Angela came into the room, handing over a small light green
envelope the size of his hand. The return address was from a C. Rafferty in Richmond in neat block print. Stee brightened.

*Connie. Well, well, well, you're just popping up everywhere, aren't
you?*

He stuck his index finger under the flap and tore through the
paper to pull out the card inside. "THANK YOU" shimmered on top of
a geometric design in green and silver. He opened it.

Dear Mr. Walsh,

If you are the one who sent me the kind gift of
River Runner Rarities, thank you very much. I've
been looking forward to listening to this and didn't
expect to be able to find a copy since they've gone
out of print. I really appreciate it.

And, if you really are Stee Walsh, I am so grateful
to you. I've had a lot of loss and sadness over the
past two years. Listening to you gave me something
to hold on to. I don't know if I would have gotten
through it all without you. Thank you for making
such beautiful, elegant music.

Sincerely,

Connie Rafferty

Her signature was purposeful: legible without being prissy. Unlike him, she signed both of her names. She wanted to be taken seriously.

Stee reread the note. He chuckled.

"Mr. Walsh" ... *"If you are the one"* ...

Then there was that word: "elegant."

That's something I've never heard anyone use to describe me in any way, shape or form.

"Why do you think it's elegant, Miss Connie?" Stee asked the note card.

He propped the note up next to his computer. As he plowed through his email, it was in his peripheral vision. Connie stayed in his thoughts.

What am I doing that she likes so much?

Now that she got some Buddy Holly, is he going to be her obsession from here on out?

Does she really *think my music is elegant?*

He checked back on the photo that Leonard had sent him previously, pulled from her LinkedIn profile. She was wearing a black suit and stood with her arms folded against a wall in some unidentifiable hallway. There was that dimple that called to him earlier, accenting a genuine knockout of a smile. Her dark hair was longer than in her driver's license photo; if he could brush her bangs back, he could figure out if her eyes were brown or hazel.

Pretty lady.

After musing about her on and off for an hour, Stee called down the hall.

"Angie? Do you have another one of my note cards somewhere?"

"Yes. Why?"

"Because I gotta write a note ... on a card."

He heard her Reeboks scuffing the hall carpet. "Here you are, and write carefully; I already put the stamp on the envelope." She left as quickly as she came. He stared at the white expanse inside the card, took a breath and jumped in.

Dear Connie,

Thanks for your note. That was really classy. I am
sorry you've had such a rough time. If my music has
been able to help you in any way, I'm honored. That's
a privilege.

Since my music means a lot to you, I'd appreciate
your help. See, I'm kind of at a standstill right now,
what with trying to get my next album off the
ground, and it's come to my attention you've bought
a lot of my music lately

He stopped. Connie didn't know he had access to her music
library. He fibbed a bit.

because I got your sales report at random.

And continued on.

I was wondering, what about my music catches
your ear? Why did you connect to it? I want to
ponder that when I'm writing new material.

He ran out of room on the inside of the card, so he drew a little
arrow at the bottom to tell her to turn it over.

Watching my mother connect to Buddy Holly
inspired me to write and play songs. Momma was a
sunny person and Buddy had a sunny sound even
for his sad songs. I saw how happy his music made
her and that's why I learned "Ready Teddy" right
away when I had my first band. I hope I lived up to
the original. When you listen to Buddy's music, tell
me how I did.

Out of room once again, he got a Post-it out of his desk and kept on going.

> I'm also partial to "Well … All Right"—Buddy's original, not the Blind Faith cover. The guitar is so pure and his voice is so honest, it almost makes you cry. I'll send you some more of his stuff so you see what I mean.
>
> If you want to find out where Buddy got his inspiration, check out Elvis Presley's Sun recordings. His labelmates were no slouches either: Johnny Cash, Jerry Lee Lewis and Carl Perkins.

On a second Post-it, he finished up.

> Enough about Buddy Holly, Elvis and all them. I have one more question about my stuff: why did you call my music elegant? Email me through the SWATRR website. Just put SEND TO STEE in the Subject line and it'll go straight to me.
>
> Looking forward to hearing more from you, and by the way, you can call me
>
> Stee

He stuck the sticky notes along the back of the card and put it into the envelope. He smeared the ink a bit as he addressed it; Angie's warning had jinxed him. He walked it down the hall.

"Put this in the mail when you go, okay?"

She looked at him warily. "Who's this Connie Rafferty and why are you writing to her?"

He shrugged. "She's a SWATRR. I'm thanking her for being a fan."

"Again?" Her eyes narrowed. "You sent her the boxed set already. What are you up to, Stee?"

"Just a little market research. Pop it in the mail, okay? And Angie, see about shipping a copy of the Buddy Holly anthology to that address, too."

Angie frowned but nodded anyway. Stee went down to his office, a satisfied smile on his face.

That was very elegant of you, Stee.

————

This is just ... a mess.

Stee—or whoever "Stee" really was—had sent Connie another card, this one with a smudged address on the envelope, written hurriedly and covered in Post-its. It arrived the same day as another boxed set of CDs, these by Buddy Holly, now gleefully hiccupping away on her Squeezebox.

The sentiment was chatty and more than a little personal. She'd felt giddy each of the seventeen times she'd read the note that evening. Connie wondered idly if this was an attempt by Amanda to do something nice to lighten her mood. However, she sincerely doubted her daughter would go through the trouble of faking the whole exchange, Malibu postmarks and all. She wouldn't waste her time.

Neither would anyone else. So it's got to be him.

Great God Almighty ...

Satisfied yet still unnerved by her logic, she clicked onto the SWATRR website and found the email button. When the blank message appeared, ready for her to fill in, her mouth went dry.

What do I say? How much do I tell him?

She set to typing.

> Thank you for the Buddy Holly collection ...
> ... if you're the one who sent it and you really are
> Stee Walsh and not some intern at your record
> company picking me at random for the perverse
> pleasure of watching me act like a fool with her
> hopes up, thinking I'm actually contacting Stee

Walsh when I'm not (shame on you!)

Connie reviewed what she had written, deleted it and started over.

———————

As Stee checked his phone for email messages in the United Red Carpet Club before changing planes in O'Hare, he scanned Leonard's constant stream, alighting on one that looked like it might have something vaguely interesting to say.

> To: stee@swatrr.com
> From: whitepines@hotmail.com
> Subject: Breakthrough for our guinea pig

Leonard, her name is Connie. "Guinea pig" ... Jesus.

> CR's been cycling through her library on a daily
> basis, even as it continues to expand: your material
> has been joined by nearly all of Buddy Holly's
> output, and a recent addition of a Sun Records
> compilation: E. Presley, J.L. Lewis, J. Cash, C. Perkins
> et al.

He smiled with pride. She'd taken him up on his suggestion.
Next I'm gonna send you some Chess recordings. Howlin' Wolf's gonna blow your mind.
Leonard then launched into his song and dance about ISPeye: how it was going to revolutionize music creation and marketing, blah, blah, blah. Stee was about to put his phone aside to catch a quick nap when a new message popped into view:

> To: stee@swatrr.com
> From: crafferty888@gmail.com

Subject: SEND TO STEE—A message from Connie
Rafferty

That was enough to get him to wake up.

Dear Stee,

Thanks for the Buddy Holly collection. It's been a
delightful discovery; it pairs well with your Rarities
collection, too. You've been so generous and I'm
not even sure why I'm the lucky girl. No matter the
reason, I appreciate all of it.

I'm a little embarrassed because you seem to think
I'm a hardcore SWATRR who can offer you valuable
insights into what sells and how to angle your next
album. I have to confess that before a few months
ago, I didn't really know who you were.

It's no reflection on you. It's probably because I'm
more of a visual person. I've been in corporate video
work for years, and in that business music is meant
to complement the story, not be the story itself.

I knew your name, of course, but your music was
just in the background, nothing I paid attention to.

Ouch.

Boy, was I an idiot.

Much, much better.

Over a year ago I got a chance to really listen to
"Come On Up" when I used it to score a video for
Tripton Reid's PharmaCares program.

Connie, Connie, Connie, please tell me you got the rights first.

Stee could care less if someone snuck one of his songs into a home video, as long as it wasn't selling anything, didn't get much airplay, and/or wasn't violent, pornographic or just plain stupid. Yet this was a corporate video and money had to change hands. Stee made a mental note to check with his legal team to make sure she had gotten appropriate permission, and went back to her email.

I had been dealing with a lot the weeks before that shoot: a major betrayal; my husband's death after several months of chemo and radiation; pulling my daughter through the aftermath by myself; moving back to Virginia without much thought about how that would go; depression and self-doubt. You get the picture: I was in a bad way.

"Come On Up" is elegant like an equation the astrophysicists search for to explain the universe concisely and beautifully. The lyrics of that song reached down and rescued me. You were telling me exactly what I needed to hear: don't give up, have some fun, you're not alone. Hearing you sing those words, my life fell back into place for a while.

According to the liner notes in the Buddy Holly collection, he was just 22 when he died. Until the plane crash he hadn't had any hardship or pain; it's no wonder he has such an innocent sound. You, on the other hand, sing like you've gone through a world of hurt, yet came out of it with your hope intact. No wonder I connect to your songs more readily than his, no offense to the pride of Lubbock.

Just keep writing hope, and I'm a fan for life.

Thanks again,

Connie

He was genuinely touched.

I'll do my best, Connie.

Stee stroked the screen with his thumb and slipped the phone in the inside pocket of his leather jacket. He pulled a notebook out of his carry-on to scribble a few thoughts down before he lost them:

PharmaCares video

Writing hope

World of hurt

Why you're the lucky girl

And finally,

I want to meet this gal

———————

"VICTORY IS MINE!"

With a muffled *ping!* eBay announced that Leonard was now the proud owner, at considerable cost, of the only surviving plaster cast of Stee Walsh's face from the "Shut Up Already" video shoot, made when he had to be fitted for a rubber zombie mask.

In your face, NoWayGirl54!

Leonard prided himself on his collection of high-quality, one-of-a-kind Stee Walsh memorabilia. He didn't bother with autographs or mass-produced items like posters or photos or even River Runner Rolling Papers; they were too impersonal. He specialized in the stuff that Stee and the band had handled, objects that still contained the imprint of their DNA. That's what had real value.

Wiping the Dorito dust off his fingers onto his right shoulder, he clicked through to his PayPal account and made it official. He shivered with satisfaction.

Stee will laugh his ass off when I tell him I bought this.

Watching Stee walk into the BetaComp conference room three weeks ago, Leonard had felt what the Wise Men must have when they clapped eyes on the baby Jesus after a long haul through the desert. The man whose music helped Leonard make sense of his life shook his hand, called him "sport" and told him to keep in touch. It was no idle fantasy. It had happened.

I have proof it was real.

In the midst of Jack in the Box wrappers in the kitchen was a specially ordered shadowbox frame he had picked up from Cheap Pete's on the way home from work, the size of a brick, wrapped in brown paper.

Leonard set his laptop on a cushion of pizza-stained paper towels and scrambled to his feet. He took the package to his bedroom and surveyed his 137 other treasures to find just the right position for the ultimate Stee Walsh memento:

The masticated coffee stirrer that Leonard had fished out of the trash can in the BetaComp conference room.

Leonard smirked with pride as he admired the strip of red plastic, mangled by Stee's actual teeth in Leonard's actual presence, now resting on tiny nails between two panes of glass.

Got one of these, NoWayGirl54?

Didn't think so ...

chapter 5

Stee tapped his laptop, and his email awoke, featuring a brief note from his lawyer:

> The Tripton Reid people got the rights to "Come
> On Up" ahead of posting the video; they're in the
> clear. Here's a link:
> www.youtube.com/keylightvideo/pharmacares

Good girl, Connie ... keeping on the straight and narrow.
The video timer spun a couple of times, revealing Tripton Reid's stodgy logo transforming into PharmaCares' heart-shaped pill, and then the screen going white. Words appeared as if they were being typed on a manual typewriter, clacking into place one letter at a time until they spelled:

> orphan disease
> 1. a disease that the pharmaceutical industry has
> not "adopted" because it provides little financial
> incentive for the private sector to make and market
> new medications to treat or prevent it
> 2. a common disease that has been ignored
> such as tuberculosis, cholera, typhoid and malaria
> because it is far more prevalent in developing
> countries than in the developed world

Larry's opening chords of "Come On Up" chimed underneath,

and then Stee heard himself sing:

You feel beat down
You been roughed up
But you got me in your corner
Lemme tell ya, I'm pretty tough.

The words disappeared, followed by the tiny, outstretched hands of a small child coming in from the left. A pair of capable adult hands entered from the right. The song continued.

I ain't gonna let you fail
You'll find your feet real soon
And when that day comes, you'll come on up
And get the good that's due to you.

Over Chad's opening salvo, the shot widened to reveal the adult grabbing the child's hands and swinging her around in a circle until they were both laughing in the dizzy sunshine. Next, the screen exploded with bright, documentary-style footage of children in a village, probably somewhere in Central America, playing soccer. In among them were adults in green scrubs, passing the ball back and forth to the kids. The scene cut to one of the adults, a balding blond man with round wire-rimmed glasses and a stethoscope around his neck, answering interview questions, speaking into a microphone held by an unseen reporter.

"I assure you, without PharmaCares' donations, many of these kids wouldn't be here today," he said as children of all ages mugged for the camera and one draped her arms around him. "Now that they've started the Orphan Disease Adoption Program, we'll be able to save even more."

Shots of an underlit one-room clinic followed, as the chorus came to the fore:

Come on up
Come on up
Get the good that's due to you

The same female reporter was talking to some guy in a suit, broadcasting from an office far away from the village:

"The Orphan Disease Adoption Program is the latest of Pharma-Cares' world outreach programs to improve the health and wellbeing of some of the planet's neediest people. I am proud that Tripton Reid has committed upwards of $25 million to treatments for childhood diseases prevalent in developing nations that otherwise would get little or no attention."

Cutting to a different angle, the exec wrapped with:

"Every sick child deserves care. That's why I'm grateful to the supporters of this program and Tripton Reid's volunteers who make this possible. I'm proud to work here."

More cheerful, hope-filled shots followed. A mother at the clinic beamed as a nurse fussed over her little boy until he giggled. A squalling baby received her vaccination, and the parents gathered her up and comforted her. A toddler in leg braces took a step or two toward her ecstatic grandmother.

Stee's voice rang out underneath the footage:

You're gonna make history, baby
You'll shine all bright and new
So come on up here, darlin'
And get the good that's due to you

There was a brief moment with the grandmother on camera, crying and gushing in subtitled Spanish:

"I never thought Teresa would walk. You saw her walk? You saw my baby walk? Thank you all so much! Thank God for you!"

As Stee and the River Runners powered through the final chorus, the blank screen returned and then the final message typed itself across the frame:

> The Orphan Disease Adoption Program saves lives
> every day because of your support.
> The world thanks you.

There was a rapid-fire montage—high-fiving kids; gloved clinicians putting on bandages; adults clapping—a crazy quilt of hands.

Through the center, the soccer kids appeared.

"Thank you! Gracias!" they yelled over the mighty crash of Bobby's pounding percussion, with Stee's war whoop capping it off.

The screen went dark and the room went quiet. Stee sat back and whistled softly.

So that's *what she does for a living.*

Stee couldn't get the first image out of his mind: those tiny hands reaching out, then the little girl being swept into the air. It reminded him of playing with his daughters on the beach decades ago when Tamara was out of town. This had been a rare Daddy's day out with the girls. Maude and Candace screamed with unbridled delight each time he swung them into the waves. They were towheaded and tanned; seven-year-old Candace's bathing suit had big red polka dots on it, and little sister Maude's was pink with green froggies.

All that afternoon, he'd marveled at the seeming impossibility that these beautiful, gleeful, carefree children were connected to his bloodline. He had never felt so lighthearted, before or since.

He hadn't thought about that day for years. It felt good to remember it now ... thanks to Ms. Connie Rafferty.

He watched the video again. The blue of the kids' uniforms against the dusty brown of the playing field was simply gorgeous. The burst of surprise on the grandma's face made him smile. "Come On Up" fit the message perfectly, and yet the visuals gave the song a new dimension he'd never considered. It was remarkable.

Shit, Connie, you sold me. Now I want to work for Tripton Reid.

He clicked on another video selection in Connie's portfolio. He watched clip after clip, grinning.

Or maybe you could work for me.

———

"Mom, could we please listen to something else? *Anything* else?"

Connie shook her head. "The driver controls the music and the air temperature. Car rules."

"Then pull over and let me drive." Amanda scooped up her

mother's Squeezebox cabled to the car stereo and clicked through the song listings. "At least you've got someone other than Stee Walsh on here for a change." She stopped short of selecting anything, muttering, "Still nothing from the 21st century, though."

"Be grateful Stee gave me some new music—new *old* music, anyway."

"You're on a first-name basis?"

"He insisted."

Amanda shook her head, a strand of pink hair falling over her face. "I can't believe you've got a rock star for a pen pal."

"I can't either, and he keeps sending me presents. I just got this Chess Blues boxed set this morning. It's like he's trying to school me up or something. He must think I'm a musical moron."

"Well, you kind of are. You couldn't tell the difference between the Beatles and Beyoncé." She deflected her mother's glare by turning her attention back to the Squeezebox. "How did he even find you?"

"No clue. He said something about seeing my Busker sales report, I think."

"Lucky." She tossed the Squeezebox back onto the dashboard shelf. "Wish someone famous would be my pen pal. Maybe he'd get me out of this burg."

"You'll be out of here soon enough. What are your top three schools as of today?"

Amanda began to count off with her fingers. "Number three: University of Hawaii."

"You and all the other kids who are sick of winter. Dream on. Next?"

"Number two: William & Mary."

"A good school, in-state tuition, all that stuff. I approve. Proceed."

"And number one: UC Berkeley."

Connie's heart dropped. "You want to go back to California?"

"Does that surprise you?"

"But we aren't California residents anymore. It would cost a fortune."

"I can live with some of my friends who're planning to stay in the Bay Area, maybe defer for a year until I can establish residency. And I can get an internship in a much more progressive law firm out there."

"It's so far away."

"It's home, Mom."

"I thought home was—"

"Virginia? You've got to be joking."

"I was going to say, wherever *I* live."

"Mom, this whole Virginia thing was a mistake. You know it and I know it. Why don't you just admit it, sell the house and go back to San Francisco?"

Connie had reasons she wasn't about to share with her daughter.

Because I'd see your father's ghost everywhere I went.

And I'm not ready to forgive him yet.

"No one's going to buy the house in this economy," Connie muttered.

"Then rent it out," Amanda demanded as they pulled into their driveway. "Or stay here. Do what you want. I'm going back to California. I'm going home." She scrambled out of the car. "And out there I can control the music."

———————

Still unsettled by the conversation in the car, Connie went to the back porch and laced up her running shoes. She pulled tight the ugly Squeezebox armband holster that mimicked a blood pressure cuff, which had been a freebie from her work years. Headphones in place, she was off and running—literally—to the nature trail three blocks over.

Landscapers had modeled the trail to look like the woods it had replaced. Its manicured version of nature was worlds away from the rugged pavement of the near-vertical San Francisco hills. On the upside, though, it was quiet and pretty and convenient, with daffodils and dogwoods ornamenting the route this time of year. She might even see a deer.

Besides, running was less for the challenge and more for the meditation. Spending time absorbing vitamin D and listening to Stee

Walsh could restore her well-being like nothing else.

As she trotted past the welcome sign, Connie clicked around her Squeezebox, scanning for her workout playlist: *Run to Me*. The leadoff song poured into her ears.

This ain't the best of times
But it ain't the worst
We've seen it all, babe
Raw and unrehearsed.

"Never You Fear" was the first song of twelve meant to wrench her back in a positive frame of mind, one footfall at a time. Chad's sure-handed guitar and Larry's bright piano underscored Stee's direct optimism, matching the warmth of the late morning sun.

And ain't that something?
We're still here.
We're alive and well
Never you fear.

Connie nodded toward the heavens.

Amen, Stee.

Connie rounded the first half-mile. Stee and Chad were tearing through "Fishing," a rockabilly goof of a song:

A long-legged cutie
In a short, short skirt
Just melts my mind
Makes my jawbone hurt
She'll kill you dead
With just one look
I'm a big-mouth bass
Caught on her hook
Just a big-mouth bass
Caught on her hook.

Connie hurtled toward a small bridge over a creek that might even have existed before the nature trail had been constructed around it. The River Runners switched gears, wading into "Solace" and its soft country wash of slide guitar and Hammond organ:

Lord, what can I do
To be free of this pain?
I come to this river
Again and again
And I search for your solace
I pray for your hand
Still I'm all alone
In this desolate land.

She slowed her pace, recalibrating her stride with the tempo. The song was quiet enough that she could hear her shoes smacking the pavement. She grimaced as the subtext of the lyric registered in her consciousness.

True that.

Living in San Francisco for so long made her hometown seem tiny and small-minded by comparison, full of people with one eye trained on the past and the other on their fussily landscaped lawns.

Years ago when she had brought Amanda to visit her grandparents, Connie had taken her over to her old elementary school to play. It was mid-July and oppressively humid, precisely the weather she thanked God she didn't have to endure in California. They took the same path Connie had followed for six years as a student, staying well to the side of the busy road until the sidewalk materialized to take them the rest of the way. They cut across the athletic field, which had been so newly carved from the existing meadows and woods when she started kindergarten that the killdeer were still nesting in the grass and gym class had to be relocated for weeks until the chicks fledged.

Before hanging a left onto the walking trail through the remaining trees, they found a freshly painted United States map on the blacktop donated by the Kiwanis Club. The plot of blue, red, green and yellow states fascinated five-year-old Amanda.

"Where do we live, Mama?"

"In California. See, on the left? That little notch there at the elbow, that's San Francisco. That's where Daddy is now, at work." Amanda placed her feet over the bay.

"Where does Grandpa George live?"

"He lives in Oregon. That's where Daddy grew up."

Amanda turned north and leaped over the border to stand on top of Portland.

"How about Uncle Andrew?"

"He's in Colorado, that square state there." Amanda cleared the Rockies easily and landed on Denver with both feet.

"Where does Grandma Sue live?"

"Virginia. That's where we are now, sweetie. See this big star here?"

Amanda eyed the star from her spot on the other side of the country and turned very serious. "I can't go there."

"Why's that?"

"I can't jump that far."

Connie winced at the memory.

Amanda's right: I made a huge mistake coming back here. I was impulsive and wrong.

Connie dodged a fat dog turd and picked up speed, urged along by Stee:

Gotta get my head screwed on straight

Make some hard decisions—

What I'm willing to lose

So I can win.

Half a mile left, and it was up a manufactured hill, barely a speed bump compared to the rollercoaster inclines of San Francisco but enough to make her legs wail at this pace. Stee and the boys pounded away at the final verse of the final song, propelling her forward:

Don't stop—nah, don't stop

Don't stop, baby—no, never stop

Blowing air through her clenched teeth, her arms slicing forward and back with her palms flat and her knees kicking out, she tore through the final yards of the course.

Do it for you, baby

Nah, nah—never stop.

The Squeezebox went silent, and Connie slowed to a walk, pinching her intercostal muscles with her fingers and gulping air as she returned to the starting point of the looping trail once more.

Thanks, Stee.

She shook out her damp hair and wobbled back to the house. She walked in the back door and slipped off her running shoes and socks to let them air out. She tore off her t-shirt and pitched it on top of the washer. Seconds after she grabbed her water bottle, Amanda stopped her in the hallway.

"Mom—your phone."

Connie's ragged expression didn't stop Amanda from pushing the cell phone into her mother's damp hand. She put it to her ear without checking the caller ID and answered abruptly.

"Hello."

"Hey, Connie—is this Connie Rafferty?"

"Yes."

"It's Stee. Stee Walsh."

Connie's eyes went really wide and any moisture in her mouth evaporated.

"Stee ... Walsh?"

"Yeah, it's me. How're you doin'?"

Connie frantically fished for a towel in the bathroom closet and swabbed herself so she wouldn't lose the call in a pool of sweat.

"I'm fine."

"You sound a little out of breath." He sounded a touch embarrassed. "I'm not interrupting anything, am I?"

Connie checked herself in the mirror, then felt like a dope since there was no way he could see her. Given that she was standing there in a sodden running bra and sagging athletic shorts, she thanked God for that.

"I was out for a run."

"Oh, you're a runner," Stee offered, apparently glad to have an entry back into the conversation. "I never got into it and now my knee won't let me. Swimming's more my thing."

"Good for you." She sat on the toilet seat, trying to clear her head enough to be able to form a coherent sentence. "Not that I'm not glad you called, but ... why did you call me?"

"Well, I figured at this point it would be cheaper if we just had a phone call; all that postage was beginning to add up." He sounded cheerful, his Southern accent plucky. Connie idly pictured one of the photos she'd brought up in a recent image search of Stee's early days. He was smiling at the right corner of his mouth in that shot, his navy blue eyes full of mischief.

"And the CDs. Thank you so much for sending them but really, you don't have to—"

"You direct videos, right? Well, in your professional opinion, should I do a music video for my new album?"

She nearly dropped the phone. "Could you please repeat that?"

Stee cleared his throat. "I mean, I've always liked doing videos but they cost a fuck—sorry—they cost a fortune outta my own pocket and I'm not sure it's worth footing the bill for them."

"With YouTube, video's more relevant than it's been in years," Connie offered, "and digital's so cheap you could get a film-quality piece for a fraction of what it cost you in the Eighties."

"Huh."

"And if you leave out all of the flying zombies and stupid shit, you'll save even more." Once the words were spoken, Connie clamped her hand over her mouth.

"Care to elaborate?" Stee asked with a tone impossible to evaluate over the phone: he might have been checking his temper or stifling a laugh.

Connie ventured back in. "I have to be honest with you: the 'Shut Up Already' video was ridiculous. I mean, your *arms* falling off? Then that 'clank' and you looking at your crotch and shrugging at the camera? The visuals cheapened the lyrics. It killed the song for me; for years I'd turn the dial if I heard it on the radio."

"Huh."

She fully expected to hear a click on the other end of the phone and never get a call from Stee Walsh again. Instead, she heard,

"You sold me. You're hired."

"Uh, what?"

"I want you to create a video for the new album."

Connie's throat nearly closed up. "Stee, I'm beyond flattered but I just insulted your most popular video. How do you know I'd do something you'd be happy with?"

"Challenging my ideas is a good way to start," he said. "You won't let me get away with crap just because I think it'll look cool."

"But you've never even seen my work."

"I *have* seen your work."

"Were you at a bridal shower I missed?"

"I took a look at your portfolio."

The bubbles in her belly multiplied; she felt like a shaken can of Coke.

"Besides, you've already done a video for one of my songs."

It took her a moment. "You watched the orphan drug piece?"

"That's the one." He sang the first couple of lines of "Come On Up," prompting Connie to babble.

"That was such a train wreck. The rain was relentless. The doctor we wanted to talk to was getting over malaria. It was—"

"Hey, relax," Stee interjected. "I like it. I really like it. Shit, I even sent those guys a check."

"Thank you." Her relief was palpable, and his enthusiasm was unstinting.

"So, you'll do my video then?"

She sat back on the bed and crossed her legs. "Stee, corporate pieces are a different beast than music videos. Besides, you can get a *real* director to do this—Michael Gondry or Spike Jonze or maybe David Fincher. I'm not the right person for the job."

There was an irritated huff. "I like your work, and you told me that you can deliver a video for a little bit of money. Why wouldn't I hire you? And shit, you're a fan. Don't you want to hear one of my new songs before anyone else? What's wrong with you, missy?"

What's wrong with me, indeed?

"Okay, I accept."

"That's great—just great!" Stee sounded relieved and a little glee-ful. "So we'll meet for dinner tonight and get this started."

"You're in town?"

"More or less. Devon County."

She processed this. "Wait, you haven't been back to Virginia in something like thirty years."

There was a brief sigh. "Something like that."

"Why are you out here?"

"Let's not change the subject. I called to ask you to dinner. You free?"

He's asking me out. Jesus H. Christ ...

"You better say yes or I'll write a song about flying zombies just to spite you."

She smiled. "Okay, fine. Anything but that."

chapter 6

I should just wait in the car. The smoke is driving me crazy.

Connie sat in a sticky wooden booth at Sweet Dreams, shelling peanuts and chucking the hulls into a brown plastic checkerboard bowl. The roadhouse earned the authenticity that dozens of theme restaurants aspired to. It was full of junk placed just so by someone who knew the origin of each piece, mostly souvenirs of Patsy Cline concerts from half a century before: ticket stubs, posters, a hand-written song list. The air was oily with the odor of fried fish and hush puppies.

It was almost 7:30 on a Friday night. A smattering of regulars sat at the bar; a couple of teenaged boys circled the pool table, cigarettes dangling from their mouths. A pair of waitresses hustled between the kitchen and the tables, looking as if they had been on since the breakfast shift. Thanks to recent coaching from Stee's CDs, she could pick out Johnny Cash on the jukebox, then Ray Charles, followed by Buck Owens.

Connie fidgeted with the skirt of her blue wrap dress, feeling con-spicuously overdressed and tamping down the sickening anticipa-tion she had experienced only a couple of times before: Christmas in eighth grade when she was pretty sure her next present was a Super 8 camera, and a few moments before she walked down the aisle.

Each time the front screen door swung open, Connie would crane her neck, then quickly retract it when the door banged shut. Two rounds of diet Coke had made her jittery, and she desperately wanted something to calm her nerves, but she figured it wouldn't be a great idea to have a beer before meeting someone whose public struggles with sobriety inspired "Recover You," one of the darker tracks from her favorite of Stee's albums, *Santa Monica Pier*. She hummed the lyrics under her breath to give herself something to do.

I shift my life to sober truth
I make my amends one by one
If you ever forgive all the bad things I've done
I might recover you.

The doors swung open once more. Connie's heart flew into her throat.

Oh my God, there he is, THERE HE IS!

And,

Old ... he's so OLD!

It was an ice-cold shock to see Stee Walsh—the fierce, fire-haired, skinny boy she expected to materialize straight off the cover of *Double Down*—in the present-day flesh: an exhausted fifty-nine year-old with a gut sloping over his waistband, thinning hair more buff-colored than red, a grizzled beard masking his wattle, and his infamous blue eyes obscured by a chronic case of crow's feet. Giving him a second look, though, she had to admit he looked a lot better than most of the musicians who shared his age and pharmaceutical history. Connie drew a steadying breath and waved him over.

Stee stuck out his hand. "Sorry I'm late; got lost driving around these parts after all these years." Connie's stomach dipped as he settled into the seat across from her.

Even in this light, his eyes are really dark blue ... that's so eerie.

"So, Connie Rafferty in the flesh," he said with a wide smile. "Good to meet you."

"Same here," Connie offered, determined to keep the conversation light rather than let her nerves overwhelm her until she vomited into her purse. "This is a great place."

"The owner is an old friend of my momma's family," Stee replied. "He used to play with Patsy and even recorded with her a couple of times. He still stops by to play now and again."

"There aren't any menus."

"Never have been. They just tell you what they're bringing you. If you come here during hunting season, you get whatever they bagged that day."

"If only it were hunting season," Connie said gamely.

Stee shook his head. "Be glad it isn't. I swear once they served us a plate of skunk."

A weather-beaten waitress shuffled over to the table but brightened when she saw Stee. "Hey, city boy!"

"Marla!" Stee stood and gave the waitress a friendly hug. "I can't believe you waited for me all this time. How you been? How's your daughter?"

Connie stayed in her seat as they updated each other on their family's history in broad strokes. Stee introduced her to Marla as a "friend," which was probably easier to say than trying to define what all the emails and Post-its added up to. Marla wiped the wet rings off the table with a yellowing rag.

"We got some whitefish tonight and pork chops. If you want a burger, we can do one or two, but we're running low on onions so put your order in for rings now."

Stee motioned for Connie to lead off. "I'd like the pork chop, please."

"You want another Diet?" Connie agreed, even as the aspartame was burning a hole in her nervous gut. The waitress faced Stee. "For you?"

"A pork chop for me as well, Marla, and some ice water, please. And we'll take an order of the rings, too." He looked at Connie and nodded. "Trust me, you'll want some."

Their waitress hauled back to the kitchen and Stee relaxed into his corner of the booth, his arm looped over the back of the seat. He, too, had overdressed for dinner, sporting a leather jacket that cost more than a month's pay for most of the rest of the patrons. She searched his frame for a shadow of the hungry young man pictured in the *River Runner Rarities* booklet, maybe across the shoulders or around the wrists.

"Hey, I know I'm not good-looking but there's no need to stare."

"Sorry!" Reddening, Connie clamped her mouth shut.

Stee's nonchalance didn't help. "It's better to be born ugly. The older you get, the better you look compared to all those pretty people who don't age well. I mean, who's the cute Beatle now: Paul McCartney or Ringo Starr?"

"It's not that. It's just I can't believe I'm sitting in front of you, of all people. It's too unreal."

"For me, too. I'm amazed a lady as pretty as you is free on a Friday night." Stee's charm might have been standard issue for every woman he met but Connie appreciated it anyway. A smile curling the right corner of his mouth, he leaned in. "You're the only person in the world who thinks my music is elegant. I had to meet you."

"I meant what I wrote."

"I could tell. Thank you." His eyes stayed on her for a couple of moments until he plucked a peanut out of the bowl and snapped it between his fingers. "So, let's get better acquainted. How about you tell me all about Ms. Connie Rafferty?"

"Shouldn't we talk about the video?"

"We have all the time in the world, darlin'. I don't have any other commitments tonight. Do you?"

"I'm all yours."

"Good to hear."

Unable to remember a single fact about herself with him staring at her, she took a different tack. "No, you first. Why did you come back to Virginia after thirty years?"

He cracked open the other half of the peanut. "What have you heard?"

"That Live Nation offered you five million dollars to open your tour at the Hampton Coliseum next year, since that was where you played your last Virginia concert there thirty years ago."

He shook his head. "It was more like a half-million, which wasn't exactly enough of an enticement."

"So what's the real reason?"

"Family."

That phrase rang a bell. Connie got a quizzical look every (single damn) time someone learned she had moved back to Richmond from San Francisco.

"Why the hell would you leave San Francisco and come here?"

After weeks of practice, she had now pared the messy list of reasons into a universally understood and airily compact answer:

"Family."

That usually earned her a word of consolation:

"Oh."

"Really?" Connie responded. "You still have people out here?"

"My brother lives up in Fredericksburg with his wife and granddaughter. Thing is, I'm not out here just to see them. My manager suggested I come out here for a change of scene. Return to my roots. Figure out what's really important. Open a closet and see what skeletons fall out."

"What do you hope to find?"

"Clarity." His steely eyes darkened briefly before he tossed a handful of shells into the bowl. "Whatever. I don't care as long as I get an album out of it because I'm sick as shit of waiting for lightning to strike and nothing happening. Enough about me. What brought *you* back to Virginia? What are you hoping for?"

"Direction, I guess. This last year, I've been unmoored."

He shook his head. "I can't imagine what you've gone through since your husband died. That's got to be just awful, especially for your daughter. My condolences."

"Thanks." She took a deep draught of her diet Coke, wishing it were straight bourbon. "It's been a journey."

"I'll bet. Not to get too personal, but in your email you mentioned a betrayal. That have anything to do with you coming back here?"

"I'm not sure that's something I should be discussing with my client."

"Sorry. I forgot this is a production meeting."

She answered his smile with one of her own. "Let's get the business part of the evening taken care of so we can get back to talking.

What's the title of the song?"

"Don't know yet."

"What's it about?"

"Don't know yet. It isn't written."

Her gut tightened. "You want me to do a video for a song that doesn't exist?"

"It will exist. It has to. I've never missed a deadline and I'm not about to now."

"When does the video have to be finished?"

"First week of June."

"Where is it going to air?"

"You know I have this Stee Walsh signature Squeezebox thing coming out in October, right? This would be the lead video on that gizmo."

She nearly swallowed her straw. "You're going to sell it? I thought this was just going to be online."

"Nope. It'll be the newest addition to my historically significant and oh so influential music video library." He caught her eye. "You okay with that?"

"What do you mean?"

"With the stuff I've seen of yours, I'm sure you're up for the challenge, but watching you twisting your napkin right now, I'm not sure you agree with me."

Placing her napkin on the table, she crossed her arms and sat up straight. "I'll do you proud, Stee."

"That's what I wanted to hear. Here's to making great art." He raised his water glass, which Connie clinked with her diet Coke. He grinned. "Whew, the business meeting's over. May I buy you a drink—a real one, with alcohol and everything?"

"A beer would be great. Thank you."

He called out to the kitchen. "Hey Marla, can you open a beer for Connie when you come back out? And some more water for me, please."

"No problem, Stee," came the muffled reply.

He turned back to her. "That's a pretty dress, by the way. The blue, the cut of it—it looks good on you."

"Thank you, but looking around, I should have worn jeans."

"Trust me: every man in this place is glad you wore the dress."

Connie laughed self-consciously. Pleased with himself, Stee took the beer from Marla's tray and passed it over. "I can't believe a bright, artsy woman like you never bought a record before now."

"I bought records, and CDs, too. I just didn't buy a lot of them."

"What was the first one you bought with your own money?"

"Billy Joel. *The Stranger*."

That earned her a guffaw. "You're not serious."

"Why wouldn't I be?"

Stee's eyes narrowed. "Maybe I don't want you to like my music. I'm beginning to question your taste."

"What's wrong with Billy Joel? He was a huge rock star."

"He was never a rock star, Connie. Pop, maybe."

"He won all those Grammys."

"Grammys are a fraud."

"You've won Grammys."

"Well, all except *those* Grammys."

"What is your beef with Billy Joel?"

"The way I see it, Billy tried way too hard to be taken seriously by the critics," Stee said, nabbing another peanut. "It bugged him that so many of them turned up their noses and that pissy attitude came through in his songs. I mean, I take my music seriously, but I don't take *myself* making that music all that seriously."

"Huh." She took a peanut as well. "I still don't get it."

"I never played music to become a star or get rich. I played music because it was all I was any good at. I was a skinny loser catching hell from my father and this close to getting kicked out of high school. Being in a band gave me friends and girls and a ticket outta Richmond. I've been lucky enough to make a living out of it—an incredibly good living—and I'm grateful, but people are fickle and times change and no one really owes me anything and the fame could all be gone tomorrow. But the music will still be around, and it still makes me feel good to write it and play it with my friends for my fans, which is more important than making some critic respect me."

He held her gaze for a moment, waiting for her response.

He may just be the most authentic person I've ever met.

Or, he might have said that a million times before.

"You didn't answer my question. What is wrong with liking Billy Joel? I mean, as amazing and heartfelt as your music is, there are thousands of people who don't like your stuff. It's a free country, right?"

He chuckled, holding up his hands in capitulation. "You're right. Who can say why a song hits you the way it does? It's like falling in love with a person: you can't explain it and you shouldn't have to apologize for it." He cleared his throat. "I mean, can you explain why you suddenly started buying my records?"

"After losing my husband, I needed a companion, I guess. I wasn't thinking about it like that when I started listening to your music, but once I listened to that first song, I wanted to hear what else you had to say. I wanted to keep the conversation going, one song at a time." She tilted her head. "Why have you been sending me so many CDs by other musicians?"

"I figured you needed to know what really good music sounded like."

"Your music isn't good enough?"

"If I'm all that's in your library, you're missing out on a lot. And maybe we'd have more to talk about."

"I'm sure we'd have plenty to talk about no matter what, Stee."

Marla was back, her arms laden with dinner plates. Connie began to tear through her chops and collards, wondering if Stee was going to let that statement just lie there.

Apparently not. "I'm sure we would. Now here's something I could talk about all day. What is your favorite Stee Walsh song?"

"Can I have more than one?"

"Shit—no! Just answer the question," he retorted good-naturedly, scooping up a forkful of apples. "Don't make this so complicated."

"Well, I guess it would have to be 'Someday.'"

"I always liked Larry's solo on that record. It's hard to play organ on a ballad without being too churchy. He nailed it."

"It's my go-to song when I'm feeling depressed. Your vocal is heartbreaking. You sound so lonely."

He winced. "Let me level with you: I deserved to be alone. I was a fucked-up drunk of no use to my wife and kids. Fact is, I didn't send Tamara away—*she* left *me*. She put all my shit in my studio and padlocked it while I was on tour with Bonnie Raitt. I wasn't allowed to see my girls again until I went through rehab. I was ashamed of myself and angry at her, so I took some artistic license to make me look like a broken hero, and 'Someday' was born."

He put down his fork. "My songs are works of fiction. A lot of people forget that and assume I'm the good guy I make myself out to be." Perhaps sensing her disappointment, he sheepishly looked at the floor. "You probably want to switch over to being a U2 fan. Take it from me, Bono's a saint."

"Are you kidding?" she blurted. "I've spent way too much money on your songs."

"And I've spent too much money on CDs trying to teach you to be a respectable music fan. So I guess we've got to stick this out a little longer, don't we?"

She nodded. "Pass the cornbread, please."

———

Long after the plates were cleared, but much sooner than Stee would have liked, Connie glanced at her watch. "I'd better go. My daughter is waiting up for me."

Stee waved her off. "She's sixteen, she probably isn't even home."

As Connie fished her keys out of her purse, she stopped. "Did I tell you how old Amanda is?"

Stee's blood froze.

Fucking Leonard.

She grinned. "Good guess!"

That was close.

Stee stood up, put a few twenties on the table, waved to Marla, then escorted Connie to her car. The black sky was full of stars that hadn't been seen in Los Angeles since the saber-tooth tigers got sucked into La Brea.

"Stee, thank you for everything."

Connie clasped her purse in front of her in both hands, not making a move toward him. Stee knew that if he wasn't famous—if he were a teacher or a hardware store manager, or anyone but *him*—she would have hugged him good-bye without hesitation. Quickly taking the lead, he gave her a squeeze and a peck on the cheek, whispering, "It's a pleasure to know you're part of the world, Connie."

"Likewise. Thanks for the best production meeting I've ever had." She hugged him back, her body fitting nicely into his. Her perfume lingered as Stee watched her car disappear down the gravel road.

Jasmine.

He got into his rental car but didn't start the ignition. Words were beginning to rattle around in Stee's head. He closed his eyes to put them into some sort of order:

Though I do not know you

You're so lonely the darkness might enfold you

His eyes wide open, Stee rifled through the glove box. Frustrated, he smacked the release button for the center armrest. Coming up empty again, he tore through the pocket of the rental car's door, growling with supreme aggravation.

A notebook. I need a fucking notebook!

––––––

It was after midnight. Stee's adrenaline had started percolating once the shell of the song had manifested itself in the Sweet Dreams parking lot, sparked by the scent of jasmine and the smile of her body curving into his as they hugged good-bye.

He pulled out his ancient Gibson Country Western from its beaten case and propped it up against his grandmother's upright piano, a fixture in the parlor even after his sister-in-law's redecoration. After hobbling up the stairs to nab his trusty notebook and pen out of the guest room, he patted his pockets to locate the cocktail napkins he had to beg off of Marla to scribble out his initial thoughts, using a golf pencil that had been stuck down in the passenger side door. They were nowhere on his person. He started to panic until he remembered he had put the napkins on the shelf at the front door with his sunglasses when he came in. He retrieved them, put on his bifocals, and took a deep breath.

He transcribed his napkin notes into the notebook, making slight edits as he went:

I'm tired of throwing good love after bad
I need a new love, better than what I've had
I'll keep on trying, until I perfect it
If I keep my mouth shut and my eyes wide open
I know I'll find love—at least, that's what I'm hopin'
It'll be there, where I least expect it
In unexpected places

The tactile pleasure of carving words into the paper was proof positive he was making progress. He read the first verse out loud, tapping out the syllables with his pen to make sure beats fell in step. He stared at the page and scribbled the next in a burst of quick, short strokes:

You are out there, and though I do not know you,
You're so lonely the darkness might enfold you,
Lost and longing for a light you cannot see.
No longer young, I might be hard to handle
But my heart burns bright. It glows just like a candle
Lighting your way here, beck'ning you to me.
In unexpected places

A melody was beginning to surface. The guitar cradled in his lap now, he channeled the tune through the strings at his fingers, the words embedding themselves into the chords.

Thing was, there was a competing rhythm jangling around his brain as well: the *kaCHUNK, kaCHUNK, kaCHUNK, kaWHOMP* of the tires bumping along the breaks in the highway pavement he heard on the way home. It wasn't an easy fit for the romantic lyrics he was crafting, but he didn't want to lose it. What to do?

Stay with the lyric; notate the chords. Don't break your stride, Stee.

Tabling the competing rhythm for the time being, he rolled his pen in his fingers until he got back into the lyrical groove.

Snow on a rocky ledge, a flower at my feet
Birds at the water's edge—they'd make my soul complete
If you were here, if you could be here
To discover them with me.

This is where he would normally fill in a third verse, but this time he let the song flow to a stop:

Their gentle, easy grace is
Lovely like your face is
I know I will find you, love
In unexpected places

Stee propped up the notebook on the piano and sang the song from start to finish, strumming the nascent melody and getting more joyous as he went along. The final words left his lips and he whooped.

"I'M BAAAACK!"

On the page before him was his first completely original song in five long, dormant years. What's more, this song was different. Stee had told a reporter once that he really only wrote three types of songs. In the first, a kid tries to sweet-talk a pretty girl into submission; he can't impress her with his looks or his wallet, so he bowls her over with his charm. In the second, a broken man watches the best part of his life walk out the door, either because she found someone better (or richer) or because he'd screwed up so royally, she'd rather be alone for life than spend one more minute with him. The third kind was a string of words that tumbled out of his mouth one day in the studio, and, because the engineer had pressed Record, it became a song that somehow got airplay. (How else to explain "Come, Come, Come"?)

This song was none of the above. It was meatier, deeper, more complex than his usual material. It resonated in a different part of his body.

Huh.

He hummed through it again to make sure it was as strong as he initially thought. Yep, it had bones—and there was one person to thank for this.

"Connie," he told the air above him, "I could kiss you!"

Suddenly, Stee's insides went cold.

What is she going to think when she hears this?

Even after all that talk at dinner about his songs being works of fiction, there was no way Connie wouldn't know this one was about her. Worse, given how the last verse played out, she might think he fell in love with her after talking to her for all of three hours.

Which just can't be true.

From what he observed, Connie was an unsentimental woman who couldn't possibly believe that that love-at-first-sight thing existed, reinforcing his stance that his lyrics were inspired by true events but were ultimately make-believe. Therefore, the song couldn't possibly be about the two of them.

Ipso facto and all that shit.

He toyed with experimenting with the rumbling rhythm he'd taken home with him from the drive back, but his adrenaline was dissipating. He was going to need to call in reinforcements to get back on track. He pressed speed dial number 3 on his phone.

"Hello, this is Angela Kinney. How may I—oh, it's you."

"Angie! Why so formal? You know it's me."

"I dunno, Stee … sometimes I wonder if it'll be the coroner."

"You're such an optimist," Stee said affectionately.

"It must be late out there. What may I do for you before you toddle off to bed?"

"How old do you think I am, Angela?" Stee protested in mock outrage. "Who says I'm going to bed?"

"Why would you stay up?" Angela dryly replied. "You're in the middle of nowhere and it's not like you've got 'company' out there."

"I'm not going to dignify that remark with a reply, Angela. I need you to track down our friend Chad and get him out to Virginia quick."

"I have his tour schedule here." Stee heard the faint clicks of her mouse. "He's in Chicago. He could come out on Wednesday, if he doesn't have other plans."

"I need him sooner."

She paused. "Stee, this might be easier if you go to Chicago. Your time is more flexible than his. I could reserve a studio."

Stee considered this. Angela was completely right but Stee was never so superstitious as he was during the creation of a new album. Connie had just been designated his good luck charm. He didn't want to risk being too far away from her in case he needed another shot of inspiration.

"Hate to pull the boss card on him, Angela. I need Chad here at the farmhouse; we don't need a studio. I don't want him to miss gigs; we can turn him around in 48 hours."

He could hear Angela exhaling in irritation. "Fine. I'll give him a buzz. Do you want me to call you or send you an email once I hear from him?"

"Uh, sure." Stee yawned.

"Which one, Stee: phone or email?"

"Sorry. Just call me tomorrow morning. I'm not going anywhere."

"Anything else?" Angela asked flatly.

"Nope, all set. Angie, you're a blessing."

"Yes, I am. Goodnight, boss."

chapter 7

As the limo driver rattled away from the farmhouse down the gravel road to meander back to Route 33, Chad Haines placed his guitar inside the storm door and his shades in a silk-lined case in the inside pocket of his cashmere jacket. He took in a 180-degree view of the front porch, noting the outsized collection of ceramic pigs, a butter churn and a three-foot-tall scarecrow, its hands made of child-sized gardening gloves, holding a calico-trimmed sign reading, "Howdy, Neighbor!"

Chad ran his fingers through his thick silver hair and sucked in his cheeks.

You better have written the next "Layla," Stee. You dragged me back to Hooterville.

Stee rushed out of the kitchen, wiping his hands on a yellow dishtowel. "How you doing, brother? Good to see you!" he bellowed, joyously grabbing him and slapping him on the back.

"Good to see you, too, Stee." Chad embraced him, surprised and relieved to find him so upbeat. Stee was not an effusive sort; even with close friends, he usually kept his delight in check. Joyousness could only mean good things after months—years—of stagnation.

He's written something.

Stee hauled Chad's luggage next to the stairs, wheeling the packing case with the amp inside the house. "Flight okay?"

"No problems," Chad replied, catching a glimpse of the bathroom. It had been vastly updated since he visited Stee's grandparents decades ago, when he had bathed in a zinc washtub in the middle of the cracked linoleum floor filled with hot water off the kitchen stove.

Stee took his silence for interest. "C'mon, let me show you what my money and Duane's muscle did for the place."

Chad followed Stee up the stairs and peeked at the master suite and extra bedrooms, the four and a half baths, and the landing outside the French doors at the end of the hallway "with a view of the plantation," as Stee jokingly described it. He continued to give his guest the nickel tour downstairs, pointing out a family heirloom here and an ancient photo there, and then waved Chad into the kitchen.

"What can I get you? Iced tea? Lemonade?"

"Tea's fine, Stee. When in Rome ..."

Stee chuckled. "You probably never thought you'd come back to visit this part of the country, did you?"

"No, I did not," Chad admitted, leaning a shoulder against the door jamb.

"Shit, have a glass of tea and your accent will come back."

Chad couldn't quite absorb what he was seeing. Here was Stee Walsh, a man who bragged about never having to do so much as peel a banana since he hit it big, busying himself in the kitchen like a pumps-and-pearls housewife from a Fifties sitcom, and obviously delighted by the task.

He's definitely got something good.

Stee pulled some cheese out of the refrigerator. "How's the tour going?"

"We're selling well. John Mayer hooked up with us for the last few dates. He's bringing in the crowds where we can't."

"Good," Stee remarked, tossing some crackers into a small basket. "He called Daniel a few weeks back. I was hoping he'd track you down. How's he to play with?"

Chad shrugged. "He's got the blues chops and can sing his way through our sets, I'll give him that. Can't say it's been perfect; he's a little too eager to take the lead, the groupies are particularly drippy, and I found a photographer holed up in our bathroom."

"Brings back memories, don't it?"

"Yeah, brother, it does."

Stee motioned Chad into the living room, placing the tray of food and beverages on the coffee table. Chad removed his jacket, folding it neatly over the back of an armchair, and arranged himself on the couch. While Stee had gone to seed after years of high living and poor choices, Chad had remained as tall and slim as the nineteen-year-old with the sideburns and bolo tie he had been when Stee first met him playing at Rodeo Ribs in Raleigh. As his finances improved, Chad's drawl disappeared and his tastes in clothes and accessories refined. Luckily, he inhabited the patrician lifestyle effortlessly. He never came off as phony; it was truly who he had become.

Make no mistake, though: with a guitar in his hands, Chad was a Southern son of a bitch to be reckoned with.

"It's Manchego," Stee said, pushing a platter toward his guest. "They make it three farms over. If my grandfather knew they were making Spanish cheese out of Virginia sheep's milk these days, he would have thought Teddy Roosevelt lost the war in Cuba.. Try it; it's good."

Chad sliced off a piece and took a bite. "You're right, it's really good." Stee beamed as if he had milked the sheep himself.

Chad chewed slowly, eyeing his partner. "You look like you're about to bust. Writing going well?"

"I'm back!" Stee declared, leaning forward on the edge of a bentwood rocker. "I got a working title for the album: *Unexpected Places*. It's about how life takes you where you never imagined you'd go. It's about finding love where you never expected it. It's about appreciating what's around you that you never see."

"How'd you come up with the idea?"

Stee cut his eyes to the floor. "Someone I met."

"Out here?"

"Yeah."

"Female?"

"Obviously."

Chad grunted. "What've you got so far?"

"I have a ballad to cruise you through, and I'm thinking about using Chuck Berry for our past masters' slot this time: 'Too Much Monkey

Business.' God knows he ended up in places *he* didn't expect."

"Jail, for instance." Chad considered this as he assembled another cheese and cracker combo. "Any overall sound you're hearing?"

"Breaking new ground by celebrating the old, I guess. I'm hoping to use your banjo and steel pedal skills; still haven't written a song that would need 'em, but there's one out there waiting for you and me to find it."

The two things Chad possessed when he extricated himself from that North Carolina trailer park were his unshakable determination to better his life and his uncanny ability to play any style of music on anything with strings, usually after a single hearing. He had amassed an army of axes and a United Nations of instruments—balalaika, ukulele, mandolin, lute, pipa, sitar—and was expert in pretty much all of them.

"Is Jonegon on board?"

Stee nodded. "Jon's been waiting to talk to us once we had a concept. Good thing he's producing this; he's got the roots sound down cold."

Chad mulled over the title, resting his head on the back of the couch. He stared at the ceiling fan circling slowly: CLICK-up, CLICK-up. It crackled like a record stuck in a groove, a 78 full of dust.

"Maybe we can open one song with an old blues record playing in the background—you can hear the needle set down on the platter ..."

"Then you take up the melody," Stee chimed, "with the rest of us building around it one by one. That'll work."

"That's what I was hearing," Chad said, suddenly yawning like a jungle cat.

"Where are my manners?" Stee said, rolling his eyes to the heavens. "You probably wanna rest and get settled. We've got how long until you fly back?"

"Twenty hours, give or take a meal or a nap."

Stee stood. "I'll give you a few minutes, then let me play you a ditty I'm particularly proud of by the name of 'Unexpected Places.'"

Stee offered up an acoustic version of the title track, which Chad greeted with total silence—a good sign, as he got lost in thought when he really liked something. Before bed, Stee played Chuck Berry's Chess recording of "Too Much Monkey Business" for Chad off his computer; he digested it quickly and laid down his own version of it, sans vocals, the next morning before Stee was even out of the shower. Stee added the vocal and bass in separate takes, then labeled the tape and put it in his carry-on bag.

As Stee prepped a fresh tape, he called over to Chad, "Lemme hear what you were thinking about with that 78 blues record idea."

Chad went back into the living room and hit a switch on the wall. CLICK-*up*, CLICK-*up*.

"Stee, can you get a mic on the fan by any chance?"

By the time they rigged the microphone with a bent wire coat hanger and several loops of duct tape so it wouldn't get chopped to ribbons by the fan, they were starving. They grabbed some of his sister-in-law's leftovers, then were back at it. Chad unleashed an up-tempo blues line he had been crafting during his solo stint of the past few months. After weeks of headlining, he was eager to take over the songwriting duties, for one song, anyway.

Stee had no issue with that. "Hoo, that's good, Chad. John Mayer teach you that?"

Chad frisbeed a sofa pillow at Stee's head. "Maybe John should do vocals on this one, smartass." Stee guffawed.

As their hours together dwindled, the two men lolled on the sofas in the living room, tossing around ideas, hoping one or more would stick.

"I'm thinking, you're rummaging through the attic of this place here," Chad suggested, waving toward the ceiling, "and you come across something that strikes a chord ... a box of records, maybe."

"I'm tired of music about music, aren't you?" Stee responded. "Folks listening to our songs already know how important music is to us … that's kind of why we exist, right?"

"Well, if you want to be pedantic about it," Chad huffed.

"*Pedantic*. Listen to you," Stee snickered. "You been learnin' those big words offa NPR or somethin'?"

Chad whiffed a *Reader's Digest* across the room so it landed in Stee's lap. "Look it up, Stee—it's in 'Increase Your Word Power.'"

Stee hooted, then returned to the job at hand. "Okay, maybe we could use the attic idea … finding a photograph you wouldn't expect. One of your mom with someone other than your dad, before they got married—or while they *were* married. Maybe a bunch of pressed flowers."

"You could make something out of that," Chad agreed. "A mom with dreams she didn't achieve—"

"So she begs her kids to follow theirs," Stee added, "like, maybe, uh:"

Her yearbook promised dreams ahead
And then she lived her life
She shelved the dreams to be instead
A quiet, patient wife
And I remember what she said
Just leave and don't turn back
That is what I say to you.
Do as I say, not as I do.
You follow your own track.

Chad parsed this silently, still amazed after all these years that Stee could open his mouth and a fully formed song would fall out. He also wondered if his friend realized how much of his past he had thrown out into the open.

"You invested in these lyrics, Stee?"

"Depends. Do you like them?"

"Write them down; it's an idea to revisit," Chad replied.

"Yeah, I hear you," Stee said, scribbling in his notebook.

"We need a 'gotta get a girl' song, Stee."

Stee was only half in the conversation, racing to get the words and chords down before they were lost to the universe. "Maybe the girl's gotta get me this time around."

"Maybe." Chad closed his eyes. "I hate to tell you this, but I'm tapped out and the car's going to show up in a couple of hours. I have a gig tonight. I gotta rest."

"Fine." Stee was understanding but perturbed. He'd hoped against hope they could crank out a dozen songs in two days and have the album all wrapped in a bow by the time they showed up at Jon Jonegon's door. It was not to be.

———————

Create a video for a song that doesn't even exist.

What have I gotten myself into?

Unable to start the project her client had hired her to do, Connie spent the afternoon surfing YouTube on a mission to cull each and every Stee Walsh moving image she could find: concert footage, interviews, other people's documentaries, even a couple of fan-created pieces that looked promising.

She watched his clips in rough chronological order. His voice had descended over time, his youthful reedy tenor settling into his tobacco-stained baritone by the mid-Nineties. His initial edginess and laser-eyed anger mellowed. By the time he had earned the right to perform with Eric Clapton and the rest of the rock-and-roll titans, he seemed secure enough to enjoy his place among them without being a jerk about it, which was refreshing.

She next pulled up *Garden Graveyard* off her Netflix queue. It was the one and only time he had acted in a major motion picture, and he had told her during their dinner meeting that it was dreadful. As she slogged through every one of its 148 minutes, she agreed; the movie was a poorly edited, precious mess. Still, Stee charmed his way through his role as a Confederate sergeant from the swamps teaching the rich plantation owner's son, played by Brendan Frasier, how to survive as a soldier.

He was being modest. He looks great on film.

He looks great.
She stood to clear her head.
Back to work.

Next up was his music video catalogue. They had been imprinted on her teenaged brain by MTV, but she hadn't seen them in decades. Watching them from a director's viewpoint, she admired how beautifully they were conceived, those music videos from the band's glory days: the day-to-night effect in "No Way Girl," the hailstorm of flowers in "Never You Fear." Her favorite was "Red Mustang." The longing in that girl's eyes searching the shabby suburban streets in the wan light for the boy who never came was devastating. Stee stood against a navy blue wall, with the effect that he was painted into the scene, unable to help her, his eyes awash in heartbreak as he mouthed the lyrics:

Driving over rocks and ruts
Reaming out the shocks and struts
Praying for a guy to come your way
In a red Mustang to take you away.
Keep on dreaming, baby.
It might come true.
It could be me
Coming for you.

The romance with a capital "R" washing over her made her wary. Sharing a meal with Stee, watching him push food onto his fork with his thumb and get crumbs in his beard, proved the guy was human. Yet time and time again, even in that little hideaway roadhouse with maybe twenty people there at any one time, he attracted attention from the farthest corners of the room. It wasn't even so much that folks recognized him as a famous singer. It was more that they were drawn to him without his doing a thing.

He was that kind of guy, the type who made each man feel more popular and every woman feel sexier just by saying hello. That's why Connie knew she'd have to be careful.

I can't let him use his magic on me.

Stee made his living off his charisma. Her husband had had that magic, too. It was what made her notice Chris in the first place when she was in a meeting with him at Tripton Reid. It was what made her feel all the more special when he asked her out and then fell in love with her: she had snagged him when so many others had failed. That assumption came back to haunt her later on when she found out about the other women, all of whom apparently were "special" to Chris, too.

I'm not special to Stee. So I can't let him be special to me, either.

She sighed.

Back to work.

chapter 8

Five down ... seven to go.

By four in the afternoon, Stee had penned another set of lyrics, written the lead sheets for two others and set the memory of his dinner with Connie on continuous repeat. The vision of her laughing at his jokes wrapped around his heart and kept it warm all day long.

Lovely.

He shook his head rapidly to refocus. He had to get to the business at hand.

Stee was a lot further along than he had been two weeks ago. He had a title, a concept and five songs written and/or demoed. At this early stage, he was even able to see an outline of the running order:

1. "Click, Click" (the working title for that blues number Chad had come up with)

2. "Unexpected Places"

3.

4.

5. "Ginny, Ginny, Ginny" (the song he conjured to take advantage of the chugging tire rhythm he'd heard on the way back from Sweet Dreams)

6.

7.

8. "Too Much Monkey Business"

9.

10. "Pressed Flowers" (that lyric he came up with for Chad in the farmhouse living room was showing potential)

11.

12.

He wrote out the list longhand and posted it on the corkboard next to the phone in the kitchen, using the guitar-shaped thumbtacks Maude had stuck in his Christmas stocking last year. Sometimes he could write songs better when he saw the holes in the lineup, even in this age of singles and shuffles when running order meant next to nothing.

He hit speed dial on his cell phone. "Hey, Angie?"

"Yessir," came the crackling reply.

"We need to get the studio booked, eight weeks out from now, okay? I'll need to meet up with Jon and the band a few days ahead of that for rehearsal."

His assistant sighed testily. "How many times do I have to go over this?"

"Over what?"

"The production schedule."

"Lemme guess: Jon's not available in eight weeks?"

"Your first masters are due to BetaComp in six."

Stee's jaw dropped. *"Six weeks?* Holy shit, Angie, why didn't you tell me sooner?"

"I told you before you went to the airport. It was part of your travel materials. It was in the daily email briefing I sent you. Daniel even texted both of us with his concerns."

I guess that must have been the one that said, "Time's a-wasting, prima donna" ...

Stee slumped against the doorframe. "Why the hell do they need them so early? It's not like they have to send records out to press or anything."

"Their Chinese manufacturer bought the titanium ore for the Squeezebox casings while it was cheap this spring, and they decided to move into production early."

"You're kidding."

"You know me better than that," Angela responded. "Do you want me to get Daniel on the line to verify it for you?"

Stee waved his hands in stunned panic. "No, no, no—the one person I don't want to talk to is Daniel right now. Let me think for a minute."

He pinched the bridge of his nose and squeezed his eyes shut. Six weeks: that was barely enough time to get everyone in one place, much less complete two songs, write seven others, and then rehearse, record and mix all twelve. *Santa Monica Pier*—his solo "rehab album"—took two years of nearly constant work, and that was mainly him and Chad rather than the whole band.

Doesn't matter what was, Stee—here's what is. It's not a problem; it's an opportunity, right?

Back then, he needed two years for *Santa Monica Pier* because he was determined to move away from the dissolute recordings of the late 1980s to create Important Work. This time around, he had a lot less to prove. If he wasn't aiming too high, six weeks could be plenty of time. Maybe an improvisational feel could take the weight out of his material. It could add back the fun of when he was first starting out and his first three albums came in torrents of songwriting and any idea turned into a great tune ... like when he wrote "Shoot Me Now" in the time it took between parking his car at the recording studio and walking in the front door.

He opened his eyes again, his jaw set and resolute. "Okay, six weeks it is then. Sorry to do this to you, Angie, but I need you to scramble the jets. We've got to get Jon and the boys ready to put this all down, and Chad's gonna have to do more heavy lifting as a co-producer if Jon's time is limited. Can you see where everyone is gonna be this month, and we'll rehearse in whatever town is the closest to the majority?"

"I can do all that, no problem," Angie said, "but can you actually have twelve songs done by then?"

"I don't have much choice, now do I?" Stee said quietly.

"Okay, I'm on it." Before hanging up, she softened. "Stee, album release dates move all the time. I'm sure Daniel can renegotiate with

BetaComp to give you a few more weeks, maybe until Christmas." Stee could tell she was worried. Her frostiness had thawed into an unusual emotion for her: genuine concern.

"I have to honor the contract, Angie," he admitted. "They don't offer Squeezeboxes to just anybody." He didn't voice what he was really thinking:

If I blow this, I'll have to retire or die ... and I'm more valuable to these people dead.

Angela clicked her tongue and sighed. "Well, if you change your mind, you know where to find me: toiling away over a telephone."

Alone with his thoughts again, Stee ran his fingers over his beard to refocus. He read and reread his running order on the wall. He'd have to attack the title song anew. It would be the lynchpin for the rest of the album, and it was the one video that had to be on the Squeezebox.

Then it hit him.

Connie'll have to start shooting in the next few days, before the song's recorded.

She's gonna kill me.

He frowned and crossed his arms. Perhaps Connie's video was an idea best left for another time. It was a whim coming off cruising YouTube late at night; he had made a snap decision reinforced by a beautiful smile hovering above the neckline of a sexy blue dress. Maybe the video was a bad idea.

Hold up. Connie's got a good eye and solid ideas. And a great smile ... and those legs ...

In that case ...

He ran his thumb back and forth across his lower lip. There had to be a way to make this easier. They could shoot it in Virginia if she couldn't leave her daughter. It would be simpler if he was the only one featured and the band stayed behind; there would be fewer schedules to coordinate, fewer bandmates to bring on board ...

Fewer people around ...

His mind was made up: the video was going to be included in the release, meaning he'd better get hopping on that title track ... and take care of a couple of other things.

Aw, shit ... now I have to book a hair appointment.

––––––––––

"ONE WEEK? We have to shoot in ONE WEEK?"

Stee couldn't tell if Connie was terrified or pissed.

"Yeah, it was a shock to me, too."

"You're still planning to include this on your Squeezebox?"

She's terrified.

"It makes sense, Connie: new Squeezebox, new album—new video for the title track."

"How can you expect me to come up with something good enough for BetaComp to sell to millions of people in one week?"

Nope, she's pissed.

"I have a good feeling about this, Connie."

"Well, *I* don't!"

Terrified. That's her final answer.

"Hey, hey there, don't hyperventilate. You are going to make something really beautiful. I know you will."

There was silence for a moment. "Connie, did you hear me?"

Her voice was shaky. "Stee, I appreciate you being a man of your word and wanting to make good on your offer to have me do your video, and clearly, your confidence in me is staggering."

I don't like where this is going.

"If this was a low-key, low-budget project on YouTube with a link to your fan site, *that* I could do in a week. If it flopped, it could be considered a noble experiment: you get credit for giving a newbie a break, and I wouldn't be ashamed to add it to my resume. But this project is too important to your career, and I love your work too much to screw it up. I'm not going to do this, Stee."

"Now hang on, sister," he interjected, a burr now wedged under his saddle. "This is not a perfect opportunity, but it's *your* opportunity to do what you've always wanted to do. You're saying this is all about protecting my reputation, but shit, you're just chickening out."

He heard her exhale sharply.

She's back to being pissed.

Good.

"You're right, Stee," she finally replied, her words clipped. "I'll make this work; not to worry."

"Atta girl," Stee purred.

"So," Connie said, clearly having decided to forge ahead, "any chance you'll be writing this song in the near future?"

"*Writing?* Darlin', it's *written.*"

Stee spun in his desk chair and picked up his current notebook. "Just let me grab a guitar."

Stee scooted across the room to nab his acoustic guitar, then came back to his seat and put on his bifocals, propping his notes against his computer screen. Hitting the phone's speaker button, he said, "I'll email you a scratch track soon. I'm gonna warn you, this just came out of my head and I haven't even played it through all the way. It's rough, but it'll give you an idea of what it's going to become, okay?"

"Okay."

He strummed an E-major chord and quickly tuned up, adjusted his glasses and cleared his throat.

"Can you hear me okay?"

"Clear as a bell, Stee." She sounded excited.

He played through "Unexpected Places" to the end. As the guitar strings rang into silence, he craned his neck toward the telephone, waiting for her positive reaction ... or any reaction.

"Uh, Connie? You still there?"

He heard her shuddering exhale. "I loved it."

Stee felt inordinately proud. "You did?"

"It was so ..."

He was grinning toward the phone. "Toss me some adjectives, darlin'."

She heaved a huge sigh. "Pretty."

That threw him. "*Pretty?*" he frowned. "Is that all you got?"

"What's wrong with pretty?"

"I mean, I *labored* over this one."

"'Pretty' is high praise, Stee. Not many songwriters do that well."

"But 'pretty' is ... a pretty average description, especially coming from you," he blurted.

"Oh." Connie seemed a touch surprised at his reaction. He scowled at himself. Neediness didn't become him.

Connie came to his rescue. "Okay, okay, how about this? The whole song just shimmers: the melody, the words, your delivery."

"Huh, good, thanks," he said gratefully. "What else?"

"I liked the candle image, and 'good love after bad' is a nice phrase."

"Thank you," he said, warming back up to the conversation. "What else?"

"'Beckoning' isn't a word a lot of people use. It fits, though."

"Glad you noticed."

She paused. "You don't usually sing about growing older." Stee sensed she had chosen her words very carefully.

"That what you think the song's about?" In his rush to get the lyrics down on paper, he hadn't given much thought to what it all added up to.

"It's brave," she replied, "and heartening. You're so confident that you'll find love at this point in your life, it's ... refreshing."

After a moment of his pointed silence, she added hastily, "Then again, you're Stee Walsh. Of course *you'll* find love again."

Then, after another beat: "I'm going to shut up now."

Stee sighed heavily and put his guitar down on the floor, leaning it against the desk. "Well, shit, I must have put that in there for a reason. I must be a little worried about getting older—being older—being old."

"You're not old," she assured him.

"It won't be long now," he mumbled.

With that, Connie burst into a fit of giggles. "Are you done? I have a week to come up with a video that's as pretty as that song or my client will be pissed."

She had him there. "I gotta warn you, your client can be a maudlin, needy bastard sometimes."

"I wouldn't know. I've always found him to be charming."

"Go earn the gazillion dollars I'm paying you," Stee commanded the telephone. "Talk to you soon."

"Take care, Stee." The line went quiet. Stee felt a ping of loneliness, then chuckled to himself.

Great gal.

chapter 9

That night, after grabbing some half-decent takeout Chinese for herself, since Amanda was once again off at a friend's house, Connie dragged a storage bin from under her bed, swept off the dust bunnies and popped open the plastic top. She dug down a few layers past art show flyers, ticket stubs and other bits of history she had intended to scrapbook at some point and unearthed a worn gum eraser, a tiny pencil sharpener with a plastic cover to catch the shavings and two soft lead pencils.

Then she discovered what she was searching for: a storyboard book. Each page had four boxes in a proper 16 by 9 ratio, with lines to the right for notes. She had used these spiral notepads by the dozen when she was in film school. Now there was only one left.

The pages were the color of weak tea around the edges and compressed by alternating seasons of humidity and dry heat. She flipped the book open and was greeted by some old friends: pages of intricate sketches, every hatch mark and half circle as familiar as the freckles on Amanda's nose.

"Hands at Work"... right where I left it.

Connie believed hands were the most cinematic part of a person, second only to the eyes. Her thesis project in film school was a study of working women's hands, moving from traditional roles—bathing a child, knitting, baking—to less stereotypical actions—performing surgery, fixing a car engine, butchering a hog. That went so well, she expanded it to include a chapter of men's hands, moving from construction, writing checks and fixing cars to hairdressing, arranging flowers and diapering a baby.

She had such high hopes for this project when she was wrapping up her MFA, but nothing came of it. She intended to submit it for award consideration, but, sidetracked by the fear that she wouldn't win anything, she hadn't bothered. The images never left her, though. When she started doing corporate work, she'd sneak hands in any time she could: helping hands, a hand up, hands down, even a hand of poker. This was her rueful inside joke with herself, the way she stayed in touch with the artist she had hoped to be.

She flipped to the next clean page.

It was a unique mark of artistry to draw a storyboard manually in this day and age and she was determined to do so to earn Stee's respect. Connie's cinematography instructor had advised her to always draw the images first: "You want characters to sit around and talk? Do radio." But a film driven by lyrics had to marry the seen and the heard.

Once she received Stee's scratch track and lyric sheet—after checking her email frantically for an hour after she hung up with him—she sketched out a basic shot list in her head suggested by the words and shaded by the texture of the melody. All she had to do was put it on paper.

Yep ... that's all I have to do.

She stared at the page.

Yep, yep, yep ...

During the intro, Stee would be looking out toward the woods surrounding his family's farm, the sunrise a brilliant circle glimpsed through gently moving trees. For the second shot, Stee's right profile would be in close-up, a stripe of sunshine across his right eye, igniting its staggering blue like a gas jet.

Connie flexed her fingers. She hadn't sketched anything of consequence in well over a decade and she wasn't very fluid. She began to fill in the first panel with about a third of the back of Stee's head and his right shoulder. She didn't bother with shading or depth, creating a line drawing with key details filled in instead: the arch of the back stitching of a denim jacket, the position of the sunbeams, the shag of hair over his collar.

One down … fifty-four more to go.

For reference, she had printed off a couple of recent photos of Stee facing right: as a pallbearer at Bo Diddley's funeral and waiting backstage at the Democratic National Convention. She had blown them up so she could see the crepe-paper texture of his skin, the encroachment of gray in his beard, even the variations in the dark blue granite of his eyes.

She slid the flat side of the pencil across the page in a few quick strokes, sweeping a curving line back toward the left: his hair was in place. Glancing again at the photos, she carefully copied the narrow slope of his nose, wondering who in his genetic background gave him such a patrician facial feature between a slab of a forehead and, frankly, a weak jawline that needed his beard for reinforcement. She framed the eyelids around a small circle, then paused.

It was going to be difficult to translate the full impact of those unusual eyes into a pencil drawing. At first when she met him, they had bored right into her. Since then, she'd noticed that when he laughed and his smile lines softened their impact, they caught the light. No matter his mood, though, she could feel electrons zipping through the air whenever he looked at her.

She firmed up his lips and roughed in his beard, setting his jaw with a hint of a hopeful smile. Following a final flick of a comma at corner of his mouth, she cast the beam of light across his eastward gaze and put down her pencil.

There on the page was the image she had seen in her head: a man, his demons at bay at last, ready to embark on a journey, unpredictable and thrilling, to find the love of his life.

That's the song right there.

She trilled with pride.

She shook out the cramp in her fingers and looked at the clock. Two panels had taken her an hour, and Stee hadn't even opened his mouth yet. She was woefully out of practice; back in the day, she could frame out ten minutes of video in that much time. Yet she was thoroughly stoked. She could see where it was going; it was only a matter of time until she'd have it all laid out before her.

Good going. Nice work.

—————

"Hello," Connie croaked into her cell phone. She hated being woken out of a sound sleep, especially at two in the morning.

"Hey, Connie—ooh sorry, you 'sleep?"

"That's okay, Stee," she responded, her voice thick. "What's up?"

Other than you ...

"I just got a look at your drawings for the video. They're really good, Connie—amazing stuff."

"Thank you," she beamed, having no further issues about being woken up. "What do you think of the—"

"Are you an artist or an animator or something?" he barreled on.

"Well, I draw. I did a lot more when I was in film sch—"

"'Cause everything you drew is so *good*," he gushed. "I mean, I could see the trees and the sun and flowers and how everything saturates with color as I walk by."

"Thanks. So, what about the storyline? Do you—"

"And me? You *nailed* me. Nobody ever gets the profile right since I had to get a nose job because of the coke. You made me look like me."

That *mystery's solved.*

"Glad you approve, I really do. But what about the story? Do you—"

"I could see the whole thing spin out; oh, man, the video's gonna be fucking great!"

Whew.

"Where'd you learn how to do that—draw that way?" He finally took a breath, giving her space for a full sentence at last.

"I've always liked to and when I went to film school, I found a way to use it. I'm glad I have an excuse to draw again; it's been a long time."

"Didn't you have to do it for your job?" he asked, sounding stunned. "Your straight job, I mean, when you were in an office and all that?"

"I might have sketched something out on a white board or a flip chart so people understood what I wanted, but that's about it."

"What *was* your job, anyway?"

Realizing this conversation was going to last a while, Connie bit the bullet and turned on the lamp. She squeezed her eyes tightly, wincing from the bright light, and propped a couple of pillows behind her as she sat up. "I was a change officer for the twenty-second largest company in the world."

"And what does that mean exactly?" Connie couldn't tell if he was being sarcastic.

Stee wasn't the first person to ask her this, though, and she had her elevator speech down pat. "By creating and directing effective cultural communications, I help Tripton Reid employees enjoy their jobs and believe they do work that's important."

There were a couple of moments of dead air. "What?"

"I help Tripton Reid employees enjoy their jobs and believe they do work that's important." Remembering she was long gone from that operation, she added, "I *helped*—past tense."

"Huh," he pondered. "So if you never worked there, all those poor people at Tripton Reid would hate their jobs and feel like they were wasting their time?"

"No, of course not," Connie said, a twinge of defensiveness coming to the fore. "It's just if you work for a huge corporation doing a front line job—being a truck driver or a lab tech or something—you might feel nobody cares about what you do. I gave those people a voice, helped them celebrate what made them special. The work they do is just as important to the company's success as what the president does."

"Uh, huh," he replied, nonplussed. "So you're saying a truck driver could take over for the president?"

"Stee, no! For God's sake—"

"I'm kidding—jeez, are you touchy. Naw, I get it. You tried to make everybody feel good about being a cog in the machine. Any luck with that?"

"Yeah, plenty." It was now 2:10 and she was not thrilled about having to justify her existence at this ungodly hour. "People told me I was great at my job."

He chuckled. "Do tell."

"Yep," she replied smugly. "I built quite a reputation." She faltered. "Well, it's all ancient history now."

"How you could love a corporate gig when you've got art in your soul like you do, I have no idea. Honey, you had to be dying by inches there at that place."

He sounded completely perplexed, which got her thinking.

He's never had to work a day job in his life.

No wonder he doesn't get it.

"I liked my job. I miss my job. I like structure; I like a regular paycheck and time with Amanda. I was able to be creative without having to be a genius like you."

"You tryin' to butter me up?"

"No, Stee, you really are a genius."

"I'm just lucky."

"And brilliant and relentless and focused. Maybe that makes you a genius at being lucky then. Not everyone can do that." She cuddled the phone to her ear. "The universe is full of stars, but there are only so many bright enough for everyone to see. The rest of us have to shine where we can."

"You just make that up?"

"Yep."

"Well, you're pretty shiny in my book, darlin'."

Hearing the fondness in his voice made her feel a lot better, if not any less tired. Connie slid into a horizontal position once more. "That's so sweet. You think I'm shiny."

"You are very shiny."

"That's *so* sweet, I'm going to let that be the last thing you say to me before I go back to sleep."

He swore to himself. "Christ, it's after two out there. Why didn't you tell me to hang up?"

"Because you're a genius rock star ... and you're sweet," she yawned. "Good night."

"Pleasant dreams, shiny one," he said softly before hanging up.

Matter of fact, she did have a very, very pleasant dream.

Connie was in the passenger seat of a red classic convertible—she thought it was a Mustang even though she didn't know cars—looking out over the glittering lights of San Francisco from her vantage point up on Twin Peaks. The top was down, and in the detached awareness of dreams, she knew she had to be cold even though she didn't feel it physically. She exhaled wisps of fog; she wasn't dressed for the weather, so she shoved her hands under her armpits to warm them as she admired the cityscape that looked like the world's largest Lite-Brite plugged in at her feet.

The driver's side door opened. "You're right. You can see for miles and miles from up here." Stee dropped into the driver's seat, grinning ear to ear. He couldn't have been more than twenty-one, clean-shaven and as unmarked by time as he was in some of the early photos Connie had unearthed online. In a moment of dream-state confusion, Connie had to ask herself,

How old am I right now?

He looked at her sympathetically. "Baby, come here." He put his arm around her and she rested her head on his shoulder, blissfully comfortable.

"See, aren't you glad you came with me?" he said as he stroked her hair.

"Uh, huh." A delicious shiver of heat roiled from her chest through the rest of her body.

"I'm right, ain't I?" he stated, crafty and confident. "Right about what you want to do?"

"You're right, Stee. You are so right."

He laughed in delight, his mouth wide open, oblivious to the cold and the throng of tourists milling around the parked cars. He was skinny and pale in the icy moonlight but so warm when he pulled her closer. They kissed and he moved his hands under the hem of her shirt. It was like his lyrics in "A Good Way to Start":

The right place at the right time
For the first time in a long time.
I was there, baby—'cuz I was with you.

———

She was jolted awake by her cell phone's blare around 9 a.m. She ran her tongue over her teeth to unstick the inside of her lips from her gums and fumbled for the phone at the edge of the desk. She squinted at the caller ID.

God, no!

She coughed before answering. "Hello, this is Connie Rafferty."

"Terri here." The thought of the icy recruiter made her lungs constrict.

Contorting her face to wake up, Connie continued. "Well, Terri, it's good to hear from you."

"I'm sure it is," the recruiter stated flatly. "Listen, I have an interview opportunity for you. Are you still on the market?"

"Yes."

"You hesitated. Why did you hesitate?"

Connie's mind raced for what to say. She wasn't about to casually spill the beans about the video, or her burgeoning friendship with a major celebrity, any time soon to anyone, much less to this gorgon.

"I am just ... thrilled to hear that someone was hiring out here."

Scary Terri snickered. "Don't get too crazy yet. Let me fill you in. How do you feel about the insurance industry?"

As she ticked off the specifics of the job description, Connie's mind raced. It was the stability and predictability she'd told Stee about only a few hours before. It was if fate was handing her a lifeline: a dependable, straight-laced corporate gig that would allow her to wallow in financial stability once more after a long, lean year.

She winced.

What fun is that?

Stee had opened a door she had shut behind her when she first took her temp job at Tripton Reid. Twenty years after her graduation, she was doing what she had been trained to do in graduate school: be an independent filmmaker. She had no idea what would happen when Stee went on his merry way once the video was finished, yet for the first time in history, the thought of instability was kind of a kick.

"So, they're seeing people this Thursday. You free?"

"I am so sorry, Terri. This week is bad."

"So that's a no?" In Terri's reply, Connie heard notes of patronizing suspicion as well. "Whatever you've got going on, it had better be life-altering and mind-blowing because if you don't come when opportunity knocks, opportunity won't be calling you at all. And my name is Opportunity."

I thought it was Scary Terri.

"I know. I'll take my chances. Thanks for thinking of me and let me know what else you find in the future."

Terri didn't stay on the line long enough to hear her final request.

To: stee@swatrr.com
From: whitepines@hotmail.com
Subject: Long time no hear from.

It was absurd in this day and age to have to use email, but Stee was old school and Leonard was down with that. It was concerning, though, that Stee had yet to reply to any of the emails that Leonard dutifully sent every day. From all the interviews he'd read and the documentaries he'd seen, he knew that Stee Walsh honored his fans and never ignored them, especially a colleague like Leonard.

Something might be wrong.

Maybe I should call him to see if he's okay.

He typed Stee's name into his phone. The musician's home number appeared, freshly pilfered from BetaComp's president's online contacts file.

Good thing his secretary has no idea that she needs to change her password every once in a while ...

Leonard's index finger readied to hit the Call button and then froze, recalling the *Mojo* interview Stee did when *Santa Monica Pier* came out, the one where he said:

"When an album is in the works and I'm trying to conjure up the muse, I become a pain the ass: trips get canceled, it takes me months to phone somebody back. My friends and family have learned not to take it personally."

Returning to his email, Leonard typed:

> Hope this finds you well and your album is rolling along. Let me know if you need to get to know the guinea pig's personality in more detail. I can help you with that. Just text, phone or email whenever, my friend.

He finished the message and hit Send with a confident smile.

He'll contact me when he can. He's just busy with the Squeezebox shit. I get it. I can wait.

I'm a patient guy.

chapter 10

"Stee, it's my privilege to introduce you to Mike Young and Ted Tejeda, our videographers. They're the guys I worked with out in San Francisco."

Be cool, guys ... please be cool.

"Gentlemen, welcome to Virginia." Stee stuck out his hand to Ted first, who gave him a professional nod of acknowledgement. Mike, however, couldn't hold back.

"Stee Walsh," he reiterated, pumping Stee's arm. "I am so totally honored to meet you."

Stee looked him straight in the eye and nodded. "Likewise, Mike. Connie's got nothing but good things to say about you, and that orphan drug piece—that's gorgeous work, man. It's gonna be great to see what you do with this one."

Mike beamed. Connie was impressed. Stee had earned the full loyalty of her cameramen in all of ten seconds by making them the stars instead of him.

Smooth.

So far, all of the pieces were falling neatly into place, in synch with Connie's production schedule. She had arrived at Stee's grand-father's farm without getting lost this time, unlike when she and the videographers had come out to get the lay of the land and nearly ended up in Charlottesville. Stee was on set, delightful as ever, mark-ing her arrival with the complete Bob Dylan anthology and a burst of roses in the dining room, which would be her command center for the next couple of days. The dollies and other equipment had been delivered and assembled. Even the weather was holding up its end of the artistic bargain, with the sun afloat in a pure blue sky awaiting the cue to cut to sunset so they could get their closing scene done that day.

Connie relaxed. She was in her comfort zone: the tightly scheduled and finely tuned video shoot.

I'M BAAAACK!

As Ted and Mike excused themselves to ensure the crane was ready to go at the west entrance of the house, Connie approached Stee. "Now that you've met the crew, I want to take you through the shot list for this afternoon."

He grunted. "That's it? That's the crew?"

She shrugged. "Well, Sara's doing makeup and hair and a friend of Ted's is the grip. We've got caterers but they're an outside vendor."

Stee scanned the outskirts of the property, counting. "You've got maybe eight people here."

"Yeah, it's a bigger shoot than I usually do, so I had to double my crew." Stee's brow furrowed and uneasiness began burbling in her gut. "Is there a problem?"

"No, no, you're the captain of this ship. You know how to run it, I'm sure."

"You don't sound sure."

"No one's doing wardrobe?" he whispered with anxious concern.

"You've got only one outfit. It's silly to have someone whose only job is to make sure you know how to button your shirt. If it gets dirty, I'll throw it in the washer."

"Where's my driver?"

"Where do you need to go, Stee? Your rental's in the driveway."

"Where's my trailer?"

"This is your grandfather's place, Stee. You're living here! Why on earth would you need a trailer?" Keeping it light was becoming a chore. She was just about to leave him to stew in his own misguided sense of entitlement when she heard him sigh, sounding wistful rather than testy.

"I know," he responded. "It's just so much ... smaller than the video shoots I remember."

She put her hand lightly on his shoulder. "Is this going to be okay? I told you when I took you through the schedule, I'm used to working lean ..."

"And traveling light. Yeah, yeah, got it." He rolled his shoulders and faced her again, pleasant once more. "All right, Madame Director and Head Wardrobe Mistress, where do I pick up my costume?"

"Your production assistant has it."

"My production assistant?" A crinkle of good humor returned to his face. "I have a production assistant?"

"You seem to think we needed more crew members; I'd think you'd be happy." A petite teenager with a pink streak in her hair met them on the front porch, bearing a bottle of water. Connie put her arm around the girl's shoulders.

"Stee, this is my daughter, Amanda."

"Mr. Walsh—"

"Stee, please," he corrected with a grin.

Amanda gave a curt nod. "Stee, it's nice to meet you."

He shook her hand and took the water from her. "It's very nice to meet you, Amanda. Your momma is very proud of you, from what she's told me about you."

"Thanks," she replied, shooting a death ray of embarrassment toward her mother.

Connie looked toward the sun. "We don't have much time before the light's in the right place. Amanda, you're his shadow for the entire shoot. Whatever Stee needs, you see to. Whatever he asks for, you get. You keep an eye on every detail—his clothes, whether he got mud on his shoe, if he needs a tissue or a touch-up. Got it?"

"Got it."

Connie turned to her star. "Amanda's yours to command, Stee. She's on walkie-talkie; she can let me know if there's anything you need that she can't handle."

He glanced over at the girl and chuckled. "I'm sure she can handle whatever I toss her way."

Connie silently agreed. "Amanda, take him over to Sara to pick up that shirt and get into makeup. Be back here by four."

––––––––

"Connie, we've got a problem."

She clicked her walkie-talkie. "What's up, Mike?'

"We have an audience."

Meandering over to the camera set ups she looked toward the driveway. Sure enough, ringing the flower bed was a group of six, their cameras of various skill levels at the ready.

Mike joined her at the periphery. "How'd they know about the shoot?" she asked.

"I dunno. Maybe one of the delivery guys let it slip."

"How'd they even get here? The main road's at least a mile back."

"Must have followed the caterers," Mike suggested. Sure enough, Connie noticed an unfamiliar SUV parked behind the van.

"Shit. Where's Stee?"

"He's still in makeup."

"Can you radio Ted and tell him to keep Stee out of sight while I go chat with these people?"

"Got it."

Stomping through the grass, Connie greeted the group with a steely smile. "Excuse me. You need to leave. This is private property and a closed shoot."

"We're part of the crew," said a pig-eyed gentleman in a Budweiser cap. "The director said we could stay here and watch."

"I'm the director."

"Cruise director, maybe," Bud Cap snickered. "Now, little girl, if you can get out of our way, we want to say hi to Stee when he comes out."

"Stee's not going to see you. You're trespassing. You have to go."

"He always makes time for his fans, lady."

She got her walkie-talkie. "Call the cops, Mike."

"Don't go and do that. Stee's not gonna like it."

"I'm in charge here and it's all about what *I* like. You all need to leave. Now."

"The cops are a couple minutes out," Mike squawked through the walkie-talkie.

Connie was unbending, and Bud Cap showed no signs of standing down even as his buddies shuffled and broke ranks. One of his friends came between them. "C'mon. This bitch ain't worth getting arrested over. Get in the car."

Bud Cap sneered at her with a level of cold contempt that spooked her. Turning on his heel, he yelled, "Hey, Stee, you better talk to your director lady. She's keeping your fans away. That's not right. That's not who you are, Stee."

Just as the SUV peeled off, Mike arrived at her side. "That could have gotten ugly."

The word "bitch" burning a hole in her pride like a cigarette, she squared her shoulders. "It sure wasn't pretty."

"Good job, standing up to them."

"I didn't think anyone even knew about this shoot, much less was going to blow by the NO TRESPASSING signs. Mike, you can't let Stee know about this. This is my problem to fix."

"What problem, Connie?"

Her star was at her side, ready for his close up. Standing against the bright afternoon sky, clad in the spiffy denim shirt Connie had chosen for him and the Stetson she'd asked him to bring from home, Stee looked like a cowboy out of a 1950s Technicolor western, all saturated blues and reds and golds. Connie's heart unexpectedly zinged.

"You look rugged," she said under her breath.

"Credit goes to Sara. She's got some sort of makeup spackle that hides a multitude of sins. I'm a little afraid to talk, though. I think it's all gonna peel right off." He looked toward the driveway. "So, does your problem have something to do with why a Devon County sheriff just pulled up?"

She sighed skyward. "We had some unwanted guests who didn't

want to leave quietly."

"They the ones who were yelling a minute ago?"

"Connie wasn't going to let them get anywhere near you, Stee," Mike asserted. "She went all Marshal Dillon on them, stood her ground and scared them off. She almost scared *me* off."

Grateful as she was for Mike's support, her credibility had suffered a blow. "This shouldn't have happened. I take full responsibility. It didn't even dawn on me that we'd need a security detail."

"Call Angela. She can contact the security team we use on East Coast tours and see if they can lend a hand."

As Mike ambled over to the sheriff's car, Stee caught Connie's elbow. "Listen, if any other fans manage to break through, tell me and I'll decide if I'm going to see them or not. Don't send them packing unless I tell you to and, unless they're waving a weapon around, don't call the cops. Okay?" His tone surprised her: not angry but unnervingly firm.

Being lectured got her back up. "It's my set, my rules, Stee. If someone's disrupting the shoot or harassing my star, I'll decide what needs to be done."

"Those are my fans, Connie."

"They're assholes."

"Assholes with Facebook pages and Twitter feeds who are busy badmouthing me for hiring a bitch to direct his video."

The word seared into her again. Catching her expression, he put his arm around her shoulders, giving them a reassuring shake. "I don't think you're a bitch by any stretch. You were protecting me and you did the right thing, the noble thing, but here's the sad fact: the only thing worse than assholes wanting your autograph is *nobody* wanting your autograph. Right now, after so many years off the market, I need all the assholes I can get."

She fumed. Either she could fight her client for supremacy or admit that he was, sadly, right.

"Okay, I'll talk to you first next time."

"Thank you, Marshal Dillon." He placed his Stetson on her head and shot her a sloe-eyed smile. "Let's get this shoot under way, shall we?"

———————

"CUT! Ted, are you okay?"

The videographer's mouth hung open. "Holy shit—did you see that? I thought that starling was going to clear the crane; it just smacked right into it."

"Is the bird okay?"

Ted shook his head. "DOA."

Connie winced. "Is the equipment damaged?"

Ted lowered the camera and stepped back to assess the damage, his mouth curled in disgust. "The unit's okay, and I think the crane is fine, but it's covered in feathers and bird guts."

Connie swore grimly into her megaphone. "How much time do you need to clean up?"

"Uh, ten minutes?"

Connie checked the sky. "Okay, get going. We can only do this one more time and then we're out of sunlight. Sorry about this, Stee."

"Nothing you could do," Stee yelled down to his director from the balcony on the second floor. "Darwin at work."

As the crew rewound and reset and Ted yelled for Mike to get him a plastic trash bag, Amanda brought out the folding chair and set it expectantly near him. Stee shook his head graciously.

"Thanks, but it's harder on my knee to keep standing up and sitting down. I need to walk around on it for a while." He leaned forward, his hands on the railing, and shifted from foot to foot to stretch his back, gritting his teeth when he put pressure on his left leg.

"Need any water or anything?" When he shook his head, she hid the chair inside the doorway and came around in front of him. "Let me check your makeup. Look at me, please." He swiveled his head and suddenly stopped smiling so as not to further crease his foundation. Amanda eyed him purposefully and caught a drop of sweat with a ready tissue before it could trickle into his ear.

"Too warm for you? I can find a fan."

"Naw, I'll be fine."

She stepped back, satisfied. "I think it can last one more take."

"Good to know." Stee looked over the railing to check the reset's progress and to watch Connie for a moment or two. In her ancient green 4-H t-shirt, a ball cap on her head and slathered in sunblock, she could have been a camp counselor. Behind the megaphone, though, she was a benevolent dictator, the troops at the ready to do her bidding.

She had no problem telling Stee what to do, either—no star treatment for him, thank God. A lot of young musicians sure didn't get that. They'd try to hide their man crushes by acting overly familiar. That's why Stee loved working with the older cats: the blues performers and rockabilly pioneers and the country old guard. They respected talent first and foremost and didn't have any use for ego bullshit. He'd show them well-deserved deference, and they'd treat him like a fellow musician, and then they'd play together. He wanted to be considered a professional, not a celebrity, and fellow professionals understood that.

Connie understands that.

As Stee watched from above, Ted reenacted the starling's kamikaze crash into the equipment with wild hand gestures. Connie looked closer at the spot of impact, and then yanked backward and shuddered with an exaggerated creeped-out gesture. Stee chuckled.

"Wuss."

He stopped stock still when he heard a sharp creak behind him. His young production assistant was perched on the folding chair in the shade of the bedroom. Thankfully it didn't seem that she'd caught him ogling her mother.

"You should get out of the sun, Stee, being a redhead and all."

"Good point." He shuffled inside and leaned against the doorjamb. "So, is this the first time you've been on a shoot with your mom?"

"Yeah."

"Did you volunteer or were you drafted?"

"I asked to come," Amanda replied pleasantly without smiling.

"Mom didn't want me to but I insisted."

"You a fan of my music?"

"I like some of your stuff, yeah."

"Huh." He straightened a bit. "So, what's your favorite Stee Walsh song?"

"Mom warned me you'd ask that."

Figures.

"So, what's your answer?"

"The *Double Down* title track, I guess. Is that an okay answer?"

He was impressed. Pretty much no one liked that song, although it was one of his personal favorites. He and Chad were determined to sound nothing like the arena schlock that was popular when they were writing their second album, so they fired up a two-minute, fuzzed-out burst of rocket fuel dedicated to being young, horny and drunk. It was an acquired taste, even for SWATRR loyalists. Perhaps it was just ahead of its time, and now the time was right for Amanda to appreciate it.

"That'll do fine." He cocked his head at his production assistant. "If you aren't really a fan, why are you here?"

"I told Mom I had to do this because it might be my only opportunity to work with a famous musician."

"So, you expect to work with a lot of not-so-famous musicians in the future?"

That earned a snort from Amanda, and Stee smiled with no small amount of pride. He had spent the last hour trying to get some sort of rapport rolling between takes, and while Amanda wasn't rude or cold, she had a serious cast to her that Stee hadn't been able to break through. Until now.

"No," she answered, casting her eyes upward in embarrassment in what Stee knew to be a very familial gesture. "I'm going to law school."

"Wow, you know that already? How old are you again?"

"You knew you wanted to be a musician when you were fourteen."

Stee was surprised. "How did you know that?"

"Mom briefed me."

"I'm sure she did."

Amanda rolled her eyes. "As if I'd never heard of Wikipedia before."

He walked around the bedroom, forcing his knee into motion no matter how much it killed him. "Wow," he said through clenched teeth, "law school—tell me about that."

The girl shrugged. "Being a lawyer seems like a good way to make a difference."

"That's an interesting take on the profession." He stopped pacing. "You know, if you're at all interested in entertainment law, I could put you together with my attorney, Marcos."

Her eyes widened. "I'm not sure entertainment law is for me."

"You might like it."

She shook her head, resolute. "I want to be a public defender."

"Well, my hat's off to you, then." Stee noticed that for all her certainty, she was looking at the floor during most of this exchange. He tried to catch her eye. "Amanda, are you sure about this lawyer thing? I mean, really, 'the law' is that interesting to you?"

Amanda raised one eyebrow, echoing her mother's signal for disbelief. "You don't believe me?"

"Naw, I'm sure you mean it. I just thought you might want to be drawing or making movies like your mother."

"Nope," she said, point blank. "Not at all."

"Ah," he said, still feeling there was more to the story than he'd get in a first-day conversation. Suddenly Amanda's walkie-talkie chirped.

"Amanda, it's Sara."

"Hey."

"They're gonna be ready to in two. How's our talent looking?"

Amanda got up and peered close at hair and makeup. "He's good to go one more time."

"Check. Thanks." She clipped the walkie-talkie back into its holster. "We're at places. Hit your mark, please."

Stee nodded. "Whatever you say, boss lady."

———

"Connie, congratulations. This is officially the earliest I've ever gotten up for anybody."

"I appreciate it, Stee."

"Even my daughters had the courtesy to be born after the sun rose. This is ridiculous."

"It's all for art, right?"

"Right. Ready?"

"Ready."

Call time had come way too soon that morning, even though Connie had made a point of driving home the night before while it was still light and getting to bed at an obscenely early hour. She'd been on the road since 3 a.m., unable to risk missing a minute of sunrise for the opening shot of the piece. Yesterday's shoot, successful as it was, only captured about fifteen seconds of the overall script. The remaining scenes lay before her and had better come together as planned that day, with foul weather slated to descend by nightfall.

Playing "Unexpected Places" on continuous repeat during that morning's dark commute, Connie was all the more committed to her vision of the song. She had cast Stee as a weary yet hopeful man searching for an honest woman. The farmhouse stood as a whitewashed symbol of safety and isolation. The girl of his dreams would be just out of reach, never in the picture but evidenced by the sights along his journey: flowers, birds, rays of light. The sun would rise and set during his journey of the heart, ending with him leaving the farmhouse behind and venturing down the road to find her and bring her home.

Poetry.

They exited the farmhouse, finding the front lawn blazing with floodlights and vibrating with activity. As they came to the porch steps, Stee took her arm. She flushed, thinking this was a gesture of their growing friendship. Then his weight shifted toward her as he stepped on his left leg, and she had to adjust her gait as they walked down the stairs out to the craft tent. Something was wrong.

He's limping.

Half of this video is him walking through the woods and the grass. Alone.

As Stee piled scrambled egg whites onto his plate, her mind clicked through each setup scheduled that day, furiously searching for Plan B.

Maybe I can find him a walking stick—no, that'll just make him look like Gandalf.

SHIT!

"Nice spread you got here, Connie," Stee said as he poured three creamers into his coffee. "Bake the bagels yourself?"

She smiled in spite of her worries. "I'm not quite that low-budget."

"You got my rider?"

"The caterers will have your carb-free lunch ready at eleven."

"Don't want you to think I don't trust you but, sorry to say, a lot of people have taken advantage of my good nature and gotten sloppy on the details."

"We've got it covered." She needed to stall for a few more moments until she had a better idea of how to modify her setups on the fly. "I didn't know you had a restricted diet."

"I have to lose weight before we shoot the commercial in the fall and this usually works. Here, could you take my coffee for me?"

He gripped her elbow and they guided themselves over to a long table and sat. Stee frowned fondly.

"Connie, you look like your cat got run over. What's wrong?"

With no other options Connie plunged ahead. "How's your knee today?"

He shrugged. "It's chilly out and it takes a while to warm up. It'll get better."

"Please level with me."

"I'll work through it."

"Cameras don't lie. If you're in pain, it'll show."

He snorted. "All I have to do is look soulfully into the rising sun.

I'll be fine."

"But that's not all we're doing today. Stee, if—"

"Ease up, Madame Director. I'll be just fine."

His nonchalance gave her no comfort. She just knew she was going to have to adjust every mobile shot on the list ... without letting him know so his ego wouldn't get in a bunch over having to downshift. She smiled, putting every ounce of her energy into being unperturbed. "Look, I'm going to make sure everything's ready to roll. Be right back."

Her star nodded and turned back to his carb-free breakfast. Connie left the tent to make a beeline for the back of the house. As soon as she got out from under the canvas, she slapped her neck.

"Ow! SHIT!"

She scowled at the pulverized legs and wings in her hand.

I don't believe this. Mosquitoes?

The sky was lightening by the second, her star was probably going to need a walker by noon ... and bloodsucking beasts were rousing themselves in the morning air.

She fumbled for her walkie-talkie, swatting the back of her knee. "Hey Mike, anyone over there getting eaten alive?"

"Funny you should mention that."

"Got any Off?"

"Negatory."

"Ask Sara. Ask Ted. Please tell me someone has something."

The radio hissed. "Sara's got some sort of no-kill bug repellent in her car. We can spray it around the porch."

"No-kill? How can that even work?"

"It makes them reconsider their options and leave peacefully, I guess."

"Get it and give it to me quick!"

Connie jogged over to the front of the house. Clouds of insects surrounded the floodlights like a black blizzard. Amanda was fanning herself with a *Field & Stream* magazine she must have pinched from the family room.

"I feel like bait, Mom."

Connie fished in her pocket and took out a wad of cash. "Take this and go to that gas station back at the turnoff. Buy up every can of bug spray you can find and get right back here. If they don't have any, keep driving until you find some."

"Anything to get out of this vampire flick." Amanda grabbed the money and sped off to the parked cars. Connie hoofed it back to the food tent, searching for a cup of coffee and a quiet corner to calm her nerves. Stee's voice boomed over the clatter of tongs and steam trays.

"You need me, Connie?"

He looked tired but game; what more could she ask for at this hour? Coffee in hand, she sat across from him. "I'm trying to get the mosquitoes under control out there before you get in place. We've got bug repellent coming."

He shrugged. "They don't usually bother me."

"After the first couple of setups we'll have to walk around the property. We'll take those at your own pace. If everything goes according to plan, we'll be done by mid-afternoon."

He hooked his thumb toward the sky. "And what if it doesn't? Like, what if it starts raining?"

She peeked under the tent flap. The lightening sky was beginning to reveal the woolly outlines of heavy clouds. Her blood ran cold.

"It can't rain now," she demanded. "The weather forecast said it's not going to rain until tonight."

He smirked. "Forget to get a signed contract from Mother Nature?"

Her head sunk into her hands. "I just don't believe this. I have everything planned down to the second ..."

"You can control the weather? The bugs, too?"

"I drag all these people up here. I rent a crane, I pay for the special food, I hustle up a security detail on short notice ..."

"And life goes the way it goes anyway." He took a knowing sip of coffee. "You're not one of those Mary Tyler Moore girls, are you? Never wants to make a mistake? Never wants to make someone mad? Needs to go lie down if something goes wrong?"

She crossed her arms, bristling at his patronizing. "I don't want to waste your time, Stee. You've got to get back to LA in a couple of days and I intend to finish the shoot before you leave."

"Give yourself a break, Con." He leaned toward her. "I admire how you want to run things but you got to let up on the reins once in a while. Let things flow as they may. See what else can happen if you give it a little more time. Maybe an extra day working on this together isn't such a bad thing."

Stee, with the same cockeyed smile and unbounded optimism as in her dream, was close enough to brush the bangs off her forehead, making her gut flash hot.

"Tell you what. I promise to relax once we get through this first setup ... if the rain holds off."

"I'm gonna hold you to that," he said with a wag of his finger. "So are Sara and her magic spackle ready for me?"

"Yes, they are."

Just like me. Ready for anything.

———————

Stee was lying on the couch, his knee propped up on a pillow, lulled by the silence into a twilight doze. He didn't want to admit how sore he was. He hadn't had a chance to swim in nearly two weeks and his joints were creaking after only a half-day walking around the property. He didn't want Connie to see him falter, and he did his best to grit his teeth with his back turned and smile whenever she was watching.

As the morning went on, he picked up on her gentle accommodation of his infirmities. She anticipated when he needed a break, signaling with a small nod to Amanda to offer a water bottle and a walking partner while they got the next scene set up. She took careful pains to avoid broadcasting that the star was an old gimp who got winded walking up a low-grade hill, disguising her protection as a need to fuss with camera angles or some such. He appreciated her discretion more than he could tell her without giving away that he was on to her the whole time.

To others, it looked like the star treatment. To Stee, it looked like maybe she was attracted to him. Given that when her fingers brushed against his hand while handing him his hat, he felt like he had touched a downed power line, it was mutual.

Great gal.

They'd missed the rain, wrapping and packing up without a drop hitting the equipment. Connie had dismissed the crew, her daughter included, so she could edit uninterrupted. He had stayed out of her way, ostensibly writing lyrics but more often than not watching her work from the other room. She was a perfectionist, swearing softly at small mistakes and smiling to herself when a scene was just so. Every once in a while she'd roll her shoulders or stand and stretch her arms to the ceiling, giving him an opportunity to appreciate the view of her backside. When he walked by, her gaze was fixed on the screen ahead of her, her head bouncing slightly to the music coming through her headphones. When he touched her shoulder to offer to get her a Coke, she nearly blasted through the ceiling. He thought it best to leave her be until she called for him ... which now she did.

"I have a rough cut of the first thirty seconds. Wanna see?"

Stee rolled off the couch to stare at the laptop screen over Connie's shoulder. As the first notes of "Unexpected Places" tinkled through the computer speakers, the opening segment unfurled with the sun rising over the trees and dawning sunbeams piercing the clouds.

"That's gorgeous."

She paused the video. "You were right about just letting things happen. I wouldn't have gotten that effect if the storm clouds hadn't been rolling in. And I've got a great contrast between the gray of today and the sunlit shots we captured yesterday. It'll look like you're moving on to better weather and a better life." She tossed him a smile. "Couldn't have planned it better."

"Told you. And the rain didn't even happen."

"Guess Mother Nature finally signed my contract."

She restarted the clip. Stee watched his back come into view, then it cut to the sunshine effect she had created by aiming a flashlight beam across his cheekbone ... and illuminating each and every wrinkle encasing his beady blue eyeball with blinding clarity.

"Whoa, hold up, stop," he blurted. "That shot's gotta go."

Connie barely had enough energy to click the Pause button. "What? Why?"

"I don't like it."

"But it's just like I storyboarded it, Stee: the sun coming up, that ray of light across your face. It's beautiful."

"It is a beautiful *concept* and I'm not faulting you for trying it out, but it just doesn't work."

"What exactly don't you like about it?"

Stee pointed at his frozen image on the screen. "I'm squinting."

Connie folded her arms, her eyebrows knotted. "You're *seeking* someone out in the distance. That's the point of the whole song."

"I look like I'm doing a two-bit Clint Eastwood impersonation."

"Well, you have a lot in common."

"What, that we both look damn good for eighty, even though I'm fifty-nine?"

"You both have that cowboy restlessness." She smoothed her hair back into a ponytail. "We're appealing to a demographic who'll appreciate that, remember?"

"What demographic would be attracted to that?"

She swiveled her chair around to face him, glowering as if she was personally offended. "You're not fooling me one bit. You don't like this shot because you think it makes you look fat and old."

Not fat *so much ...*

She barreled on. "Guess what? This is as good as you're gonna look and as young as you'll ever be, and if you'd just stop expecting to see a red-headed teenaged string bean for a minute, you'd see I have captured a very sexy man on that screen."

In all the time he'd known her, Connie had never said a word to him about how she saw him, physically anyway. Scrupulously professional when fully rested, she was apparently too pooped to keep her guard up. Stee was fascinated.

"Sexy?"

Coloring slightly, she persisted. "If you can embrace where you are in your life right now, so many more people will relate to you. You've always stood up for who you are. This is no different." She turned to the screen and traced the line of the light, her fingers shaking from fatigue. "That's what I see in this shot, that self-confidence ... and the amazing blue of your eyes."

A sheen of sweat and sun block greased her nose. Her hair was lank from the humidity and it looked like her lips had gotten sunburned. She had a couple of nasty mosquito bites on her left arm. She was pissed off and tired and vulnerable and more than a little sexy herself.

He kissed her temple before he could stop himself. Startled, she cast him a wary look.

"Does that mean the shot stays?"

"It means I should never have doubted you." His lips hovered near her ear. "How about we go get some dinner?"

"There are leftovers in the fridge from the caterer. I'm too tired to go out and I have a lot of work to do."

"You need to take a break."

"I'm almost done." She was clearly off-kilter, scrambling for a way to cope with his being so close. He was going to have to act fast to calm her down.

"At least come outside with me for a minute."

———

The early evening was heavy with the scent of freshly mown grass, and the meadow was silvering in the twilight. Stee came out with two Cokes in glass bottles in the crook of his arm and handed one to Connie, who was sitting on the back stairs.

"I hope you weren't expecting Diet. Duane stocks a Co-Cola machine on the porch with what our granddaddy used to have. There's

Yoo-hoo and Grape Nehi in there, too, if you'd rather."

"This is perfect, Stee. Thanks."

Stee sat down next to her on the steps, resting his forearms on his knees. She wasn't on the defensive now and was willing to chat.

"What did your grandfather grow here?"

"Corn and alfalfa mostly, for animal feed," Stee said, rolling the Coke bottle between both hands. "He'd have sheep sometimes, maybe thirty or forty, for meat more than wool. My grandmother wanted to put in an apple orchard, but he didn't want to have to climb all those trees, so he planted one tree here near the back so she could take care of it."

Connie rubbed her upper arms.

"You cold, in this weather?"

"Just keeping the mosquitoes off me."

"Here." Stee put his arm around her and, to his welcome surprise, Connie rested her head against his chest. They could have been little kids; they could have been a hundred years old. Then she sat forward.

"I think I might have seen a lightning bug."

He cozied up to her, looking out over the meadow. "I don't re-member them coming out this early. I think we used to see them in late June."

"Chalk it up to global warming," Connie said dreamily. She soft-ened her focus out toward the grassy shadows. The two of them fell silent, until,

"THERE!"

A tiny green glow flashed several yards in front of them.

"You've got a good eye, Connie."

"You just have to be quiet and patient, and they come to you."

"Ooh, there's another one!"

There were two little lights now, flashing in tandem and coming closer to the stairs. Connie cupped her hands and clasped the air. She made a small peephole in her fist and looked inside.

"Got 'im!" she exclaimed. "Here, take a look."

She held her hands at Stee's eye level, and he peered in, his eyelashes brushing her fingers as the light flickered. He could just make out the firefly's thin black legs when its abdomen glowed.

Connie took one more peek, and then she opened her hands, letting the insect fly off. "You know," she said, settling back against him, "the male flashes first, hoping to get a female's attention."

"Does he now?" Stee said, his nose close to her collarbone, trying to latch on to her perfume among the fading scents of sunscreen and bug repellent.

"I read somewhere that the females like the males who can flash the brightest and longest."

"Good news for me," Stee said, nuzzling her neck.

"Of course, those flashy males attract predatory females, who eat them after they mate with them."

"Well, I'd better feed you right quick," he said, nipping her ear.

"Yeah, because you'd taste terrible," she agreed as their lips met.

Connie brought her A Game to that kiss. It wasn't trying too hard; it wasn't a mouthful of pheromones and desperation. It was sweet and hot and honest. She made a delicious humming sound as he pushed back her hair. When her hands alighted on his chest, he got light-headed.

She smiled. "I take it back. You taste pretty good."

Glorious.

He needed her closer. With a sweeping gesture, he reached around her and pulled her onto his lap in one move. As she slid happily into place, a bolt of the most searing pain he had ever experienced shot through his leg.

"*shhGAH!*"

"Stee—what's wrong?" Connie scrambled back onto the step.

His eyes twisted shut. "Muh ... knee ... CHRIST!"

"I thought you had it wrapped up and it wouldn't be a problem ..."

He shook his head wildly. "No, it's not the arthritis—it's like something popped."

Connie was on her feet. "What can I do to help? Do you have

painkillers—can you *have* painkillers? Do you want an ice pack?"

His head bobbed up and down. "Ice—ice pack, please! And drugs—upstairs in my bag. Prescription bottle."

She disappeared into the house. He could hear her rustling around in the ancient refrigerator's freezer section, ransacking the drawers and cabinets, and then she came out, carrying a Ziploc bag loaded with ice. "I'll be right back." She went back in and quickly returned with a tall glass of water and a couple of small white pills.

"Here you go."

Stee took a mouthful of water, popped in the pills, and swallowed. Still wincing, he gave her a half-hearted smile. "Better living through chemistry."

Connie looked at him sympathetically. "Let me help you inside onto the couch. Would you do better with a pillow under your knee?"

Stee nodded, teary-eyed from the pain. Connie got in front of him on the stairs, and he braced himself on the railing with his left hand. She took his right and helped him stagger upright. She joined him on the stair and supported him as he hopped and dragged himself into the house, going from countertop to chair back to doorjamb until he was close enough to the sofa to pitch over onto it, his knee angled in the air like a grasshopper's.

Connie piled the sofa pillows under his leg and gently lowered it so his bent knee was supported and his feet were on the armrest. She retrieved the bag of ice, wrapping it in a hand towel before placing it on his kneecap.

"There. Is that better?"

"Yeah, that's better." Stee wasn't seeing stars anymore. The ice was beginning to slow the throbbing, and he knew in a few minutes the medicine would kick in and he could relax.

Connie had left and returned without him even seeing her do it. She had a pillow from the bed upstairs, and she tucked it underneath his head. She stroked his hair off his forehead and pulled up a chair so she could talk to him as he lay supine before her.

"Well, that was embarrassing," Stee said ruefully.

"How're you doing?" She took his hand in both of hers. He noticed she had iridescent nail polish, like she had been blowing soap bubbles in the sun.

"I need to call my doctor."

"I'll get your phone." She was slipping back into her professional, untouchable director mode. He didn't want her to just yet. He didn't really want her to leave the room.

"I must look like a rickety old man," Stee said plaintively as she walked away, trying not to sound as pitiful as he felt. She turned and smiled.

"No, you were pretty heroic. You risked life and limb to kiss me. That was nice."

"Is that the best you can come up with: 'nice'?"

Her dimple was out and he was suitably awestruck. "Nice kiss. Nice man. 'Nice' fits the situation pretty nicely."

———————

Where are you, man?

Leonard stared forlornly at his laptop, the screen ablaze with Stee's Facebook fan page. Having waded through weeks of generic postings that stank of a PR campaign, he was hoping to see a line or two from Stee himself explaining what he was up to ... why he had been unable to answer even one of Leonard's daily emails and text messages ... and perhaps a mention of a little program called ISPeye that might be of interest to anyone who loved music, psychology and figuring people out without having to get to know them personally.

There was no word from the Great Man here or anywhere else.

This is not good.

He toggled over to the live feed from the lone security camera he had tapped into. He hadn't observed any unexpected activity at Stee's mansion over the last couple of hours, just the usual comings and goings of FedEx trucks, pool service vans and an occasional high-end suv. He hoped to glimpse the red Mustang convertible speeding out of the gate in the direction of Jon Jonegon's studio, but there was no sign of it. The car never went anywhere. It was as if Stee hadn't left his house in days, or had gone into hiding somewhere no one could find him.

Writer's block's a bitch, I guess.

Stay strong, man—I'm here for you.

chapter 11

Home at last after his Virginia sojourn, Stee stood in front of his set list, posted to the bulletin board in his office.

He had been a very busy man since the dam broke in Virginia and his creative output started flowing once again. With only days to go before the first day of recording with Jon and the full band, the running order was finally filling in:

1. "Click, Click"
2. "Ginny, Ginny, Ginny"
3. "Unexpected Places"
4. "Shot Glass"
5. "So I Go"
6. "Cold Comfort"
7.
8. "Too Much Monkey Business"
9.
10. "See You Cry"
11. "Pressed Flowers"
12.

"Click, Click" had no lyrics. It didn't need any. The ceiling fan percussion would lead into the rumbling blues of Chad's mighty guitar. For the first time, Stee Walsh and the River Runners would play an instrumental number in a general release album: the lead-off number, in fact.

Something old, something new ...

"See You Cry" was completely kickass. As he orchestrated it in his head, he imagined a galloping bass line worthy of Caldwell's talents and Larry playing saloon piano—what could be better? Stee wondered how long it would take the critics to figure out he had summed up his entire marriage to Kayla in three minutes and eleven seconds. It would be worth the snarky speculation to pound her out of his system once and for all.

Then there was the flip side of the divorce saga: the chilling loneliness. "So I Go" wasn't his personal story, although he could certainly relate to it. It came from an image Stee got in his head while he was swimming last Sunday, a mental picture of a guy driving down a mountain covered in snow.

He also had a couple of other ideas knocking about his brain that had to shake out soon. There was an image that didn't fit into "See You Cry" that intrigued him:

I was looking down the barrel of a shot glass ...

That was all he had, but it had a cleverness that harkened back to his first couple of albums. He was sure it would jell if it drifted in his subconscious for a while.

Then there was what he had dubbed "Pressed Flowers," the snippet of a family saga that he started back in Devon with Chad on the couch, about a photo that captured a mother's faded dreams of her own happiness: *his* mother's story. No mystery there: Chad saw it in seconds from the look on his face.

Stee was still on the fence about this one, though. Since his career began to take off, he'd made a hard-and-fast rule that he would never use his family as subject matter. He was the one who had agreed to being in the public eye—not them—so he would protect them as much as possible. (Of course, once the divorce papers were signed, an ex was fair game.)

Stee shrugged. Perhaps he could give his mother a little fame and recognition after all those times in the early years driving him to gigs and sewing his outfits and worrying about him making a living. Still, "Pressed Flowers" needed work: the chorus wasn't bad, but the rest was too sentimental, too literal. That was a job for another day, as was "Cold Comfort," a song he was wrestling with that was a lot darker than his usual material.

Breaking some of his self-imposed rules had helped end his writer's block, that was clear. He had survived returning to Virginia, and was working on putting some issues from his past to rest in song. He was collaborating with a girl, if you could still call her a girl when she was north of 40. He was even dating that girl, if that's what you could call taking her to dinner once and surviving an exasperatingly bad night after a fantastically great first kiss.

Connie hadn't abandoned him, though. She'd set him up in the guest room on the first floor, fetching his sleep t-shirt and toothbrush. She'd helped him stumble to the bathroom and back again, staying by the door with her head turned while he did his business. When he'd shuffled into the living room the next morning, he saw she hadn't gone upstairs to a spare bed, sacking out instead on the couch, staying within earshot. She had not been too tired to smile when he woke her up, either, which made his world of troubles fall away.

I'm liking this girl. A lot.

She had edited well into the night in order to present him with a thumb drive containing the rough cut she'd promised to deliver before he flew out that morning. His song and her story threaded together naturally, and it was simple and strong and striking. He even looked comfortable in his own skin when he was hiking around, "seeking." She nailed the empathy and the desire without making him look dopey.

Connie kept him safe, not just on camera. There he had been, out in the middle of nowhere without any of his usual guardians at hand. He had lost all dignity, like a dying cockroach with his legs in the air, and she was ready and willing when he turned his pride over to her for safekeeping. This wasn't just keeping his bloopers off the internet. This was holding what happened between them, between them.

Like that kiss.

They hadn't kissed again before she trundled him into the Town Car so he could go to the airport. That distressed him. She had been friendly but distant all that morning, packing up her equipment, wrapping her cables, checking bathrooms and kitchen counters for any stray belongings. Since he wasn't steady enough on his feet to plant one on her without her help, he couldn't initiate anything, so he left with a wave and a smile, feeling like he'd failed an audition.

Maybe she didn't want to tell me good-bye.

He mulled this over on his flight back to LAX and while he waited in his orthopedist's office. As usual, his doctor gave him a steroid injection and told him now was the time to seriously consider total joint replacement surgery, and as usual, Stee said now was *not* the time since he had work to do.

Which he did. And he needed to go do more in a few minutes.

Having swallowed a couple of Aleve and wrapped his knee securely, Stee grabbed his keys and slipped on his shoes. He was due at Chad's place to hash through the existing songs and bring Larry up to speed. He put the set list in his pocket and brightened. He was toying with improvising the final track once he got to the studio. Winging it could be a good way to get everybody back in gear after so many years apart.

Chad and Larry would tell him if he was crazy, but he wasn't worried.

————————

"You're fucking crazy, Stee."

Larry Mulholland was perched behind the banks of keyboards in Chad's home studio, his arms tightly folded across his concave chest, glowering beneath his faded Dodgers baseball cap. The older he got, the more he looked like a light bulb with a mustache.

"And why is that, Larry?"

"I'm not worried about me. Give me an opening chord and I can take care of myself," he blithely offered. "Chad, of course, will do fine, and Caldwell will clock in, and Bobby will eventually do a passable job if we can get him into the studio with a clean tox screen. I'm worried about *you*. It took you forever to get seven decent songs on paper, and now you just want to see what happens in the studio, for the final cut on the album? That'll be a colossal disaster."

Stee didn't take this too much to heart. Larry had a major dooms-day streak courtesy of his parents, an actuary and an accountant, who nearly kept him from joining the band in the first place by in-sisting he complete dental school before pursuing his "hobby." Even though he quit school eventually, he was determined to nail down every possible fuckup ahead of time and not leave much to chance.

Stee decided to defer to the calmer head in the group. "Chad, what's your opinion? How fast and loose do you want to be in the studio?"

Chad's eyes narrowed as he thought this through. "Stee, I'm with Larry. I'd feel better if we had the melodies and lyrics worked out."

Stee didn't let his surprise show. "And why is that, Chad?"

"Because it's been a long time since we've been in the studio, brother."

Stee frowned. "You saw how I was in Devon. Don't you trust me now?"

Chad shrugged apologetically. "I don't trust the muse, Stee. She shows up when she wants to and doesn't when you need her to. It's not like you can call her up and make her come out here from Greece or wherever muses live."

Call her up.

Why didn't I think of that before? I just have to get Connie to the studio.

This might pose a problem. Stee Walsh and the River Runners had a virtual "Girls Keep Out" sign on their studio door. The locker room atmosphere helped them survive the brutality of 28-hour recording sessions and months of farting into the seat cushions of a tour bus. It wasn't that they didn't like women; given there were nine marriages among the four avowed heterosexuals in the band, they obviously *loved* them. They just didn't have a place in the band.

While they had shared the stage with a couple of remarkable ladies—he wasn't about to say no to Emmylou Harris or Joan Jett—there had also been a couple of studio debacles. Making a pop single with the all-girl band Candy Buttons in 1984 was not the sorority romp Stee had anticipated. They were shrill, coarse and lousy musicians. To add insult to injury, they treated him like he was three hundred years old. He didn't like feeling quaint. It killed him that the song had charted so well.

Later, one of *Come, Come, Come*'s many (many) problems was the use of female back-up singers, given that the lyrics took a number of wrong turns during the call and response, like in "My Way or the Highway":

You're up my alley (up my alley)
The top of my tree (ooh, ooh, ooh)
Since my old lady (my old lady)
Shafted me (shaft me, shaft me)

He joked much later, "This is your producer on drugs." Stee had been the producer; he'd know.

He had never asked Tamara for her ideas when he was songwriting because neither of them considered that to be her job. Kayla? Her talents were few and narrow at best. But Connie was different. She helped him frame his thoughts and gave him a lot to think about. She had been his good-luck charm for this whole project, and if his most trusted collaborators were having doubts about this album, he needed her here.

Stee looked at his bandmates and bit his lip. He wasn't ready to spill details about Connie yet. He'd need to introduce her at the right time ...

Like when I break it to them I'm doing a solo video ... and it's in the can.

A ruse was needed. Stee theatrically patted his jeans pocket. "Shit—cell phone. Hang on, fellas. I gotta take this."

Leaving Larry and Chad befuddled, their hands idle on their instruments, he scooted out of the studio and hit speed dial as soon as he was out of their sightline. Two rings later, Connie answered.

"Stee? Wow, you called before I was in bed. I'm going to mark this day in my calendar."

He shivered with pleasure. "It's so good to hear your voice, Connie." Her tone had this warm, honeyed quality that told him, second kiss or no, she was glad he had called.

He forced his head to clear. "Let me cut to the chase. I need you to come to LA for a few days."

"How soon?"

"Thursday. We'll start recording and I want you to be there."

"I have to check my schedule and get back to you."

His eyes went wide. "Connie, you have to be there. It's important."

"Amanda has finals soon. My brother would have to keep an eye on her and the house. I can't just cut and run."

Her reluctance seemed preposterous, unless he had really screwed up somehow.

He sighed. "Connie, why are you holding back? Did I piss you off?"

"No." She sounded surprised by the question.

"Then why can't you come out here?"

"Stee, what's wrong? You sound panicked."

"No, no, I'm good," he bluffed, squeezing his eyes shut. He wasn't ready to tell her how much her life had been sparking his creativity, so he flailed around for any plausible excuse, no matter how bogus. When he found one, he jumped back in. "I've decided to use the band on the 'Unexpected Places' track."

Her response was immediate and indignant. "You can't!"

"I'm considering it."

"You swore the acoustic version was the final version. I synched the whole video to it. You change the track at all, I'll have to start over."

"I guess so, yes." He didn't want to make her upset but he needed her within an arm's reach again, by any means necessary.

"But the video has to be in to BetaComp by the first of the month."

"All the more reason for you to come out to the studio to work this out now, isn't it?"

Stee held his breath. He could practically hear her brain melting over the phone. After a moment, she sighed, barely masking her fury. "Changes this late will cost you. I'll have to reassess our contract."

"Understood."

"You're going to have to tell the band I'm coming to the session. I may need to grab some shots of them playing if it's no longer just you."

"Okay."

"And getting a flight on short notice is going to cost a fortune."

"Connie, this is on me; Angie'll do your reservations. So, you're coming?"

"I have no other choice, do I?"

Stee did a silent victory dance. "Great! I'll get Angie on it right away."

"I can't believe you're doing this, Stee." She sounded worse than angry. She sounded disappointed in him.

"I'll make it up to you, I promise." She hung up without saying good-bye.

Stee frowned at himself for not being up front with her. Then again, once she got there, he was sure he'd be able to bring her around once he told her that he had "re-reconsidered" and "accepted her first version" and "Hey, since you came all the way out here, let me show you the sights and take you up to the house and all that."

That prospect cheered him up again. He returned to his perplexed bandmates, beaming.

"Worry not, my friends. I just spoke to the muse and she'll be at the studio."

———

Even though Stee had proven to be a charming guy and a spectacular kisser, that wasn't going to make up for the fact that he was demanding that Connie fly across country to jack up her video. All the more reason she needed to end this little romance right here and now ... no matter how much she liked him.

She had become incredibly fond of "Unexpected Places" as he had recorded it in the farmhouse dining room only a few days before she arrived. Stee was a much better guitarist than she'd given him credit for, and that oversized acoustic guitar of his was mellow and deep. "Pretty" didn't adequately describe it anymore; she could no longer find words for how it made her feel.

She had become equally protective of her video concept, which only worked if he was truly alone. With other instruments joining the chorus, that went out the window. He couldn't be shored up by his band. He needed to be lonely and vulnerable. Otherwise no one would believe that a woman could mean that much to him.

Because you're a jackass, Stee. A vain, controlling, indecisive jackass.

She sighed sullenly, knowing that wasn't true. Stee had been nothing but kind and generous with his patience and his pocketbook, as she felt her way through her first high-profile shoot. He seemed happiest when the people around him were having a good time, which meant the crew adored him. He even got Amanda to laugh once or twice, which Connie couldn't do much anymore. Even when he complained about the opening scenes, he listened to her and gave over to her direction.

Then I called him sexy ... and we kissed on the porch.

Following a sleepless night on the couch with that kiss rolling over and over in her brain like wet laundry in a clothes dryer, she'd convinced herself it was a mistake to even imagine getting involved with Stee Walsh. He was flying back to California without a need to ever see her again. She'd be left in the suburbs with a shelf full of CDs and months of boneheaded regret.

Besides, she couldn't fall in love with a guy like Stee, with whom the whole world was in love and who seemed to love the whole world in return. If everyone was so special to Stee, then no one was.

I've married that man once. I need to be the special one this time around.

She was turning to a clean page in her storyboard book when her cell phone went off. She had programmed the name and number into her phone so she wouldn't be taken by surprise again. The *Psycho* ringtone helped as well.

"Hello, this is Connie Rafferty. What may I do for you, Terri?"

"What flawless phone etiquette. It's as if you've been practicing for a job interview."

"Is there something new?"

"There always is for the right candidate. Are you the right candidate right now?"

"What's the job?"

Terri rattled off the main points of a job in Arlington, which was a hell of a commute, but "in this economy, you should buy a tent and sleep in the parking lot if it means steady employment."

"Sounds great," Connie lied. "When would they want to see me?"

"Thursday."

Oh, of fucking course.

Maybe this was a sign she should cut her losses. Her dream project as a videographer was over and done, and she would be better off packing it in a box and stuffing it under her bed so she could work a real job once again. That approach would solve her romantic dilemma as well: she'd end it on her terms and tell Stee where to stick his reshoot.

"Name the time. I'll be there."

chapter 12

"What ... *is* ... this shit?"

Stee's jaw clenched. "Not impressed, Bobby?"

"Why the fuck should I be?"

The River Runners' first full rehearsal at Chad's, a mere two days before Jon would join them at the studio, had been excruciating, with full credit going to drummer Bobby Brewer. Once he'd arrived, three hours late, it quickly became clear that he was incapable of keeping a beat. Bobby would pile-drive over the melodies, and his sticking was sloppy. Stee and the rest dragged him through the up-tempo numbers and gritted their teeth, knowing that time was in short supply.

Yet when they'd tried out "Pressed Flowers," Bobby stopped playing altogether ... and here they sat.

"Bobby, just play the goddamn song," Caldwell hissed, exhausted and edgy.

Bobby wouldn't let up. "First those chugga-chugga Johnny Cash ripoffs and now this gloppy ballad. When did the River Runners lose its edge?"

"This is good material, solid songwriting," Larry sniped from behind the keyboards. "If it doesn't sound right, the problem is you."

Relentless, Bobby looked from player to player. "We've been out of the spotlight forever, dudes. We gotta prove we haven't changed, we can still get the party started—that we're still the best *rock-and-roll* band out there. This soft-serve shit is gonna kill us for good."

"Don't listen to him; he's high," Chad muttered to Stee.

"What's that?" Bobby barked. "Speak up, Chad!"

"He said you're high, jackass!" Caldwell shouted, heading toward the drum set with his bass slung behind him and his fingers clenched.

Stee stepped between them. "Caldwell, cool it. Bobby, take a break. Go outside. Now."

The drummer sneered. "You're all a bunch of pussies, you know that? Especially you, Stee." Bobby tossed his sticks to the floor and stalked out. Robbie the Roadie, who had been paging through a comic book in the corner of the studio, stood up.

"Want me to keep an eye on him, Stee?"

"Yeah. Make sure he's back in five—and the only thing he's smoking out there is tobacco."

"Yep." Once Robbie left, every man in the room cursed Bobby in his own way.

"Fucking cranked-up *asshole!*" Caldwell sputtered.

"He looks awful," Chad said. "He's all scabbed over."

Larry shook his head. "He's reduced to doing meth? How the mighty have fallen."

"Bobby knows he needs this job," Stee said. "He's gonna snap to when he comes off of break."

"Puh-leese," Larry said. "He's probably passed out in the parking lot. He's hopeless."

"Hey," Stee said sharply. "He's always had problems, but put some pressure on him and the work gets done. This is our comeback album and I want all of us on board."

"Doesn't matter what you *want*. It's about what we *need*," Caldwell said flatly. "Bobby is in no shape to play, and no amount of time or pressure is going to change that. He's got to go."

"I'm with Caldwell," Larry said, frowning. "Bobby's too far gone this time."

Stee turned to his guitarist. "Chad, want to weigh in?"

"We've got to move on without him, Stee."

Stee's eyes widened. "You're that sure—forty years in?"

Chad sighed heavily. "Look, he was there for you when you needed a meal and a couch and a deadbolt between you and your dad. But you paid off that debt a long time ago." He moved closer to Stee so only he could hear him continue. "And you know better than anyone here, you're not doing him any favors covering for him. If he never hits bottom, he'll never get better and we'll all get sucked down with him."

Stee felt sick to his stomach. It wasn't simply processing how truly dreadful Bobby had become, so far gone he smelled like spoiled milk. It was like looking at an out-of-focus photo of himself from seventeen years back: the arrogance and denial so thick he couldn't perceive how thoroughly he was destroying the people he loved.

Robbie opened the studio door and Bobby shambled in, wired and tetchy. Stee got in front of him before he could pick up his sticks.

"Bobby," Stee said evenly, "we've gotta move forward with rehearsal now because Jon's here day after tomorrow. You're in no shape to play and we're on a deadline. You gotta leave."

"You're shitting me."

"I speak from experience, man. You gotta get some help and get cleaned up. You're not any good to anyone like this, least of all to you."

"You kicking me out?" he snarled. "You want me to leave?"

"We all do," Stee replied, motioning to the rest of the band.

"You can't kick me out, Stee. I'm a founding member."

"I'm not kicking you out of the band, but you can't work with us until you're clean. That's it."

"Who are you to tell me to get clean? You nearly torpedoed the act back in the Eighties."

"Then I stopped."

"Yeah, and I can stop when I want to, too, you know."

"That ain't gonna happen before Jon comes into town. We've run out of time." Stee's throat went dry. "You're off the album. I'm sorry, man."

Bobby's eyes darted from man to man. Finding no sympathizers, he jerked to his feet, threw his sticks at the high-hat cymbals as hard as he could, and hauled out the studio door.

"You can't fire me. You'll be sorry you tried. Fuck you, Stee!" Bobby continued his tirade down the hall as the soundproof door slowly suctioned shut.

Larry and Caldwell stood staring at the closed door in silent frustration. Chad sat in an armchair and began drumming the body of his guitar with his fingers. Stee rubbed his face with his hands and muttered:

"Ladies and gentlemen, *Bobby Brewer and the Insiders!*"

————————

"Ladies and gentlemen, *Bobby Brewer and the Insiders!*"

Whenever Bobby's drum solo went on too long or too wild, or he missed an entrance, or the cymbal crashed unexpectedly, that's what Stee would announce over the microphone. He did it in recording sessions; he did it in performance, too, if the mistake was one the audience could hear. Then Stee would throw his head back in a full-throated laugh and Chad, Larry and Caldwell would crack up. Right on cue, Bobby would always stand, spin his sticks in the air and take a bow ... even though he never thought it was very funny.

Stee should have figured that out by now.

I deserve better, after all I've done for him.

Freed from the studio bullshit and back home, Bobby sought out a tiny package of a small white crystal in the pocket of his bomber jacket. He dumped a cruddy pipe onto the coffee table and crouched on the edge of the loveseat with his lighter.

Maybe some respect.

Bobby was hardly the guy you'd expect to have a problem earning people's respect. He looked like he could have played football in high school: six-two, square-jawed, long limbs. He had a swagger. Girls dug him.

Even though sitting behind a drum kit for four decades had contributed to his current gut and butt spread, at this point in his life—fifty-nine this year, thank you very much—he was still the best-looking dog in this pack of mutts. He wasn't a cue ball like Caldwell; he wasn't a no-chin wonder like Larry; he wasn't gay like Chad. And he wasn't the moth-eaten redneck Stee had been all his life, either. Yet here he was, expected to bow and scrape like some clown in a circus.

Yeah, I deserve better.

It stuck in his craw that the reporters never got it right when they chronicled the history of Stee Walsh. Fact was, Stee wasn't the original bandleader, and the River Runners weren't the original band. Bobby had methodically planned the band's success. First priority was the lineup. Their bassist from their high school days got drafted, leaving a hole in their rhythm section. Not long after, they found Chad at a cheese-ball country and western bar at the North Carolina border and Stee moved to bass. There was also this keyboard guy Chad knew—Larry, up from Savannah during summer break from dental school—who could step into their Doors numbers as needed.

Next was the song list. Bobby saw to it that they had a solid set list of covers, which he knew the kids really wanted to hear instead of new stuff. He threw Stee a bone by playing two or three of his songs each set; it was rare to find a bassist who could sing, so Bobby was willing to keep him happy.

Final step: get a record deal. That was going to be the result of Will Corrigan of Majestic Records standing at the back of that smoky Baltimore concert hall in 1974. With Bobby at the helm, the Insiders were going places.

Corrigan was a cubby roughneck with a hefty beard and sunglasses permanently attached to his nose, even indoors, even at night. When Bobby caught up with him after their set, he had his arms folded like a bouncer, sucking on a toothpick, lost in thought. Bobby put out his hand. It was ignored. Bobby barged ahead with a shrug and a broad smile. No matter how much of a prick he was, Corrigan had the keys to his future.

"Hey, man, thanks for coming to the gig. So, what'd you—"

Corrigan started walking away without even looking at him. "Where's Walsh?"

Bobby's smile froze, as if he hadn't heard him correctly. "The bass player?"

"The songwriter," Corrigan snapped, searching the crowd.

Bobby caught his arm. "I head up this band. You talk to *me*."

Corrigan shrugged off his hand with a violent jerk. "Look, dick-head, I don't care who you *think* you are—"

"I'm the leader of the band, goddammit! I'm the *drummer!*"

Corrigan laughed in Bobby's face, which was a feat since he was a head shorter. "Oh, the *drummer*. How could I have missed you all the way in the *back?*"

Every muscle in Bobby's body went rigid. It was all he could do not to deck this guy.

"Stee Walsh is the guy Gregg told me I had to see. He writes your stuff, right?"

"Yeah, a couple of numbers, but—"

"Why isn't he writing *all* your numbers?" Corrigan demanded. "And why is he stuck on bass singing backup? If he played rhythm with that freak-of-nature guitarist you got on lead, Walsh would be able to sing. Then the band would *work*. Then you'd be going places."

"*I* sing lead, buddy," Bobby shouted, thumping his chest for emphasis. "The band is Bobby Brewer and the Insiders, not Stee Walsh and the Shit Kickers. I sing lead and I run the lineup, or we don't go anywhere."

"Let me tell you something, sweetheart: you *aren't* going anywhere. Not unless Stee takes over. Stee's got the spark, man. All eyes go to him, and the other guys, Chad and that cat on keyboards, they play in spite of you half the time, and that's a shame because you're a good drummer." He shrugged. "Look, man, if you want off this college town merry-go-round and a record deal, you have to step out of the way and let the real talent lead you there."

Corrigan walked over to where Stee, Chad and Larry were packing up the instruments and equipment with help from a teenager named Robbie who'd attached himself to the band over the past few weeks. Corrigan put out his hand, and the boys popped down off the stage to meet him. Everyone was all smiles.

Bobby wasn't pissed anymore. He was caved in, like he had taken a grenade to the chest.

After a night of pot-infused reflection, Bobby realized that a small percent of something was better than a large percent of nothing. Not long afterward, Bobby signed the Majestic recording contract without a peep of protest, giving Stee sole songwriting credit and a larger cut of the profits. With a stroke of his pen, Bobby Brewer and the Insiders died in a broken-down club in Baltimore, and Stee Walsh and the River Runners rose from its ashes.

That cocksucker Corrigan was right: putting Stee out front got them noticed and made them stars. So Bobby stayed year after year—sitting all the way in the *back*—putting in his beats, cashing his growing paychecks and living the rock-and-roll dream: girls, music; girls, touring; girls, MTV; girls, partying; and, oh yeah, girls. Not a bad gig.

Good thing, because home life was a joke. He had quit after three marriages and figured ladies on the road were always better than living with a vampire in a house that wasn't going to be his after a divorce anyway. If the girls at the show, even the fat ones who were usually easy pickings, weren't up for any fun, he could find someone he could pay to play.

1992 was not a banner year for Mr. Bobby Brewer, though. His second ex-wife had just sent him to the poorhouse because, like an idiot, he forgot to make her sign a pre-nup, having learned nothing from his first ex-wife. Up to then, he had been able to forget his troubles with Stee, but his drinking buddy had shipped off to rehab for 45 days and had to prove he was on the wagon to see his kids again. Stee had to leave the Santa Monica pad for good, so the party would have to be wherever Bobby was, whenever he could afford it: his house; his apartment; his agent's guest cottage; his cousin's guest room; a hotel room; a motel room.

Over the last seventeen years, Stee had gone solo more and more often, leaving Bobby behind. Fucking 12-steppers probably told him to stay away from his old friend—his *true* friend, who kept it secret whenever Stee crashed at his place until his black eyes healed after his dad had given him a workout.

Work with other bands dried up—and no, the rumor wasn't true that no one wanted to hire him because he had a bit of a substance abuse problem now and then. It's just he didn't feel connected to the material, not like the old days. If the music didn't *speak* to him, he wasn't going to play it.

Now that Stee's music had turned to shit and his oldest friend treated him with nothing but contempt, it was time to leave the band for good.

The smoke was furling in the pipe. Bobby breathed it down deep. He wished his royalty check had arrived that morning; he would have had enough cash for a hooker, too.

"Here's to the next chapter of my life," he said to himself. He wiped his mouth, searching for a bolt of inspiration from the hit.

I know; I'll open a bar.

"I'll call it The Bobby *Brewer-y*!" he exclaimed to the empty room. "That's pretty fucking funny." Then he reconsidered.

Naw, it needs more class.

"The Insiders," he said definitively. "That's it, of course." Then the second hit went right to his head.

———

"Stee? Hey, you're calling early."

"Connie? Are you coming out here tomorrow? Please tell me you're coming."

"I left a message with Angie earlier. I have a job interview tomorrow. It's what I should be doing with my life right now, so if I have to do reshoots they'll have to wait until—"

"Connie, Bobby's dead. They just found him—"

"Oh God, Stee ..."

"He was doing meth and his heart gave out—he was just in rehearsal this morning—oh fuck, he's dead, what am I—he's—"

"I'll be there, Stee. I'll fly out first thing. Shh ... it's okay ... it's going to be okay."

Stee, dude, I am so, so sorry about Bobby.

Yeah, he was a thorn in your side from the beginning, with his half-assed playing and his whoring around and drugging and all that bizness. That must have been so hard. I know how much you treasure true friends and how much sorrow you carry when people you love let you down.

I've been there. My dad ran off when I was three. The only memory I have of him was when he sang your music. Then he was gone. At least I still have your music.

My phone is on 24/7. I'm here for you. Really, call me, man. Consider me a true friend.

Leonard

chapter 13

In the blinding Malibu sunshine, framed by the archway of Stee's rambling mansion with the Spanish tile roof, Connie's luggage looked no better than cardboard boxes held together with duct tape.

She was trying to absorb the enormity of the place. The uphill approach to the gated front entrance circled around the back of the property, and she had gotten a glimpse of the churning Pacific reflected in two stories of floor-to-ceiling glass before eucalyptus and palms occluded the view. She tried to estimate the number of rooms by counting the windows; she stopped at 30.

What was I expecting: a two-bedroom condo with clubhouse privileges?

Once he took out her laptop and video equipment and slammed the Town Car's trunk shut, the driver whisked her ratty Costco rollaway to the front door with the same care as if it had been a vintage Louis Vuitton. The heavy wooden door appeared to be old-growth redwood hewn into lumber for a Spanish mission centuries ago. The driver rang the doorbell.

The door swung open with some effort. When Stee appeared from the darkened entryway, a sudden, relieved smile completely illuminated his face.

"Connie."

She couldn't move. She was taking in so much so quickly: how sad his eyes were; how drawn he looked; how seeing him again knocked the wind right out of her.

Stee nodded to the driver. "Hey, Munny, how's it going?"

"Mr. Walsh, it is going so well, thank you for asking. Would you like me to put the luggage in the north guest room?"

"Naw, just put it inside the door here. I'll move it later." He reached over to a small alcove near the entrance and grabbed a voucher. "Here you go; Angie's seen to your tip."

The driver touched the shiny bill of his chauffeur's cap and pocketed the receipt. "Ms. Rafferty, please enjoy your stay. Mr. Walsh, much good health to you."

Connie heard him step back to the car across the cobblestones behind her as Stee drew her through the doorway as speedily as he could before shoving the door shut behind them. He pulled her tight against him, his tears wetting her cheek.

"Thank you for coming, Connie."

"I am so, so sorry," she whispered. He didn't let go of her for some time, silent until he escorted her across the marble-floored foyer to a sunken living room facing the ocean. She picked up on Willie Dixon coming through the sound system, his voice heavy with sorrow.

"I'm glad you got here between phone calls," he explained, sitting them down on a chocolate suede couch set near a striking granite fireplace. "Since none of Bobby's family has anything to do with him anymore, it's falling on me to get him buried after the coroner's done with him."

"You're a good friend," Connie said, squeezing his hand.

He looked at her wearily. "No, I'm a terrible friend. I didn't know how bad things had gotten. Shit, he was practically living in his car."

"How awful."

"I should have known; I saw it coming." He shook his head. "When I went to rehab all those years ago, I knew I had to cut ties with the people I used to party with to stay clean, and one of them was Bobby. I just couldn't cut him out completely. I mean, we'd known each other since we were eight years old. He was a River Runner; he created our sound just as much as Chad or me. As much as it killed me, though, I had to keep my distance a lot of the time; he was ... unrepentant. Now here we are."

Stee hunched forward, his elbows on his knees and his face

resting against his palms as if he were praying. Connie put her arm around his shoulders. Nothing she could say would make him feel better before he was ready to feel better. She knew from experience that the best thing she could do was stay quiet and present.

The doorbell broke the silence. Stee stood and helped her off the couch.

"Stee?" A heavy-set woman with long frosted hair appeared at the fireplace. "Marcos is here. Do you want to meet him in your office?"

"Yeah, Daniel and Chad are down there already. I'll be there in a minute. Thanks, Angie." The woman turned on her heel and walked back to the entryway.

"That's my lawyer," Stee muttered. "He's been trying to find a cemetery and figure out what we're gonna tell BetaComp about the album. Sorry, this might take a while."

Connie suddenly felt uneasy as the next couple of days played out in her imagination.

"Stee, I'm going to call a cab and go to a hotel. You have a lot to do, and you need to be with your friends and family right now. I don't want to be in the way."

He looked terrified. "Don't go. I want you to be here."

Connie heard low voices move from the foyer down the hallway. "Have you told anyone about the video yet? Have you told anyone about me?"

"No. Why?"

"Well, how do you want me to introduce myself to your friends, to the band? As a videographer? As your friend? Do you want to have to explain all this right now?"

"I want you here," he pleaded, looking haggard, "because you lost someone close to you and you know what I'm going through. Because you're not so deep in all of these people, all of this history, you can help me keep some perspective. Please stay."

Connie flashed back to her isolation when Chris died, and how bone-chillingly lonely it was when she couldn't find someone she knew and trusted she could speak to about her anger and grief.

If I can spare him that ...

"Okay, I'll stay," she said. "We just need to agree on a game plan really soon, okay?"

"Thank you, thank you, thank you." He kissed her cheek and grinned as he headed toward the hallway. "I'll send Angie to get you set up in your room. Everyone's meeting for dinner at Chad's about 7:30 and we'll drive over together. I'll find you before that, I promise. Make yourself at home." Then he disappeared.

She was now stranded in that enormous living room, her thoughts swirling with the surf out beyond the wall of windows.

Why did I fly out here?

Because he said he needed me. I canceled an interview, shipped Amanda off to my brother's and came out here without thinking it through, because he said he needed me.

She took in the aerial view of the enormous lap pool and Tuscan-tiled terraced patio a level below her, with landscaping and furnishings like those in some aristocrat's mansion on the Italian coast.

I've only known the guy for a month. Would I have flown out here if he wasn't famous?

She looked out at the ocean, heard the faint caw of the seagulls gliding above the water.

I came because he was crying ... I never thought I'd hear Stee Walsh cry. That killed me. Guys like him don't cry.

I don't want him to cry ...

While collecting photos of Stee when she was storyboarding, she discovered hundreds of pictures from grade school, high school, hippie beginnings, New Wave success, European tours, album covers, red carpet portraits, benefit concerts, award handshakes, official portraiture, and candid shots. Yet she never came across an image as fragile as he was when she said she'd leave a few moments ago ... and none so joyful as when she said she'd stay.

Maybe he needs me.

Maybe he thinks he loves me.

Maybe I came here because I think I—

"Ms. Rafferty?"

Connie jumped. It was the frosted-haired woman she had seen earlier. "Stee asked me to get you set up. Could you come with me, please?"

"Sure, thanks." Connie walked to the foyer behind Stee's assistant. She glanced around for her suitcase. "Excuse me, where's my luggage?"

"It has already been moved to your room, Ms. Rafferty," she said curtly, not even looking over her shoulder to talk to her directly. Connie was taken completely off guard. She always considered herself someone everyone liked, or at least someone no one disliked. However, she could feel the chill coming off the woman's cold shoulder across the three paces' distance she was being forced to keep.

"Are you Angie?"

"Angela."

Brrr.

"Sorry—*Angela.*" Connie tried to identify the musicians in the framed photographs along the main hallway but they were speeding along way too fast. She decided to keep trying to warm things up. "Stee told me how much he relies on you."

"That's my job, Ms. Rafferty," she replied dully as they reached a spiral staircase. "Making accommodations, keeping people at bay." Angela worked her way upstairs, and Connie scurried to keep up.

"Please call me Connie." She got no reply.

They arrived at a mahogany door with a brushed steel handle. Connie followed Angela in, and then stopped dead in her tracks.

The north guest room was in reality a suite, with a view overlooking the ocean peeking behind the greenery. The decor was modern and unfussy, with a massive Hockney positioned over the fireplace as the centerpiece of the room. The bed faced the water, with linens the colors of sand and blue sky. A yellow orchid with bat-shaped blossoms possessed the coffee table. The space was opulent and quirky all at once.

Angela finally faced Connie for the first time. Her words were clipped, her expression devoid of humor. "Ms. Rafferty, given that you are a first-time guest here and I haven't been told what your role is going to be over the next few days—"

That makes two of us ...

"I will now go over the rules of the house. Please pay attention; I will only review these with you once. This is the north guest room, and you are permitted the run of this suite and the adjacent hallway and stairs down to the first level. Do not enter the other guest rooms as they may be occupied. The first level is a common area; you may use the entertainment equipment, the library and the kitchen 24/7 as long as you observe proper noise levels, and you are allowed to take whatever food or drink that is not labeled with the exception of alcoholic beverages of any kind. You are also not permitted to bring any alcohol, illicit substances or weaponry onto the property, for your own use or anyone else's. The south wing of the house on all three floors is off limits as it is reserved for the Walsh family only. You may only go to the basement-level rooms, the pool or the gym if you are accompanied by Mr. Walsh or one of his family members over 21. Going offsite is permitted, but all vehicles—including but not limited to automobiles, aircraft, watercraft and two-wheeled transportation—belonging to Mr. Walsh and his family are not to be touched. If you plan to explore the grounds or the beach, please contact me as security will need to be told to stand down. You are also advised to heed all buoys and other markers delineating Mr. Walsh's portion of the waterfront; his neighbors to the north use dogs to patrol their property and cannot be called off by anyone on our staff. If you need off-site services such as a taxi or dry cleaning, you contact me and I will process your request as soon as it is feasible. During your stay, you are allowed to access Wi-Fi service—the password changes every 24 hours, so contact me well in advance of your use—and to use your personal cell phone, but no photographs or recordings are permitted at any time. Any phone in the house will reach me if you dial 2; no outside lines will work unless I dial you out. I will remind you that you are also bound by the nondisclosure agreement you signed as part of your video contract, meaning if you break these rules, you will not only removed from the premises to be prosecuted for trespassing, you will also nullify your contract and will be required to return any funds already paid to you. Finally, for God's sake, do not blog, Facebook, tweet, or otherwise 'share' details of your visit with your 'friends.' Not only is it an invasion of Mr. Walsh's privacy, but it also completely cheapens his hospitality. Finally, please remember this is a home, not a resort, and although you are a guest here, nothing provided to you is free, so no swiping a bottle of shampoo when you leave. Do you have any questions?"

Connie could come up with nothing other than, "How long did it take you to memorize that?"

"Ten minutes," she said, her monotone unwavering, "following eleven years of learning from bitter experience."

"What happened eleven years ago?"

"Warren Zevon brought Hunter Thompson over for a visit. There're three square yards of grass out front that won't grow back no matter what the gardener puts on it, and we're still hollowing bullets out of the eucalyptus around the pool."

Angela moved to depart but Connie stopped her with another question.

"Angela, may I ask your advice about something?" By the ever-so-slight change in the carriage of her shoulders, Connie sensed that she didn't get asked her opinion often enough.

"You can ask; I don't know if I have any advice to give."

"Stee is taking me over to Chad Haines' house tonight for dinner, and I know he hasn't told him about the video yet."

Angela grunted in disgust. Connie thought she heard her say, "Stee, you coward."

"I don't want to look like an interloper. Do you have any ideas on what I could bring as a gift for the host on short notice? What do they like?"

Angela spied Connie's sorry suitcase. "I'm guessing an appropriate bottle of wine might be a bit out of your price range?"

Taking her expression as a signal that it would be, Connie nodded.

Angela pursed her lips for a moment. "Chad and his husband just got a puppy, a dachshund. Named it Marlene. They are goofy as shit over that dog."

"Do you have a picture of Marlene?"

"I have hundreds. They email me new ones almost every day."

Connie brightened. "I have a great idea for a gift, if I could possibly get your help." As she described her plan, Connie was unaware that she was witnessing a truly rare occurrence: Angela smiling.

chapter 14

"What's in the box?"

"Host gift for Chad and ... Randall, is it?"

"Yeah, Randall." Stee was impressed. "You even made them a card?"

"Thanks to Angela."

"Angie helped you?" Now Stee was even more impressed, but maybe not surprised. Connie had proven to be a remarkable lady in so many ways, and it was little wonder that he could now add lion-taming to her list of abilities.

When he called her yesterday, desperate, broken and lost, he didn't expect she'd actually fly out on such short notice. Yet she came right to his side, with open arms and soft words, lovely and smelling of jasmine. Good thing, too: he was nearly doubled over by the desire to drink away his sorrow. Knowing she was right there got him through another minute, another hour.

Another day at a time.

Stee found his car keys on the kitchen desk next to the laptop. Connie was finishing a glass of water. "You ready to go?"

"Just about."

In Stee's professional opinion, she looked amazing. She was wearing a black one of those Indian-style long-sleeved shirts with white embroidery around the neck, and some white pants that hinted at the smooth curve of her calves, and a pair of sandals with a bit of a heel on them. Her hair was clipped up; her earrings were a scramble of silver threads with crystal beads. Stee felt like a total dope but he couldn't look away from the sweep of her neck as she ransacked her purse to find her compact and lipstick, the left earring dangling like a raindrop ready to fall.

"Connie?"

She looked up, her dimple winking at him. "Yes?"

"I meant to give you something when you got here." He kissed her before she could powder her nose.

Her mouth was cool from the water she had been drinking. He didn't want to mess up her hair—actually, he wanted to *really* mess it up, but he knew he shouldn't—so he kept his hands low around her waist. If she had been Tamara, she'd have been swatting him away, yelling, "Don't do that! All you have to do to this shirt is look at it and it wrinkles, and we're late enough already!" Connie, in contrast, was contentedly stroking his shaggy head, happy to stay right where she was.

She's definitely not *Tamara.*

As marvelous as this was, traffic was going to be a bitch. He dotted a couple more kisses across her cheek and grabbed his keys. "Don't forget your present."

"Uh-huh." She was putting on her lipstick, her mouth open and soft.

Stee had to turn away or driving a stick shift would soon prove awkward.

———

At Chad's door, Connie suddenly swore.

"What's the matter? Forget the gift?"

"We didn't decide how you'd introduce me. What do you want people to know at this point?"

"I don't think we need to make a big production outta this, Con. Just play it by ear. Relax."

Connie was not in relaxation mode. After years in corporate America, she knew she could pitch successfully to any audience as long as she knew something about its makeup ahead of time. To-night, she didn't know the room at all, so she feared the worst. To begin with, this was a somber occasion. Also, there could be a lot of talk about the future of the current album and the Squeezebox deal, which involved her to a tiny degree, and her involvement in the project on Stee's word alone probably wouldn't make her particularly popular if emotions were running high. What's more, everyone coming tonight had had a long relationship with Bobby and each other for decades. She had never met the deceased, Stee would be the only person she knew in the room, and they could count their relationship, such as it was, in weeks.

Stee opened the door.

Here goes nothing.

She followed him into an enormous kitchen, outfitted for people who loved to cook. A huge assortment of pans and pots hung from a hammered copper hood suspended over a central island with a glass-top range, a sink and charcoal-gray granite countertops. Connie wasn't much of a chef, but she had seen enough Food Network programs to know that the refrigerator alone cost as much as her car.

A tall, willowy woman in a crisp white shirt and flowing black pants was mixing a salad near the sink. Next to her was a well-built man in his early fifties pulverizing salad dressing ingredients in a blender while giving the woman detailed instructions about how to plate the course; this would be Randall, Connie assumed. And the silver-haired gentleman in a black chef's apron stirring a pot of fresh tomato sauce with pancetta was—

Oh my God, it's Chad Haines.

Well, of course it's Chad Haines. It's his house, genius.

"Hey, brother."

Chad looked over his shoulder to acknowledge Stee, with Connie half hiding behind him. "Hey." Once he noticed Stee hadn't come alone, he wiped his hands on a towel and came over to them. "Uh, hello, I'm Chad."

"Connie Rafferty," she said, shaking his hand. "It's a pleasure to meet you, although I am truly sorry about the circumstances."

"Likewise." Chad cast a quizzical glance toward Stee. "She with you?"

"Yep," Stee answered with a slyly confident expression.

"Oh, okay." He shrugged and went back to the stove.

"Told you you could relax," Stee whispered in Connie's ear with a small kiss. He called over to his friend's husband. "Hey, Randall, what's going on?"

"Trying to get dinner on the table for 100; just another day at the ranch." Randall came over to the couple, bearing a club soda and lime for Stee, which he placed on the edge of the counter. He gave Stee a hug and a peck on the cheek, sighing. "I am so sorry this happened. Bobby and I may not have had much good to say about each other, but he was your friend and a member of the band, and his death is a true loss."

"Thanks." Stee guided Connie forward. "Randall, this is Connie. She's a new friend of mine. She directed the video for the new album."

"She did what now?" Chad didn't turn around. His tone was offhand, like he thought he might have misheard.

"She directed the video for the album," Randall repeated loudly. He briefed Connie. "He has selective hearing when he's cooking. It's like when he's playing guitar: he doesn't like anything to break his focus so he tunes out everything else. It took me years to figure out he wasn't giving me the silent treatment; I had just assumed I pissed him off all the time. What'll you have to drink, Connie?"

As Connie put in her order for a vodka tonic, Chad slowly turned to Stee, his head cocked to one side. "When did we do a video?"

"*I* did, solo, using an acoustic version of the title track," Stee said matter-of-factly. "We have so little time before it all has to ship, I figured me doing it alone was going to be easier than dragging everyone back to Virginia."

"Virginia?" Chad folded his arms across his chest. Connie didn't think he was upset exactly, just trying to make sense of a situation that wasn't easily adding up.

"Yeah, we filmed it in Devon, at the farm, soon after you left," Stee continued. "It fits the tone of the album so far, don't you think?"

"I guess so." Chad's eyebrow went up. "Larry's not gonna like this."

"So what else is new?"

"I brought my equipment," Connie interjected, "so we can incorporate footage of the River Runners recording the song in the studio."

Chad's other eyebrow raised. "We're playing with you on the track now? I thought you wanted it to be you, solo and unplugged."

"Maybe—no—I don't know," Stee spluttered.

"You told me you wanted the band to play the track, so I was planning to come to the studio tomorrow." Connie added, uneasy. "Isn't that what you wanted, Stee?"

He looked caught out. "Uh, I'm keeping my options open."

Not knowing what was up yet not wanting to put Stee on the spot at a time like this, Connie broke the awkward silence by presenting the gift bag to Randall. "To thank you for giving me a seat at your table, sight unseen and on short notice, I've put together a tribute to the newest member of your family. You can take a look at it when the time is right."

Randall opened the bag and pulled out a DVD case bearing the title, "An Album for Marlene." A hand-drawn tiny dog with long ears and button eyes wagged her tail below the lettering.

"Maybe the right time is now. God knows I need a break." Randall walked over to a computer in a hutch near the pantry and popped in the disc. "Chad, can you spend a moment with our guests over here?" Chad put the spoon on the counter and turned down the heat.

Stee moved surreptitiously to her side. "What is this?" he asked under his breath. "A demo?"

"More of a sign that I come in peace," Connie whispered back.

The DVD loaded and a leader with large numerals and a sweep hand counted down to the beginning of the video, steeped in the pops and wandering vertical lines of a 1930s film. Then a mournful string introduction cued up a very familiar voice singing a very familiar tune:

Falling in love again
Never wanted to
What am I to do?

Can't help it

What followed was a lushly presented photomontage of one incredibly lucky wiener dog. Connie had cut together a few dozen shots from Angela's email cache, featuring Marlene in a remarkable assortment of doggie bling, narrated by Dietrich's world-weary paean to the love-addled. With each pan and fade, Randall cooed and Chad chuckled with parental pride. Stee stopped watching the screen after a few frames to get more entertainment value out of watching his friends behave like outright idiots.

As the final "cahn't help it" wheezed over a picture of Dietrich's canine namesake asleep between her two daddies, a large cream satin heart came to the fore, pulsed lovingly for a few beats, and then disappeared into the crackling black of an end title card embossed with "The End" in lavish script. Connie held her breath.

The applause was deafening.

Connie bowed her head appreciatively toward her hosts, and then stole a glance at Stee, who was staring at her in profound admiration.

"You put this together this afternoon?" he queried.

"Well, I had some time on my hands while you were meeting with Marcos." Stee squeezed her hand, and at last Connie relaxed.

Soon, the house was teeming with key players from the career of Stee Walsh and the River Runners. He squired her around as best he could, making introductions before or after tearful greetings and stunned conversations, but eventually he was pulled in another direction and Connie was left to take in the scene from a perch in the living room near the Basquiat. There were a few people milling about she recognized on sight: Larry Mulholland and Caldwell Miller, of course ... and Jon Jonegon ... and ...

"Yep, that's Bono," Randall said when he found Connie staring goggle-eyed at the chap with the wraparound glasses helping himself to a mushroom bruschetta across the way. "What's a wake without an Irishman?"

Her mouth opened and closed a couple of times without any sound coming out. Randall put a reassuring hand on her shoulder.

"You haven't been seeing Stee very long, have you?" She shook her head and he nodded sympathetically.

"I could tell you're a civilian. It takes a while for all of this to look normal."

Connie finally found her voice. "This is normal for you?"

"Not everyday kind of normal, but I've gotten used to it. It's just part of the rhythm of life around here," Randall said, relieving her of her empty cocktail glass and muttering a request to a passing waiter.

"How long have you and Chad been together? Are you a musician, too?"

"Lord no, I can't play a note. I was a fashion advisor on a photo shoot they had with Annie Leibovitz back in '83. Chad came for a fitting, one thing led to another, and here we are decades later with a house and a dog and a marriage license and Bono in our living room."

"Congratulations!"

Randall took a fresh vodka tonic off the returning waiter's tray and handed it to his guest. "Before we're parted by a sea of celebrities, I want to tell you two things. One, I like you and I wish you and Stee all the best."

"Well, thank you," Connie replied, her cheeks brightening. "I barely know Stee at this point, so—"

"You're a marked improvement over other dates I've met, although that's not saying much. I'm so glad he's moved out of the Junior Miss section." Before Connie could quip her way through her awkwardness, Randall barreled on. "And two, Stee is one classy redneck."

Connie wasn't exactly sure how to interpret this. Thankfully, Randall filled in the blanks.

"When Chad and I started getting serious, the River Runners were all over MTV. In those days, gay was okay only if you were a transsexual novelty act. It would have killed the River Runners' following if we were found out, but Stee said he would be there for us when we wanted to go public. We didn't come out for the longest time because we figured people would assume we had AIDS, which we didn't, thank God. Well, at Freddie Mercury's memorial concert in '92, it seemed like the right time to take a stand. Stee made sure he was photographed with us both. There were even some pictures that got some press of him kissing each of us full on the mouth. He made it clear that if anyone wanted to give us shit, they'd have to go through him first, and they left us alone. Totally badass. God, I love that man."

Connie watched Stee's red head move across the room. He caught her looking at him, and he smiled in a way that told her he wished this could all be over. Randall continued in a much more conspiratorial tone.

"All of these people here, they could care less about Bobby," Randall whispered. "He was a bitter, lowlife addict, but Stee loved him like a brother and did all he could to help him. Stee'll do right by people in need, even when they don't deserve it. He gets them gigs or pays their medical bills, puts a word in. He's good-hearted like no one else I know in this business, even Chad, and that's saying something. Now they're all here to return the favor."

Someone in the crowd whistled to get everyone's attention, so Randall and Connie stopped to listen. Stee, who had ended up a few feet away from them, cleared his throat.

"Can you all hear me? Okay, good. I thank all of you for taking time to be with us this evening to remember and pay tribute to Bobby Brewer. Before I forget, let's all thank Chad and Randall for hosting us and feeding us. Thanks, gentlemen."

Once the applause died down, Stee continued. "I'm not going to gloss over the fact that Bobby was a man who made few friends during his career. Bobby was difficult, he was ungrateful, he was obnoxious, he was loud. Bobby was all of those things because he loved rock and roll and he was never going to be satisfied with anything less. That's why we started playing together in middle school. That's why he formed and led the Insiders. That's why we spent over 40 years arguing and getting loud and playing incredible music together. That's why I loved him even when we were at odds. No matter what, he'd square his shoulders and become the music.

Without Bobby, without his talent and confidence, we wouldn't have been a band in the first place ... and now that he's gone, the River Runners have lost our heartbeat."

Stee's eyes were wide and his breathing shaky. Connie's heart broke for him. She could tell he wasn't accustomed to getting emotional in public and didn't quite know what to do. Stee sighed and continued.

"Seeing so many people here, so many musicians he admired, would have made Bobby suspicious. 'What are you guys *up to?*'" Stee imitated Bobby's bug-eyed incredulity and the audience chuckled. "I want to send him off with some of the songs that inspired him and the music we made together. Let's get some more to eat. Then those who want to can sing and play for a while. So when you hear the guitar, come join us. For now, I ask everyone to find a glass and raise it. To Bobby Brewer, drummer extraordinaire and my oldest friend: may you have peace at last."

As the glasses clinked and the "To Bobby" chorus died down, Stee caught Connie's eye. He maneuvered over to her and pleaded, "I need some air."

Stee led them out onto a deck off the kitchen, which had steps down to the terraces a level below. They moved down and away from the guests who were grabbing cigarettes on the deck, although Connie noticed that Stee inhaled a deep lungful of second-hand smoke and blew it out before going down the stairs.

Stee put his arm around her to steady himself as they slowly descended, his knee clearly still bothering him. They touched down, and Connie walked them over to the edge of a Japanese koi pond. For a couple of minutes they stood with their arms linked and his hands in his pockets, silently watching the fish trace languid figure eights in and out of the watery light.

"That was lovely, what you said about Bobby."

He stared into the water, his shoulders up like he was cold. "I meant to have a funny story about when we started but I just couldn't think of one. I've been too mad at him to think straight."

"You'll probably be mad at him for a while, and you'll feel guilty about being mad about him dying. I've been there."

Stee started nodding as her words settled in. "Look at what he did to the band, Connie. He did this stupid, selfish thing when we're minutes away from recording an album. Now we've got no drummer, and Jon's got a commitment in New York right after us so he may not be able to reschedule our studio time."

"That's tough."

"Do you know how pathetic Bobby was?" he demanded, starting to pace. "I called his ex-wives to let them know he died, thinking they'd at least want to tell his kids and maybe take them to the funeral, to finish that chapter. Sandra laughed. Julie wouldn't talk to anyone but Marcos and her only question was if she could still collect child support. I couldn't even reach Maureen because she lost her house and had her phone cut off. *That's* Bobby's legacy: women who are poorer for knowing him, and children who'll never even speak his name."

"That's really sad."

"I just had to face a roomful of people who know he's a fuckup and try to make him into some misunderstood rebel. He made me look like an idiot."

"You didn't look like an idiot. No one thought you were an idiot."

"I should have known better. I'm an addict myself. I'm an idiot because I believed I could change him. Everyone else had more sense."

"You loved him and did all you could for him, all that he could accept."

He sat down heavily on a wrought-iron bench. "What's happening? I was handling this so well this afternoon, making arrangements, sticking to business. Now I can't stop shaking. I gotta go start the jam session and I don't think I can even go back up the stairs." His eyes were flickering with panic. "I can't lose my shit in front of all these people I respect. What am I going to do?"

She joined him on the bench, her arm in his. "You can sit here with me as long as you need to. They can wait."

He rested his head on her shoulder. When the tears came and

he fell into great, gulping sobs, she held him fast, and thankfully, no one came near them. When he sat up, rubbing his eyes with the heels of his hands, he flinched when he saw her tunic was a mass of crumpled wrinkles with a wet patch on her shoulder.

"Aw, shit, I messed up your beautiful shirt," he said, touching the spot sorrowfully with his thumb.

She gave him a small smile. "It'll dry."

Stee took a couple of deep breaths and ran his fingers through his hair. He sat back on the bench. "I don't know how you got through this, Connie. Bobby was someone I hated as much as I loved, and I feel like someone beat me all to hell. But you lost a husband. There's no comparison. How long were you married?"

"Sixteen years."

He grunted sympathetically. "Even though my marriages ended badly, I miss being married a lot of the time. The good times stay with me more than the bad. Are you there yet?"

"What do you mean?"

"Where you can focus on the good times again?"

"Not yet." Her throat tightened. This wasn't supposed to be about her. She pressed her lips together and prayed she wouldn't have to say anything else.

Stee winced. "God, I'm getting you upset. Misery loves company. I—"

"Chris cheated on me. A lot."

Stee's mouth dropped open. "Oh. I'm, I'm sorry."

She watched the fish, swimming together without a care. "A couple of years ago I found out about three women, and there were probably others throughout our marriage that I was too naïve to know about. He and I went to counseling—not that it was worth much at that point but just to say we tried—until one night we didn't go because he wasn't feeling well. I figured it was guilt over what he'd done to me and Amanda. Nope, it was pancreatic cancer, and not the Steve Jobs kind either. He had only a matter of weeks to get his life in order and surround himself with friends and family. And do you know who he chose to be with?"

He frowned, disgusted when he figured out the answer to her question. "His latest girlfriend?"

"He called her the 'love of the *rest* of his life.'"

"Bastard."

"It was like he'd rather have died right there and then instead of being with me one more minute." She tried to muster a sneer but her heart wasn't in it.

"He didn't want to be around Amanda either? Did she know he was running around?"

"I didn't go into all the details but I had to tell her the truth."

"I can't imagine ... shit ... how could he walk out on his daughter without saying good-bye?"

"I told her because of his medications, he didn't know what he was doing. I think she believed me. She'll never say."

"Did you see him again before he died?"

"His little girlfriend dumped him in the hospital when his health took a nosedive and she couldn't cope." Connie's attempt to be stoic was failing miserably and she hurriedly wiped away a tear. "He begged me to forgive him. I said I did."

"Did you mean it?"

"No, but what else could I tell him? He was terrified and in pain. I couldn't add to his misery. I loved him."

"So that's why you like 'Someday' so much," Stee said quietly. "It's what you hope Chris was doing: sending you away so you wouldn't see him at his worst."

Connie froze. "Oh my God, of course. Why didn't I see that before?"

"I dunno. Maybe you were so busy hating him you didn't realize you were trying to forgive him at the same time, to put it all to rest." His voice was gentle. "It's hard to accept that some people in the world—Bobby for one, and maybe your husband, too—just aren't able to accept the gifts life gives them."

His arms around her felt good. "And you're a gift, Connie; a great gift."

––––––––––

"Test, test, test."

In front of the living room fireplace, Stee sat with his Gibson Country Western on his lap, Chad seated to his right with his acoustic at the ready. Larry was to one side of the Persian rug, running scales on an electronic keyboard. Caldwell was standing on the opposite side tuning up, his bass plugged into a small amp. Robbie the Roadie taped down the cabling for the mic in front of Stee, and two standing mics were at the ready for guests.

In the center was a full drum kit, draped in sheer black fabric.

Connie perched on the arm of a leather chair occupied by her new best friend, Randall, and trained her full attention on Stee. Once she had successfully steered him back upstairs, she made sure she remained directly in his line of sight in case he needed an extra dose of moral support.

Larry ran a few scales to make sure the keys were firing on all cylinders. Stee coughed, checked in with his mates and addressed the group.

"Okay, friends and loved ones, we've had some people generously agree to be a part of our brief set tonight and they'll be joining us soon. I'll start with one of ours, though. Bear with us because it's been a hard couple of days." He counted off and Larry began the church organ prelude to "Solace."

Connie closed her eyes.

That's perfect.

"Solace" was the prayer of a heartsick man, and in this night's context, it elevated the mourners as well as the mourned. There were few dry eyes in the house as they went through the second verse, with Stee singing the closing harmonica line as a melody without words. During the applause, he looked at a point on the ceiling for a moment, then granted a thank you to the audience and moved to the next song. Connie could swear that his guitar was glowing, burnished by the movement of his fingers and the caress of his hands.

For the next hour, Stee described the man he had known so long in song, from his rebellious beginnings to his lonely end. Knowing how worn out he was, she was surprised his voice was so smooth and his phrasing so completely connected to the meaning of the lyrics. Then again, this was where Stee lived most of his life, with a microphone catching his every breath. It was where he was most at home and most secure.

Connie watched the River Runners play, transfixed. They stayed in synch using nothing short of telepathy: one picked up another's cue like married people finishing each other's sentences. A key would change, or a solo would start, harmony would arc over melody, and even if it was a song that was new to them, there would be no hesitation, no obvious missteps.

She tried to figure out how they did it: a nod here, a quick glance there. Sometimes Stee would name a chord and the band would follow him there. After decades of working as a unit, it was as routine as breathing to them ... until there was a drum solo and the well-oiled machine slipped its gears for a millisecond. Then, Stee would thump his guitar, Caldwell would beat-box, or Larry would throw in a synth rhythm line—or they'd just let the silence reverberate.

Toward midnight, the show wrapped. Stee concluded his master of ceremonies stint as graciously as he began it.

"Thanks again to everybody who joined us up here to say goodbye to Bobby. Before you go, I want you to know we've established a fund for his kids. If you're interested in contributing, please catch Marcos on your way out or call Angela tomorrow. I appreciate whatever you can do, from the bottom of my heart."

Stee caught Connie's glance for the first time since he started playing. She smiled at him, and he nodded to her before continuing.

"Tonight we honored the dead. Tomorrow we return to living. Be sure to hold those you love close to you tonight and let them know how much they mean to you. With that, here's our final song. Thanks for being here."

This ain't the best of times
But it ain't the worst
We've seen it all, babe
Raw and unrehearsed.
And ain't that something?
We're still here.
We're alive and well
Never you fear...

The guests left in groups, paying their respects to their hosts before filing out to the valet out front. The catering team tidied up; Larry and Caldwell made their exits with their wives and children; Robbie the Roadie broke down the instruments and equipment, with his seventeen-year-old nephew (Ronnie the Roadie in Training) helping him. It took nearly an hour for everyone to clear out. Stee was determined to be an extra set of hands for Chad and Randall, and Connie was determined to help him be helpful. She toted chairs; she wiped down counters; she chatted with the men. She did all she could to show them she was a good-hearted gal.

At last, Stee was at the wheel. Connie fought to stay awake and talk to him as they cruised down the winding road through the canyon and back out to Malibu. It was all she could do to get out of the car and be escorted to her guest room door.

She yawned mightily. "It's five in the morning my time. I just pulled an all-nighter. Haven't done that in a while."

"You need some sleep," he concurred. "You should rest."

"So should you."

He pushed a loose piece of hair off her forehead, his fingers glancing off her skin. "Connie, I wouldn't have made it through tonight without you. You're ... a good friend."

"I'm glad I could be here."

She was totally spent. Holding him close, she could feel waves of fatigue and sadness rolling off him. It was all they could do to stand there, leaning into each other. It was all she wanted to do.

So tired.

"Stee, I'll see you in the morning, okay?"

"Okay." He kissed her, long and deep. She no longer had enough energy to think in complete sentences. All that ran through her mind were fragments.

So nice

So tired

Don't stop

Must stop

Better to stop

So, so tired

"Goodnight, Stee."

chapter 15

Orchid—fireplace—Hockney.

It took Connie a few moments to process her situation after she opened her eyes.

Why am I in a hotel?

She pressed her palm to her forehead.

Right, this isn't a hotel. I'm in Stee's guest room, and that print's the real thing.

Her eyes widened.

Am I alone?

She slowly cast her eyes to the opposite side of the bed.

Yes, I'm alone just like when I went to sleep. No funny business.

She yawned and shook out her facial muscles, and then looked at the clock at the bedside.

6:43 a.m. Pacific Daylight Time. 9:43 at home. Four hours' sleep.

She stared at the ceiling.

What am I supposed to do now?

That was a stumper. She wasn't sure what her host was up to right now and Angela's house rules had flown out of her head, given all that went on yesterday.

Start by getting my ass out of bed, I guess.

After giving herself a basic once-over in the bathroom and deciding it wasn't worthwhile to do the whole shower thing until she figured out what was what, she threw on a pair of shorts, a t-shirt and sandals, and went down the spiral staircase to the main floor. She walked slowly around the main entrance, absorbing the art on the walls that she had sped by the day before—Native American textiles, a Chuck Close self-portrait, contemporary ceramics—and found her way back to the kitchen.

Coffee was already made and two mugs were waiting next to the coffee maker.

Am I allowed to drink the coffee? Yes, that was on the list.

She poured herself a strong one and padded into the living room to take in the view. As she watched the ocean warm up and the sky begin to brighten, movement on the patio below caught her eye.

Stee was in the pool, swimming laps freestyle. He wasn't fast, but his strokes were even and his rhythm didn't vary; he had obviously put in plenty of practice. He'd get to the end of the pool, do a neat flip turn and continue steadily on his way. It was so methodical, almost meditative; from this aerial view, he looked like a redheaded otter, totally at home in the water. Connie smiled into her coffee and watched him for a while, then she dropped off her mug in the kitchen and headed down to say hello. When she got to the stairs, she stopped suddenly.

Crap, is the pool included in the unrestricted area?

Oh, fuck it, I'll be out of there before Angela even gets here.

On her first journey down the hall on the lower level, she overshot the exit. She cursed when she ended up at the opposite staircase, and turned around for another go. She unlocked the door and walked out onto the tile. Stee was still immersed in his regimen, so she perched on a chaise lounge and waited. Soon, he tagged the wall on the shallow end of the pool and stood, sputtering the water off his face.

"Good morning, early bird."

She didn't mean to startle him but did so anyway. After splashing defensively for a moment, he squinted toward the horizon of the patio and broke into a toothy grin.

"Shit, Connie, don't scare me first thing in the morning. That's prime heart attack time."

"You look pretty indestructible to me, Stee." She leaned toward him. "Nice pool. I got lost coming down here and I was afraid Angela would jump out and send me packing."

"Did she give you the whole 'rules of the house' speech?"

Connie nodded. Stee frowned. "I've got to get her to cut that out. Sure, I have a guy who watches the gate, and there's a camera on the front entrance and one down near the beach, but guard dogs and all that mess? Angie's just trying to scare you."

"Well, it worked."

He swam to the side closest to her chair and propped his chin on the side. "Didja bring your bathing suit?"

"No," she confessed, a little disappointed. "I packed for a funeral, not a pool party."

"Well, of course, you don't *have* to wear a suit, you know," he offered innocently.

"Nice try," she tossed back. He pushed up with his arms and flipped around to sit on the edge of the pool with an *oof!* He turned around and staggered as he got to his feet with her help.

"Dammit," he hissed, shaking his left leg.

"Your knee?"

"It feels like I took a bullet."

"How long has it been hurting you?"

He limped to the other end of the patio to find a towel. "I dunno ... three or four years."

"Ever thought about surgery?"

He shook his head rapidly. "No, no, no—no knives, no hospitals. The pain killers take the edge off when it gets really bad."

Connie got a good look at his profile. "You've lost some weight. That no-carb diet's working."

He patted his belly and smiled. "You inspired me." Before she could blush at the thought that he was trying to look more attractive for her, he added, "Seeing myself on camera told me I have some work to do."

Oh.

"Besides, I have to start going into training for the tour soon."

"A tour? When? Where you going?"

"After the New Year we'll work our way toward the East Coast, then we'll be in Europe by the summer."

"That's exciting."

"I am pretty excited," he concurred, swiping the towel through his hair and dropping it on the tile. "It's been way too long since we've had the whole band go out together ..."

His banter skidded to a halt as Bobby's absence floated back into his memory. Connie grabbed his robe off a peg and brought it over, wrapping it over his shoulders.

"It'll be good for you to go on tour, I think. It'll give you and the guys a way to come back together and create something new."

Stee looked at her intently. "Bobby was a blast on tour. He was so glad to be out in the world, he enjoyed every place we went, no matter how podunk. On the bus, he would get us all laughing and throwing shit and messing with the driver, like kids going to summer camp."

He turned his attention to putting on the robe and securing the sash around his waist. "Did you ever see the band on tour?"

"I never saw you play live until last night."

He grunted in small disbelief. "Really? You've never seen us in a concert hall or an arena or anything?"

"New fan, remember?"

Stee got two bottles of water out of a small fridge hidden behind a serpentine marble bar off to one side of the pool. "Well, sorry you had to start your concert-going career in Chad's living room."

He offered her a bottle, and she scooted over so he could share her chaise lounge. "Worked for me. I never thought in a million years Bono would be singing 'Walk On' practically sitting in my lap."

"Yeah, we crossed paths enough times that when he started the One Campaign, he got me involved. He was in town for the *Tonight Show,* got the news, came by. Good guy."

"Very polite, too. He gave me the last ravioli." She took a swig of water. "Nice Jim Morrison imitation, by the way."

He rolled his eyes. "I was pathetic."

She hadn't expected to laugh so hard the night before. When Stee and the band tried to dope their way through "Touch Me" in homage to Bobby's early obsession with the Doors, Stee failed so miserably on vocals that Larry completely cracked up, and Stee had to ask the audience to sing the *bump-bump-baa-de-bump-bumpa-da-da* keyboard line so they could finish the damn song.

When the poolside conversation experienced a companionable lull, it seemed like a good morning kiss was in order. He stayed at a chaste distance in his wet trunks, but she nestled in anyway. Minutes later, he gazed at her face and down and back again, his eyes a little unfocused, his smile curling the right corner of his mouth.

"So," he drawled, "are you rested?"

She answered the question—the one he was really asking her. "Yeah."

He stood and extended his hand. "Me, too."

"I have to get to the studio so I can set up, though," she said, straightening the collar of his robe.

"Well, about that," he replied, fussing with the hem of her t-shirt. "I've, uh, reconsidered and, well, I'm happy with the acoustic version of the song. The video is perfect as is."

She stopped his hands. "What?"

He smiled as if he'd told her she had just won a million dollars. "See, this is great. You don't have to reshoot anything, and now you can just come be with me at the studio. Won't that be great?"

"*No!* For God's sake, it took you until now to make up your mind? Why didn't you ..."

His face fell and she stopped mid-sentence, regrouping as she remembered how much had happened to him over the last few days. "Fine, I'm going to assume you were going to talk to me about this before but then Bobby happened and you weren't thinking clearly."

"Yes," he said quickly.

"Because I don't think you're the type of person to make up something on a whim just so I'd drop everything and rush to your side, right?"

"Right," he said, faster still.

She sighed. "Look, since I already hauled all my equipment out here, how about I shoot anyway? We can use the footage on the website, maybe a sneak preview for the album or something."

"Now you're talking."

Before she could step into the house, he slung his arms around her waist.

"What's the rush?"

"We're back to Plan A. I gotta get my stuff."

"We can get there a little late," he cooed. "Don't forget: I'm the boss."

"You also told me you've got a song to write in the next 24 hours."

"I need some inspiration first."

She eased into his kiss, his Southern charm chipping away at her work ethic. When they stopped, he looked at her placid expression and nodded.

"That gave me a few ideas."

"Care to share?"

Stee looked inordinately pleased with himself. "Not just yet. Ask me when we get back from the studio."

————————

It was 1:42 a.m. by the clock on the nightstand. From what Connie could tell, she had fallen asleep about an hour ago, and Stee had been snoring for about 57 minutes of that time. He was splayed on his back, his mouth agape, another log sawed through with every intake of breath.

Connie rolled over on her side away from him, chuckling quietly. *So this is the life of a groupie.*

She sifted through the precious details of the last few hours: how the recording session ran late, then back to Stee's place for takeout and some friendly petting, then staggering down the spiral staircase to the master suite and, well, *this.* Throughout it all, even with the bum knee and spare tire, Stee was—*Stee:* delightful, focused, and really good with his hands.

He knows his way around a woman, that's for damn sure.

Glowing, she flipped over again so she could appreciate Stee in profile: the authority of his brow giving way to the slim slope of his nose, his soft lips wide as if he was singing full-throttle. She liked this so much, the intimacy of sleeping with someone. Sex is an exercise in trust, sure, but falling asleep in someone else's presence leaves you completely vulnerable. Then again, sleeping in someone's arms is the safest feeling in the world. She hadn't remembered how much she had longed for that again until he gathered the covers around them when she could barely keep her eyes open.

The rumbling continued. More ticked off now than enamored, she stuffed the pillow in a ring around her head.

Enough already. Chris never snored, ever, not even when he had been drinking.

Her heart froze.

Oh ... Chris.

Since Chris died, Connie assumed she'd have sex again at some point, maybe even have a boyfriend or remarry. She'd been without him long enough—and angry at him longer than that—for the time to be right to move on. Still, she'd expected to feel something profound when another man made love to her for the first time. Instead, it was just her and Stee.

This feels ... really right.

Her stomach began to churn.

Now what?

She had scrupulously avoided thinking about what would happen in the morning when she and Stee went their separate ways, the video all but complete. Now, she could think of nothing else.

This was probably his way of saying good-bye.

She shivered. He had hummed a lullaby for her before she dozed off. She hadn't said anything for fear that she was dreaming it all.

That means something, doesn't it?

She was shocked to hear ... nothing. Stee had rolled over onto his side, and the lumber mill shut down. He was drawn up in a fetal position with his back turned to her, his game left leg stacked on top of his right. Connie sidled up to him, gently so as not to wake him, hooking her knees behind his and resting her arm around his stomach, her cheek pressed against his shoulder.

Please don't let this be over after breakfast.

chapter 16

Stee felt great.

Tremendously great!

He didn't even mind limping back from the bathroom, his knee giving him grief due to the workout last evening. He paused for a moment to appreciate the beauty of the scene before him:

The morning sun filtering through the skylight …

a soft breeze streaming through the window …

and a warm brunette colonizing his side of the big round bed, dead to the world.

Life is good … and there's someone I want to make sure is awake to enjoy it with me.

He sat next to her and spoke softly so she wouldn't be startled.

"Good morning, sunshine," he whispered.

Connie uncoiled and stretched. She opened her eyes and took in Stee's goofy-assed grin.

"Hello yourself."

"You're like a morning glory turning toward the sun," he said, dazzled. "You bloom."

She snorted. "Wow, poetry at this hour of the morning."

"You inspire me."

She stroked his face. He was glad that she could cope with the whole beard thing and didn't tug at or skritch it. He moved in for a kiss but she ducked him.

"Bathroom—toothbrush—hold that thought!" Connie trotted away and closed the door. Soon, she popped back out still wearing nothing but a bright smile.

"All better."

"I agree." He held up the covers and she clambered next to him once more.

Stee breathed her in and exhaled the grief tightening his chest that had crept up on him unannounced when she walked away. His mouth traced the trails he had blazed across her body the night before, stopping here and there to revisit a particularly beautiful recreational spot. He was already feeling the tug of her impending absence. It hurt.

"Don't go back to Virginia," he murmured into her navel. "Stay here with me for a few more days. Please."

"I wish I could." She didn't sound like she was kidding. He sure hadn't been.

This meant he had to have *that* conversation with her before she left. Given what he knew about her dog of a husband, it wasn't going to be easy.

I have to find out what she can handle before we go any further.

His gut clenched and then relaxed as she pulled him toward her.

Oh well, might as well enjoy this now, while I still can.

"So we're talking, what—a thousand girls? You've slept with a thousand *different* girls?"

"That's pretty conservative, but let's go with that."

This was not the breakfast conversation she had expected on the heels of a supremely satisfying night and morning in Stee's strange, round bed. When Stee said, "I have to tell you something, and I don't know how you're going to react," Connie thought perhaps he was going to say he was out of eggs.

For a musician, his timing needs work.

"Look, you gotta remember I lost my virginity when I was fifteen, and I was twenty-six when I met Tamara, so right there you got eleven years. Then I had six years between my divorce and my next marriage, and it's been seven years since Kayla. That's twenty-four years of time when I wasn't promised to anyone. That's more than half my adult life."

"You never cheated while you were married?"

"Nope, I moved on only after the papers were served."

"Wait—how do you define 'cheating'? No kissing on the lips? No intercourse? No falling in love? I heard all of those from Chris, and believe me, he cheated."

His eyes cut away from her. "Well, Tamara and I had an agreement."

"Oh, I bet *you* thought you did, but I'm not so sure *she* agreed to it, if she's like any wife on the planet."

"It was a long time ago, and I was an alcoholic. I wasn't being fair to anyone back then and I'm not proud of how I treated her. And Kayla cheated first, so that was permission enough for me, I figured."

"Have you been tested for HIV lately? Any STDs I should know about?"

"Every six months, and I'm clean. As you saw last night and this morning, I keep Trojans in business."

"Any possibility of there being a child out there you don't know about?"

"My brother taught me how to use a rubber before he left for Viet Nam, and once Maude was born, I got snipped."

"Any sex tapes out there? Porno photos from parties you forgot you went to?"

"Christ, no, Connie, who do you take me for?"

"Someone who cheated on his wives and slept with more girls than I've met in my entire life, Stee!"

"Well, we're not talking Gene Simmons' numbers, you know."

She was in no mood for humor. "Jesus, how could you *do* that? Are you a sex addict?"

He looked stunned by the question. "No, I'm a rock musician."

She was incredulous, and his eyes narrowed. "I was on the road 250 days a year doing 80-city world tours. I was playing to packed houses full of very enthusiastic fans. I had a lot of ... opportunity."

She licked her lips nervously. "How did that all work exactly? You have your crew scout the crowd for you? You call room service: 'Send up a skinny blonde with big boobs and a fifth of Jose Cuervo'?"

"You really want to know?" he snapped. "I can tell you if you do."

"Did you ever hire prostitutes?" she fired back.

"They were from a very discreet escort service," he said matter-of-factly, "and I booked girls only twice: once after my first year of sobriety because I needed practice before dating without booze, and a second time about a month later because I wanted to find out if I hated the first experience so much because I didn't like the sex-for-hire thing or I just had an off night. It was the former; I never did it again."

She stayed icily silent, and he threw his hands in the air. "This is my history, Con; it's made me who I am today. I can't go back and change it, and at the same time, I don't think I should have to."

Connie sniffled but didn't look away. "What am I supposed to do with this information, Stee, welcome it? What if the shoe was on the other foot? Would you be okay if I told you I had slept with a thousand men?"

"I guess I'd have to be okay with it, now wouldn't I?" he said after a split second of consideration.

Connie didn't say anything. Stee looked at the ceiling, shaking his head. "This is why I knew we had to talk about this before we go any further."

"I like how you bring this up now instead of last night before we went to bed," she said pointedly. "Was that a road test?"

"No, of course not," he replied, a little wounded. "Last night was just beautiful, and I really don't want this to be the last time I see you. Otherwise there would be no reason to have this conversation."

Connie was not yet ready to concede that point. He sighed heavily.

"My past history, that's going to be a deal breaker, isn't it? Especially since Chris did what he did."

She couldn't squelch her tears any longer. "I was just beginning to let myself believe that you might possibly think of me as someone special, but now it's clear I'm an idiot."

"No, you're not. Connie, honey, please don't cry." He grabbed a tissue off the kitchen counter.

She dried her eyes and sought a small, quiet space in her brain to sort this out.

"Am I just 1,001 to you? Is 1,002 waiting in the garage for me to leave?"

"No," he softly insisted.

"What assurance do I have that you're telling the truth?"

"You don't have any other than my word. You have to trust me. You can trust me."

"Why should I?" She was so dreadfully uncomfortable she could no longer look at him.

He tentatively took her hand. "Connie, there may be no way I can talk about my past and have it come out right, so please hear me out and know I'm being honest with you. My tomcat ways pretty much petered out after that Kayla mess years ago. Sleeping around left me feeling old and emptied out and unhappy. That's not what I want anymore. I want to be with someone I care about."

Connie smiled weakly, which Stee took as a cue to continue.

"My past is past. This, with you, makes me feel good, better than I've felt for a long time." He traced the back of her hand with his thumb. "I want to make you happy, baby. That's all I want. Can I do that? Could that happen?"

He stared at her, dead serious, awaiting her response. She didn't know what to say, because that was either the most romantic thing she'd heard in years ...

Or the lyrics to one of his songs.

———

"You didn't like that either, huh, Jon?"

It was hard to tell. Stee's producer hadn't moved since they started their twelfth take twelve takes ago. The engineer was gesticulating wildly, pointing at the board, then at the band, then at the clock; the musicians were mercifully unable to hear his bellowing, as they were on the other side of soundproof glass. In the midst of this, Jon rose out of his chair, left the booth, and pushed the exit open with a grunt.

Stee, Chad, Larry and Caldwell silently watched the door until the rubber soundproofing caught it with a plunger-like *snork*.

"Did he just quit?" Caldwell asked sharply.

"Guys, Jon wants to see you in the lounge." The intercom popped off and the engineer bolted to the alley for a smoke. The band removed their headphones and hung them glumly on the music stands. Larry took off his Dodgers cap and tossed it dejectedly on his keyboard.

"It's my fault, Stee. I'll sit out the rest of the session."

"Christ, Larry, this is *not about you*," Chad groaned as Robbie the Roadie relieved him of his guitar.

"Well, it sure as hell ain't about me," Caldwell groused, setting his bass on its stand. "I'm not even in this number until the third verse and then I'm just doing that 'bum, bum, bum' crap you stick me with when you put me in a song just to be polite."

"Not now, Caldwell," Chad warned, arching his eyebrows in Stee's direction. The three of them turned attention to their leader. Stee was staring at the Oriental rug beneath his feet, shaking his head slowly back and forth, his face drawn. He didn't even look up when he spoke.

"This is our best number, my best song. I'm killing it."

Chad shrugged. "It sounds tentative, like the spark went out of it. Like you lost faith in it."

Stee sighed heavily. "What if Bobby was right? Maybe this album's flawed and I'm not able to hear why. He could always tell when something was off; he had a great ear for a hit."

"Bobby wasn't in his right mind last time we saw him, Stee," Chad said quickly. "Trust me, this is a good song. It just hasn't found its way yet." He put a guiding hand on Stee's shoulder. "C'mon; let Jon have his say and then we'll get it in the next take."

The four of them limped through the heavy studio door like football players who had gotten the stuffing knocked out of them in the first half, steeling themselves for the coach's tirade. They plunked down on the squishy green sofas, tossing several tattered grocery store tabloids and sandwich wrappers to the floor. The place stunk of stale coffee and congealed tuna salad. Dinner would be brought in soon, but until they got the album's final track in a better place, it would stay untouched.

Swathed in an emerald-green Hawaiian shirt, Jon was planted in a swivel chair, his arms resting on his stomach. He eyeballed his star grumpily. "Stee, it isn't there yet after a fuckload of takes. I bet I know why."

"I'm all ears," he said wearily.

"Because you're a lousy actor."

Stee actively ignored a hoot from his bassist. "What?"

"This is a song about being certain about something, and you're not sounding very certain, bud."

Stee waved him off. "I'll get it on the next take, Jon. I know we only have so much time before you're going to New York. I want all this laid down before you light out."

Jon sized up his musicians and nodded definitively. "Stee, let's try this take solo. C'mon." He rolled to his feet and motioned toward the door to the studio. Stee glanced at each of his bandmates, seeking any disapproval; finding none, he followed his producer.

Stee sat in the broad wooden chair in the center of the studio floor, his acoustic guitar in his lap. Jon balanced on a listing plastic chair a few feet away.

"Stee, this is going to be a great record," Jon began sincerely. "I hear it; the heart's beating; it'll get there."

"Thank you," Stee said with palpable gratitude.

"We've just piled way too much on top of this song. It's delicate and personal. That doesn't come through with the full band."

"Yeah, you're right. I heard it in my head as a solo number, but now that everyone's together—"

"You wanted backup to ward off the ghosts." Stee felt his breath catch while Jon continued. "Larry told me what happened in that last rehearsal with Bobby. You've faced life and death and final reckoning shit these past couple of days. You sure you're up for this?"

Stee nodded, his jaw set. "What else am I going to do?"

"All right, then. Here's what I'm thinking. Rather than singing like you're the guy who knows everything will be okay, sing like you *want* to comfort the girl, but you really need her to comfort *you.*"

Stee revisited his last moments with Connie before the driver took her to LAX; she was so overwhelmed and wary she couldn't even kiss him good-bye.

What if this could bring her back?

"This girl in the song, is she real or some figment of your imagination?"

"You met her yesterday."

"The chick with the video camera?" Jon coughed, nonplussed. "Huh. Figures. No matter. Where did the song come from?"

"Connie lost her husband. My music helped her deal with her loss. That inspired me; I started writing songs again the night I met her."

Jon smiled conspiratorially. "Love at first sight, huh? You gotta love how the universe works sometimes."

Stee wasn't going to argue the details about when exactly cordiality turned to interest, then friendship, and now ... whatever it was at the moment.

"It's debatable if she even wants to talk to me right now."

Jon perked up. "Even better. You can use this song to get her back."

"Uh ..."

"Close your eyes, Stee."

Stee wrinkled his nose. "What are you, my shrink?"

"No, your acting coach."

Stee hissed through his teeth in amusement. "The director of *Garden Graveyard* liked my acting well enough."

Jon grinned. "Hillbilly Horace isn't singing this song. You are. Now close your eyes."

Shrugging, Stee complied.

"Stee, take a few deep breaths. I want you to clear your mind, okay? Just listen to the quiet in the room." Stee struggled for a couple of minutes but at last was able to hear nothing but the low buzz of the lights, the hum of the air conditioning and his own breathing.

"Good. Now, I want you to see her in your mind's eye: that girl, the night you met her. Imagine her looking at you. Really see her."

Stee's shoulders relaxed. Connie was standing in the dim light of the roadhouse parking lot, the cool breeze fluttering the skirt of her sweet blue dress. The thought of her pierced his heart.

"You see her?" Stee nodded slowly. "You want to tell her something?"

"Yeah."

"What?"

"Stay with me. Make it all right."

"I'm sorry, I couldn't hear you. Say that again, Stee."

"If you stay with me, it'll be all right."

"Great. Now open your eyes and keep that in front of you when you play the song."

Stee's eyes readjusted to the lights and the reality of the room, and Jon ensconced himself back behind the mixing board in the booth. The engineer slated the take, and the song was finally released from its prison:

Babe, there's no shame in crying.
Just share your pain with me
You've had to live through dying,
And I can set you free.
I can't erase your past from you
That's part of you for life
But on the path ahead of us
I'll cry with you, I'll laugh with you,
I'll sing with you,
Companion, true for life.

You've traveled through a world of hurt

Walked paths I'll never know
You need a hand up from the dirt
To let your feelings go
I know that soon the clouds will part.
Reveal the shining light
That burns within your beaten heart.
I'll walk with you, I'll run with you,
I'll dance with you,
Companion, true for life.

The future is an open book
Of pages new and white.
And as you write your tales, just look:
I'll walk with you, I'll run with you,
I'll laugh—I'll laugh a lot with you,
I'll live with you, I'll be with you,
I'll love you,
Companion, true for life.

The guitar strings stopped vibrating. Stee looked up at the booth, wearily hopeful. Jon leaned in and hit the intercom button.

"Nice work, Hillbilly Horace."

————————

"So how was the trip, Mom?"

Amanda was still behind the wheel after picking Connie up at the airport. Connie was too out of sorts to drive, having spent the last seven hours mulling over the morning's events as she flew homeward, debating what to say if pressed, wondering how she really felt.

She started off vague and noncommittal. "Stee took me to the studio yesterday to shoot b-roll of the band while they were recording."

"That must have been cool."

"Yeah." Of course, it had been more than cool. When she had walked into the studio with Stee, she could barely take it all in: the dozens of guitars strung along the walls; the stacks of monitors; the musical history the room had witnessed. Jon Jonegon was already in the booth, a bearded mountain in a ruby-red Hawaiian shirt. Once Stee had found her a chair and stepped out to get a bottle of water, Jon fixed her with an unforgiving stare.

"We're here to make an album, not for you to make a movie. Stay out of our way."

She nodded obediently; she wasn't about to argue. She worked quietly, shooting snippets of Stee and the band playing over the next ten hours, absorbing how Stee translated what he heard in his head into directions for the band, orchestrating on the fly. It wasn't all that different from directing a video: knowing what you wanted walking in, but staying open to welcome happy accidents, too.

She got footage of the drum kit, with its vacant stool and a set of headphones looped over an empty music stand. The engineer provided a steady computer-generated beat just to keep the songs in line; Stee couldn't yet bear to have another drummer record with them.

She also covertly filmed him when she found him hunched into a corner of a couch, his back to the traffic moving through the lounge. He was carefully inscribing lyrics and chords into a spiral notebook, stopping every few words to tap his pen against the page to work out the beats and dislodge the words pent up in his head. She knew if he saw her, the spell would break, so she stayed out of his line of sight, catching him in the act of creation.

Watching him through the lens had given her an excuse to indulge in all she admired about him: his professionalism, his humor, his musical mind. Then admiration would segue into attraction: she'd focus on Stee's hands, or his eyes, or his mouth and it was all she could do to keep the camera steady.

Then they had ended up in bed, and it had been so lovely until—

"That's all? 'Yeah'?" Amanda demanded. "God, Mom, you sound like me when you ask, 'Did you have a good day at school?'"

"Sorry. This whole experience has been surreal. I walked off the plane Thursday and that night we went to the wake at Chad's house—Chad is Stee's guitarist—"

"I know who Chad is, Mom. Give me some credit."

"Seems like Stee's worked with every musician on the planet, so they all came to the wake."

"Like who?"

"Elvis Costello sang 'My Love, My Dear,' which was heartbreaking."

"That's nice," Amanda said, underwhelmed.

"Ry Cooder was there ..."

"Okay, him, I don't know."

Connie figured her daughter wouldn't appreciate that David Crosby dropped by either, so she swung for the fences.

"Then Bono sang a—"

"You met Bono? *Shut up!*"

"I met him in passing at the pasta table. It's not like we exchanged phone numbers or anything."

"You *met Bono* and you're talking about it like you ran into Aunt Samantha at the grocery store!" After the shrieking subsided, she added, "Well, that's Stee's life, I guess. Hanging out with famous people."

"It wasn't hanging out, honey. It was a funeral."

The word "funeral" was a loaded one in their household. Even though her father had kept his infidelities completely hidden to the outside world, Amanda had been convinced her friends somehow knew the sordid details, and she had to be dragged to the funeral home after a long, painful argument. Connie had few friends who weren't also her husband's, meaning she had to suffer their tears and memories without having the heart to challenge them with the truth. Since Connie's relationship with her in-laws was frosty at best, she didn't want to make things worse by ratting him out. What would it have gained anyone now that he was gone?

What was worse was Connie's fear that any number of Chris' girlfriends might appear, lacking the good taste to mourn in private. She'd kept an eagle eye on the funeral home door, and at the graveside, so that Amanda wouldn't have to endure any further humiliation, ignoring how humiliated she felt herself. Thankfully, none did.

The worst time of their lives barely described it all.

"Mom, do you like Stee?"

"Of course. He's a good guy."

"No, Mom—do you *like* him?"

Connie turned to take in her daughter's expression to gauge how much she'd figured out, but Amanda had her eyes on the road. "It would never work out, Mandy," she answered quickly.

"So you do like him."

"It's complicated."

"Not really. He's your idol and you've got a thing for him."

"I've gotten to know him pretty well over the last few weeks. It's more than just a crush."

"He obviously likes you."

Connie felt the blood drain from her face, wondering if something about her appearance tipped her daughter off about her night with Stee. "Why do you say that?"

"He was watching you from the balcony whenever we were between takes at the farmhouse."

"That was because I was the only woman on set."

"Sara was there. She's younger than you."

"Thanks."

"He didn't make a pass at me."

"Thank God."

"So it had to be he was interested in you."

"Honey, he's interested in a lot of women."

That sentence might have struck an ominous chord between them as well, but Amanda let it pass, her guarded optimism leading the conversation.

"If he has all those women and famous friends, why did he ask you to fly out there?"

"He wanted some moral support from someone who'd been through a death in the family."

"Wish we could have had someone there for us," Amanda muttered.

"Me, too."

"It was horrible. It's still horrible."

"I know."

"And I still miss him so much, Mom."

"I miss who your father was," Connie admitted. "Who I thought he was, anyway."

"He really was that person, Mom," Amanda insisted. "He had to be. He loved me. He loved you. He would have left us so much earlier if he didn't."

"Are you still angry at him?"

"He was sick. He was acting crazy. He didn't mean to hurt us."

Amanda took the exit off 64 to the West End. "I like Stee, Mom. And I know he likes you, and you don't have to pretend you don't like him back."

Connie sighed. "It doesn't really matter. Now that the video is done, and the wake is over, he doesn't have any reason to stay in contact. I'll just have to make my peace with that."

They pulled into their driveway. The air was buzzing from the residual heat of the day. Moments after Connie struggled up the stairs with her suitcase and carted it to her room, the doorbell rang.

"Mom, the door," Amanda yelled.

"Could you please answer it? I'm unpacking."

With Amanda's flip-flops slapping down the hall as an affirmative, Connie unzipped her suitcase. Lying on top of her clothes was a CD, Elvis Costello's *North,* topped with a note in Stee's handwriting on a Post-it:

Thinking of us.

"Flowers, Mom. He sent you a boatload of flowers!"

Amanda laid a long white box on the dining room table. Popping open the tape, Connie was greeted by at least two dozen orange roses.

"They match his hair!" Amanda snickered as she meandered back to her room. Connie instantly knew there was more to the color choice than that. Through her wedding video work, she knew flowers were symbols.

Orange is a mixture of yellow and red: friendship turning to love.

There was also a note. She opened the envelope and stared at the card, her heart racing, her eyes glistening. All it said was,

1,001 and I'm done

I miss you to my very soul

Please call me tonight

Stee

chapter 17

"Mom, the door!"

Connie switched off the vacuum cleaner and slung her headphones around her neck like a stethoscope. "Why do you always yell for me? Can't you ever just answer it?"

"Because it's never for me," came Amanda's muffled reply through her bedroom wall.

Connie sighed testily. She had been completely engrossed in putting her house in order following her sojourn to California and delivering the video to BetaComp. As tired as she was, doing housework was her own weird reward for putting in so many late nights. It helped her regain control of her life again. She didn't like to be interrupted.

Glowering, Connie combed her bangs with her fingers and prepared her "no, thank you" speech for whatever Jehovah's Witness or Boy Scout was hawking salvation or peanuts on her doorstep at 11 a.m. on a Saturday. She yanked the front door open and nearly swallowed her gum.

"Stee! What are you doing here?"

He was wearing his customary shades and curlicue smile, bearing a vase the size of a fishbowl bursting with lilies. "I was just in the neighborhood and decided to drop by." Connie spied a black Land Rover consuming her driveway and saw the glint of a familiar bald head through the windshield.

"Is that Roland from the security detail in Devon?"

"Yeah, he and I go back a ways. It's always handy to have a six-foot-seven guy on call."

Connie nervously wiped the film of sweat off her brow with the back of her hand and put on her best game face.

"Uh, does Roland want to come in and visit?"

"Naw, he's got other appointments. I'll just call him when we need him." Stee turned and waved at the car, which immediately pulled out and motored toward the intersection. He turned back to his astonished hostess and grinned. "So, may I come in?"

"Well you'd better. Your ride just left." She stepped back as Stee ambled into her living room. Connie did a quick scan up and down her block to see if any of her neighbors had witnessed his arrival in suburbia, and then she closed the door. He handed her the flowers.

"These made me think of you."

"Thank you. They're gorgeous."

"Like I said, they made me think of you."

"Those roses lasted more than a week. I just tossed them out yesterday."

"They'd better for what I paid for them." He kissed her cheek. "Ooh, salty."

"Sorry, I wasn't expecting company. I ran earlier; I've been cleaning. I haven't even taken a shower today."

He licked his lips and winked. "Tasty."

Her cheeks burning, she buried her nose into a lily's trumpet and noticed a copy of The Byrds' *Sweetheart of the Rodeo* taped to a stick in the midst of the flowers. Touched, she set the arrangement on the marble-topped table in the entryway and was at a loss for what to do next. Stee walking unannounced into her home completely upended her. There was nothing wrong in his doing so, of course. If he were anyone else, it would be a natural step to have him come over, two months after they first met, to see where she lived and kick back for an afternoon.

But having Stee Walsh in the flesh in her tiny ranch house in her mundane neighborhood, she felt like there wasn't enough space to contain him. Seeing him, the Rock Star, standing in front of her fireplace—her nondescript, non-granite fireplace—was like looking at him through a telescope. He was enormous and up close, and she felt incredibly insignificant.

He peered to his left to take in her family room, and then right to view the dining area. "You have a lovely home, Con."

She helped him ease out of his denim jacket. "It's where I grew up. It's what my parents could afford. It's small."

"Doesn't look it." He pointed to the series of oversized photographs of hands anchoring the living room. "Those are spectacular."

"Thanks. I took those to promote a documentary of mine that, uh, never got further than the poster art."

He held up his hands, mirroring the positions in the photos. "Maybe you should revisit that project."

"Maybe." She hung his jacket in the hall closet and whipped the vacuum back in there as well. When she came back, he was looking at the family photos on the mantel, pausing in front of each one. He took down Amanda's school picture and smiled broadly. "I gotta tell you again, Connie, she's a great kid, really sharp and focused. The apple didn't fall far from the tree."

She sidled up to him and admired the photo, one of the few that caught her daughter's old-soul smile. "It amazes me how moving here opened her up. She made new friends, got into her schoolwork, settled into the whole Southern 'yes ma'am' and 'no sir' culture without a problem."

"Is she home?"

"She's in her room studying for finals. I'll let her know you're here."

Stee put the portrait back in its spot, next to her wedding picture. Once the image of Chris and Connie as happy newlyweds registered in his line of sight, he quickly looked down at the hearth. She looped her arm into the crook of his elbow and gave his bicep a squeeze.

"I'm glad to see you. Talking to you on the phone this week has been good but not the same as talking in person."

"When you answered the door, you looked spooked."

"I have to say, you were the last person I expected to be on my front porch. It was so out of context it took me a moment to realize it was you."

He searched her expression. "So, is this okay, that I'm here?"

"Yes. I missed you."

Her honesty earned her a smile and a hug. "I should have called. I have some business in Memphis on Monday so I came out early to surprise you."

"Mission accomplished," she said before she kissed him. He started to pet her hair but abruptly pulled his hand away. Connie laughed, bumping her forehead against his chest. "That's what you get for not calling ahead. My hair's disgusting and I stink."

He tried to make the best of it. "I know people who pay a ton of money for that messy-hair look."

"Give me twenty minutes to make myself presentable. Then we can figure out what we're going to do, okay?"

"Deal."

"Do you want anything to drink, a diet Coke or something?"

"That'll work."

She grabbed a can out of the refrigerator and tossed a few ice cubes into one of the few glasses that wasn't chipped. When she walked back into the living room and handed him his drink, she noticed his guitar case propped by the front door ... next to an expensive overnight bag.

"Planning on staying over?" she queried, not altogether pleased. "That's a little presumptuous, don't you think?"

"Let's just say it never hurts to be prepared," he replied lightly.

"Stee," she said quietly, "you're welcome to stay the night if you sleep in the guest room. I wouldn't feel comfortable otherwise with Amanda here."

He half smiled, not sure if she was joking. "Amanda's sixteen, right?"

Connie stayed firm. "It's not about her age, Stee. I haven't dated anyone since her father died. I want to ease her into this."

"But she's met me," he protested. "She knows I'm not some creep."

"Then let's make it clear to her that you didn't just cruise by for a booty call," she retorted. After his derisive snort, she blanched.

"That's still the term, right—booty call? Am I showing my age again?"

"I came here to spend time with you both, especially to get to know Amanda better. But part of that is being together around her, making it clear we're not just friends."

"I couldn't agree more. Being affectionate around her is one thing. Us in bed together in the next room is a lot for her to take in."

Stee frowned and capitulated with a shrug. "Look, you're her momma, and I'm not gonna contradict you in your own house."

"Thanks." She took his hand and kissed his palm, and then she put it up to her cheek. "I'm so glad you're here."

Stee's face turned crafty. "Any reason we can't make out on the couch at some point?"

"How is your knee doing?"

"Wrapped and ready."

"Well then, as long as we keep the noise down."

"That'll be up to you. You get pretty loud."

Her eyebrows arched. "Do tell."

His eyes twinkled. "Go take your shower."

————

"Stee?"

"Well if it isn't my favorite production assistant!" Stee clicked off ESPN and struggled off the couch. Amanda hugged him briefly like a family friend, the top of her head barely reaching his chin.

"What are you doing here? I thought you flew home after the shoot."

"I have a gig out this way on Monday." He caught her smiling. "What?" he asked good-naturedly.

"I just never thought I'd see Stee Walsh sitting on our couch."

"Why not?"

"Because you've got better places to be than Richmond."

"There's no place I'd rather be right now." Amanda rolled her eyes and he grinned.

No lie.

"So," he said, settling back down onto the couch, "you're studying for finals on a Saturday? Practicing for law school already?"

She sat in the wingback chair across from him, hanging her leg over one of the arms. "Chemistry and world history on Monday, pre-calc and American Lit on Tuesday. Then I can cruise through art and psych the rest of the week."

His ears perked up. "Art? What, like art history or are you learning how to be an artist?"

"It's Honors Art," she stammered. "We do painting and sculpture and drawing."

He smiled. "So you *do* take after your folks. What do you like most?"

Caught out, she had to answer. "I like to draw. Cartooning, actually; pen and ink."

"I'm sure you're good at it, too." Seeing her shyly look down at the floor, he continued. "Can I see some of your work?"

"Sure." She soon returned with a couple of sketchbooks and the two of them sat side by side as she introduced him to *The Adventures of Princess Valley Ant.*

"Like Prince Valiant, right?"

"Nothing gets by you, Stee."

He was floored. The strips were a parody and an homage to the 1930s serials, with stalwartly designed characters and mystical backgrounds. The details were rich and finely wrought. It was like the work of someone three times her age. There were hours of love in those notebooks.

"You learned how to do this from your mom?"

"More Dad than Mom. He was with DC Comics early in his career."

"Well, you're doing him proud. This is incredible."

When she replied with a quiet "Thank you," he was puzzled. Usually when he complimented people, they were doubly glad for the praise and the fact that he was the one giving it. Not Amanda.

He shifted on the sofa to face her. "Have you thought about doing this professionally? I mean, look at all this. That's from a deep well of talent."

"I told you, I'm going to be a lawyer," she said firmly.

He pointed at the notebooks. "Look, I may be out of line saying this, but I find it hard to believe that you'll ever have that kind of passion for being a lawyer."

She looked him straight in the eye. "Believe what you want; it's what I want."

"Fair enough," he said gingerly, "and you're free to live your life as you see fit. I just think it's a shame to see someone so young put that kind of talent on the shelf to take a job that's kind of ordinary."

"Have you ever been a lawyer?" she asked, her mouth a firm line.

"No."

"So how do you know it's ordinary?"

"I don't know that," he conceded, "but I do know what it's like to have an artistic soul. If you can't do what you really love to do, you walk around all the time with a big piece of you missing."

"My dad did okay for himself," she replied curtly.

"If your dad was anywhere as talented as you are, that might have been tough."

"You don't know me, and you sure didn't know my dad," she said so coldly, Stee wished she had yelled at him instead.

Stee nodded guiltily. "You're absolutely right, and I apologize. This isn't my business, and I should have kept my mouth shut."

"Yeah, you should have."

Stee heard the water turn off. Connie would soon be gliding into the room, sleek and showered and wondering what her boyfriend had done to piss off her daughter in the space of ten minutes. He had to act fast or this was going to be a very long couple of days in the guest room.

"Can we start this morning over?"

She eyed him suspiciously. "What do you have in mind?"

"Let me take you and your momma to lunch at your favorite restaurant. Any kind of food, anywhere within driving range. Can I do that for you?

Amanda shrugged. "I guess so."

"Well, what are you thinking? Chinese? Mexican? Pizza?
She thought for a moment. "You like corned beef and bagels?"

————————

As the signage for the Monarch Mall came into view, Roland asked, "Are you sure this is where you want to deploy, sir?" His tone was steady, but his clipped speech betrayed his unease.

Stee was unconcerned. "This is where Amanda wants to eat," he stated simply, "so this is where we're going to go."

The driver's neck stiffened. "This is a crowded shopping mall midday on a Saturday, sir. It's going to be difficult to enter and exit without incident."

"Stee, there are dozens of places to eat around here," Connie interjected. "We can go somewhere less public."

"Don't worry. This will be fine," Stee scoffed, and then he leaned forward to whisper to Roland. "Help me out here. I'm trying to score points with Connie's daughter. Can you see any way to make this work?"

Roland's jaw tensed and released. "Let me call mall security. Maybe they have a back entrance through the kitchen."

The SUV came to a halt in the parking space furthest from the front entrance. With the motor still running, Roland whipped out his cell phone and punched in 411. Stee relaxed back in his seat and grinned confidently at Amanda by his side and Connie at the other window.

Amanda was mystified. "What's going on?"

"Stee has to be careful in public places," her mother stated, "because of the paparazzi."

"It's not like I'm Paris Hilton," Stee said with an embarrassed snort. "I'm probably not gonna have a bunch of professional photographers up in my face, but I haven't been out here before so I don't know what reaction I'm gonna get from the people here. Roland wants to have an escape plan in case some well-meaning fans won't leave us alone."

"I think we'd get less attention if we go through the front entrance," Amanda offered. "It's weird to see people come through the kitchen and take a seat."

"That may not be the best option," Connie clarified.

"It's a better option to have a huge ninja bodyguard leading the way?"

"Amanda!" Connie hissed while Stee snickered.

"That's got to be pretty cool," Amanda continued on a tangent. "People recognize you and ask for your autograph and tell you how much they like your music. I bet it feels really good."

Stee smiled. "Can't deny that it does."

"Honey, he's got a right to be left alone when he wants to be," Connie said quickly, "which is why I'm going to ask you to turn your cell phone off now. No texting about this, and please ask your friends to be discreet, okay?"

Amanda sat back, folding her arms. "Then why go out at all?"

Connie hissed under her breath but Stee stepped into the breach.

"Amanda, you're right. If we don't make a big deal about this, we should be fine." Stee tapped his driver on the shoulder. "Roland, tell you what."

The driver quickly closed his cell phone. "Yes, sir?"

"Just drop us at the front door of the restaurant and leave us on our own for lunch. You don't need to go in."

Roland cleared his throat. "That's not recommended, sir. We don't know what the locals will do."

Stee chuckled. "Christ, Roland, we're grabbing a sandwich. We're not invading Iraq. I'll call you when we're paying the check."

Roland squared his shoulders and accepted his orders. With a curt "Yes, sir," he circled the car to a pair of doors painted with a rabbi and a leprechaun clinking pints of beer, overhung with an awning announcing the entrance to Blarney Goldstone's. As he reached to release his seatbelt, Stee stopped him, announcing, "I got this, Roland."

Stee shoved his Braves baseball cap down on his head and adjusted his sunglasses. He exited the car, chivalrously loping to the other side to help the ladies out of the vehicle and into the restaurant. He gave Roland the high sign and the SUV pulled away.

Once indoors, he put his shades in his jacket pocket and took in the scene. In all his travels, Stee had never been to a place remotely like Blarney Goldstone's. The hostess station featured a five-foot-tall 3-D fiberglass version of the rabbi and leprechaun, here chomping bagels. On the walls, photographs of Irish pubs were interspersed with pictures of Depression-era delis in New York City. Dublin soccer jerseys shared pride of place with what purported to be Sandy Koufax's ball and glove. He noted that the servers were wearing shirts with panels of blue and white on the front and orange, white and green on the back.

Hoo boy.

Amanda was clearly delighted to take her seat near the center of the restaurant, where she could watch for her friends coming and going from the mall who, text-free, would have no idea she was there otherwise. Stee glanced at Connie, who took measure of her daughter's glee and smiled with relief. He settled in with a self-satisfied smirk.

Good call, Stee. Good call.

A server zoomed over with a basket of hot bagels, butter and cream cheese, and buzzed to the next table. Tickled, Stee picked up a pumpernickel bagel and tore off a hunk. "I can go off my diet for one day, I guess," he declared with delight. Chewing mightily, he put on his bifocals to page through the oversized menu, marveling over beer-battered bagel rings and the Schmaltz and Shillelagh™ chicken soup and corned beef sandwich combo.

"So, what do you recommend?" he asked. "The Reuben O'Reilly, maybe?"

"With a side order of CPR," Connie muttered, scanning the salad listings.

"I like the turkey club," Amanda said. "It comes with great potato salad."

"Then my choice is made," Stee said, hoping to cadge a conciliatory smile out of Amanda. None came, but she was talking to him, so that would do for now.

They were soon joined by a middle-aged waitress: Trish, according to her nameplate. She wore her uniform proudly, flashing dozens of badges on her chest with sayings like "Oy, vey! Have it your way!" and "Faith and Begorra! We'll never ignore ya!"

"Good afternoon, folks!" Trish gushed, setting the water glasses at each place, her badges clacking. "Have you had a chance to look at the menu?"

"Yes, ma'am, we have," Stee replied for the group.

She looked him in the eye, her smile electric. "Then what can I get for you?"

He ceded the floor to Amanda. Once they had all placed their orders, Trish took a good look at Stee.

"Excuse me, but you look really familiar."

He looked back at her, his face less animated, his voice quieter. "I get that a lot."

"No, I've seen you somewhere. Did you used to be on TV?"

"A bit during the Eighties." He purposefully kept his tone pleasant but took the energy out of his response, hoping her interest would dim.

Trish brightened back up.

No such luck.

"I knew it—you're famous! Who are you?"

Undaunted, Stee leaned in, smiling flirtatiously up at the waitress. "I'm a customer who wants to see that this poor, hungry girl gets her turkey club right away, darlin'. Thanks for putting in our order as soon as you can."

"No problem," Trish trilled, and then she spun out of view. Stee watched until he was sure that she was out of sight, mildly irritated that his cover was nearly blown so soon. He caught Connie's eye; she squeezed his knee empathetically.

Amanda, by contrast, was intrigued. "Why didn't you tell her who you were?"

He shrugged. "It can't go well. If she knows who I am, I look like I'm trolling for attention. If she doesn't know who I am, then I look like an asshole."

The girl nodded. "I see what you mean."

"So what are you doing in Tennessee on Monday?" Connie asked.

"T Bone Burnett is producing a tribute album for Carl Perkins. I've been asked to cover one of his numbers out at Sun Studios."

"Is the band meeting you there?"

"That's the plan. It'll be nice to take a break from the album and do something fun."

"Do you have a drummer yet or will you just go with a session guy?"

"We got Icky Sticks."

"Shut up!" Amanda gasped. "Icky Sticks from Pynchon?"

"Didn't think I was that cool, didja, Amanda?" Stee tossed back.

Pynchon had lit a fire under the asses of many a complacent musician with their 1991 debut album, *Read MN Weep*. No surprise for a punk outfit, they made lots of noise, but it was noise with a dark purpose. The three boys making the noise—Newt Tucker, Johnny Dietz and Icky Sticks (born Melvin Lefkowitz)—were determined to rid the world of hair metal, prefab pop and classic rock, one furious song at a time.

They damn near succeeded, which was enough to scare Stee into resurrecting his career. When he came out of rehab, Stee knew he had to up his game to keep up with the new punks on the block; *Santa Monica Pier* was the result.

"Hold on," the girl added, distressed. "Does that mean that Pynchon broke up?"

"My manager says they're taking a creative hiatus for the next twelve months. Since he's with our label, Icky can record with us in Memphis and step in to finish the album with us over the next couple of weeks. Could even join us on tour next year if things work out in the studio."

"This is the guy with the teeth, right?" Connie queried.

Icky had the biggest mouthful of choppers in the history of rock and roll: a perfectly matched set of Chiclets top and bottom. When he maniacally banged on his kit, it looked like he could chew the oxygen right out of the air.

"Yeah, Mom, the guy with the teeth," Amanda huffed. Her mood quickly shifted back to sardonic awe. "Icky Sticks—with him, a lot of new people would listen to your band."

"That's the hope."

"*I'd* even listen to your band," she added, her eyebrow askew. Stee gave her a jokey shove and she chuckled in reply. With barely enough time to pat himself on the back for how well the bonding experience was going so far, he spotted Trish coming toward the table followed by a couple of other servers and a fellow in a tie with a paunch as round as his big bald head. They were craning their necks around the indomitable waitress, trying to get a glimpse of her customers.

Connie spied the procession and whispered, "Smiles, everyone, smiles."

Trish put her hands on her hips, grimacing playfully. "You're Stee Walsh, you stinker! Why didn't you say so?"

"I didn't think it was important," he answered with a wary smile.

The paunchy fellow put out his hand, *Kevin* glinting on his name-plate. "Mr. Walsh, I'm the manager here. We are so pleased you came to our franchise today."

Stee shook it firmly but perfunctorily. "Well, this is my friend here's favorite restaurant. She likes your food. She likes to eat here." Out of the corner of his eye, he saw that Connie caught his emphasis on "food" and "eat." These subtle hints were sadly lost on the crew. The male servers, whose ages probably added up to the low eighties, were gawking admiringly. Trish was fishing in her apron for a cell phone.

"We'll get your sandwiches out in a moment," Kevin announced, "and they're on the house, by the way."

Even as Stee pleaded, "Thanks, but you don't have to do that," the manager waved his hands, perishing the thought.

"No, no, no; it's our pleasure." There was a pregnant pause, the manager rocking on his feet, the servers still gawking, Trish peering down her nose to focus on the little buttons on her cell phone, prob-ably trying to remember how to turn its camera on. Resigned, Stee waved them closer so he could speak quietly and firmly.

"I'll make you all a deal. If you can keep it to yourselves that I'm here and give us some time alone—and if those sandwiches can land on our table in the next five minutes—I'll be happy to pose for photos and do autographs and all that once we've eaten. Okay?"

"Gotcha!" the waitress gushed, giving his shoulder an uninvited tweak. She shooed her coworkers back down the narrow aisle between the tables. Stee did a quick scan of the restaurant. Sure enough, Trish and Company had made enough of a disturbance to catch people's attention, and customers were rubbernecking toward their booth to see what the source of the commotion was. A couple of brave souls were actually coming over to see what the fuss was about, and their eyes lit up when they recognized him.

Stee slumped in his seat.

Fuck me slowly.

"Well, at least the food was free, Con."

"If only we could have eaten it."

Even into the fourth decade of his notoriety, Stee found that the mob mentality was incredibly hard to predict. Inevitably when he just wanted to get a lot of shit done, he attracted all kinds of unwanted attention at traffic lights and crosswalks and drive-through lanes. Then again, when the sales for *Come, Come, Come* were in the crapper and he purposefully went to Venice Beach to trawl for autograph hounds to feel wanted, he could have run down the street naked and on fire and no one would have batted an eye. This afternoon, he was camouflaged as a regular Joe and he got pinned into a booth on both sides by people who thought manners were optional when a famous person was involved.

If Roland hadn't come to the counter to get a sandwich, and then rushed over to hustle them out through the kitchen's back exit, Stee might be nothing more than a stain on the bagel-shaped tiles of the Blarney Goldstone floor.

Returning in the Range Rover, Roland had the professional courtesy not to say "I told you so." Stee looked grim and Connie stayed silent, the two of them looking out of opposite windows. By contrast, Amanda smiled like a goon all the way home and went straight to her room to begin tapping furiously at her keyboard.

"Do you want me to fix you something?" Connie called over her shoulder, filling a glass of water for herself in the kitchen. He shook his head. She drained the glass and folded her arms.

"I'm a nervous wreck, Stee ..."

"I was an idiot, thinking I could handle this myself ..."

"People were elbowing me out of the way, pushing at Amanda ..."

"I didn't think anyone could pick me out of a lineup anymore. I bet it's because I played the inauguration. That got a lot of attention ..."

The phone rang.

"Hello? Oh, good afternoon, Mrs. Compton." Connie put her hand over the receiver and mouthed, "From across the street."

As she digested what her neighbor was saying, Stee figured she wasn't being asked for a cup of sugar.

"No, ma'am, everything's fine. That's not the police in my driveway. No, Amanda's not in any trouble."

She pressed the heel of her hand between her eyes. "Thank you for being so concerned, Mrs. Compton," she blurted with all the civility she could muster. "I have someone visiting from out of town and we have limo service for the day. Sorry to make you worry." She hung up and groaned.

"Problem?" Stee asked.

"She thought Amanda had been busted for drugs," she said without a trace of good humor. "The fact that this was the first scenario she thought of pisses me off." Connie quickly opened the living room curtains and then shut them. "Dandy. She's got her binoculars out."

The phone rang again. Stee stood dumbly in the living room as Connie had a second tersely friendly interchange with a neighbor. She hung up with a grunt.

"That was Bill Nielsen from the corner checking to see if there was a home invasion in progress."

"Nice that your neighbors are looking out for you," Stee said.

Connie cut by him and checked the lock on the front door. "This is a disaster, Stee," she muttered. "Now I'm trapped in my own house."

"Nonsense," he countered. "You can come and go as you please. *I'm* the one who's trapped here."

She pursed her lips.

"Okay, okay, let me start to make this right." He fished his phone out of his pocket.

"Roland? Hey, look, you can have the rest of the afternoon off. I'll call you later on—oh, and next time you come by, could you drive up in something a little less, I dunno, conspicuous? Thanks a million."

A few seconds later, they could hear the Land Rover rumbling off. Connie still looked shaken. Stee extended his hand.

"C'mon, let's sit and talk about this for a bit."

He was grateful that she sat next to him on the couch and didn't shrug off his arm when he put it around her shoulder. He was even more thankful when she let out a little laugh.

"I had no idea that they'd be so interested in me dating again."

"It's nice they're ready to defend your honor."

She hooted and laid her head back onto his shoulder. Stee busted into a grin.

"I love hearing you laugh, Con."

She rolled her head toward him, her eyes liquid. "Then just keep me laughing."

Clearly forgiven, Stee breathed easier. "I'll have Angie book dinner reservations someplace nice for the three of us, and this time, we can have Roland check out the place first."

She looked at him pensively. "Is this what will have to happen whenever we go anywhere?"

"No," he said, nudging closer to her. "This probably wouldn't have happened out by me. Musicians are a much more common sight in LA and we could go out and about pretty much like anyone else. When we need a little extra peace of mind, I have security guys who work with me all the time who can give us a safety zone. You wouldn't even notice they were there."

She looked at her hands. "So we could only have a social life if we're in California, then."

He studied her. "How much do you like living in Virginia?"

She shrugged. "It doesn't matter if I like it or not. I'm committed to staying here until Amanda finishes high school next year."

He toyed with her hair. "Well, when I start to come out here to visit you more often, I'll fade into the background."

That got her attention. Connie looked him in the eye for a long time, and Stee looked right back. He had put an offer on the table and wasn't about to back off, even though he felt like he was skydiving and wasn't sure if he'd packed his parachute.

"You want to visit me more often?"

"I do."

"Here?"

"Yes."

"Why?"

"Because I'm in love with you."

There we are.

She closed her eyes and exhaled. "Oh, God."

"What?" It was all he could do not to have his voice crack, wondering if he had, in the space of a sentence, nipped his happiness in the bud.

She shook her head. "This is going really, really fast."

"That's bad?"

"It's not good."

He touched her face, guiding her gaze his way. "Why? Don't you trust how I feel?"

"It's scary."

"I'm scaring you?"

"Yes," she said quietly. "I don't want to get too deep too fast. It might flame out. It might end too soon. I like this too much. I don't want to get hurt."

He drew close to her ear. "So, I'm scaring you because you're in love with me."

She didn't reply so he assumed he was right. He kissed her cheek and sat back.

"Baby, I'm sixty years old come the first of August. My oldest friend just died. I'm in recovery for the rest of my life, my knee is shot, and the moral of this story is, life is short ... and I don't have to tell that to you, of all people."

She nodded. He kept going.

"The way I see it, Con, there's no guarantee that love will last or people will stay, so if your heart tells you to do something, you'd better just go ahead. You leap out there without looking first, what's the worst that can happen? You fall down. What's the worst that can happen if you wait? You fall anyway—and you lost precious time at the start when you could have been happy."

She still wasn't saying anything.

Then again, she usually didn't when she was kissing him.

————

"Hey, Mom, I—*holy shit!*"

Amanda yanked herself out of the doorway, completely disgusted. That was one image she wasn't going to be able to erase from her brain ever:

Her mother making out with Stee Walsh.

Stee had her pressed down onto the arm of the couch, bracing her leg around his hip. She was stroking his back with one hand and caressing his red hair with the other. They were making a slurping, cooing sound like in the movies. They didn't even hear her come in.

EW! EW! EEEEEW!

Amanda sped to her room and closed the door firmly without slamming it. She didn't want to give her mother the satisfaction of knowing how disgusted and completely freaked out she was. In less than ten seconds, though, there was a knock.

"Amanda, I'm coming in."

"Don't you ask for permission anymore?"

"Ain't no way I'm not coming in, sweetheart."

The door opened. Cold eyed, Amanda looked her mother over. She had smoothed her hair back in place and pulled her shirt down since she last saw her—*EW!!!*—but her mouth was pinker than usual and her face was flushed.

Amanda was not going to start this conversation. She had nothing she really wanted to say right now, other than

EW!!!!!

Her mom sat on the edge of her bed, sliding a calculus textbook to one side. "So what are you thinking right now?"

"He's so ... short, Mom," she spat.

"That's not what I thought you'd lead with." Amanda knew her mother was flailing inside, trying to come up with the perfectly communicated Mom Speech, yet only able to cough up lame retorts.

Good.

She stayed adamantly silent, hoping her mother would give up without saying another word ... like that ever happened.

"Amanda, let's start talking about this now rather than me pestering you to a slow and certain death."

Amanda fixed her eyes on the floor in what her mother had dubbed the Burning Vacant Stare.

"You know if you don't start talking, I'll keep on until I've said my piece, right?"

Like you always say, Mom: silence is assent.

Her mother blew a gust of air out of her nose, less like she was angry and more like she was relieved. "I apologize. Stee coming all the way out here this weekend was a total shock. If I'd known about it, I would have brought you up to speed about our relationship ahead of him showing up on our doorstep for a weekend visit. You deserve that."

Amanda sucked her teeth because she knew it drove her mother insane. She plowed on anyway.

"I'm also sorry you found out by seeing what you did. I can't even imagine how I'd feel if I'd caught my mom fooling around in the living room ..."

Thanks, Mom. Another indelibly gross image burned into my brain: Grandma and Granddaddy getting it on ...

"... much less my mom and a new boyfriend."

Along with an image of Grandma getting it on with some other old wrinkly guy. Mom, STOP IT!

"I'll stop now. I'm probably grossing you out even more."

BINGO!

"Anyway, honey, Stee is decent and kind, and since we make each other pretty happy, we're probably going to be seeing a lot more of each other. He wants to get to know you better, too, and given who he is, having him around is probably going to attract a lot of unwanted attention and be really strange and awkward and take a long time to become normal. All I ask you is, don't hate him just because things are weird right now. Please give him a chance."

They sat in silence for a moment or two. "So, what did you want to tell me when you came into the living room?"

It took Amanda a few seconds to remember. "Chelsea invited a bunch of us to have a weekend study group and sleepover. I was going to ask if you'd mind if I went, since Stee's visiting."

Her mom nodded. "You can take the car after dinner. Stee's taking us out."

"This time with the big ninja bodyguard, right?"

"Right."

The AP Government notes had been abandoned six seconds after Amanda showed up at Chelsea's house. There were more pressing issues to discuss than the Articles of the Constitution. Rushing to the rec room and plopping onto the nearest couch, she filled her friends in on the melee at Blarney Goldstone's and dinner and the creepfest she witnessed in her living room. They were rapt.

"I can't believe they were—*EW!*"

Leah swallowed some vitamin water and snorted. "That happened to me when my dad started dating, and he wasn't just making out either. He couldn't figure out why I asked to move down to the basement."

"That's got to be better than the alternative," Chelsea offered, downing another handful of M&Ms. "My mom and dad barely touch each other anymore. It's like they're co-workers or something. It's really sad."

"Are you afraid Stee's trying to take your mom away from you?" Leah asked.

Amanda's eyes widened as she shrugged. "I dunno. At dinner, the two of them were talking about commuting on the weekends and me visiting with Mom sometimes out at Stee's house."

"Where does he live?" Sophie passed the popcorn bowl to Amanda.

"Malibu."

"Whoa, that's money talking." Amanda shot Chelsea a look. She had a penchant for stating the obvious.

"He's some big-shit rock guy, right?" Sophie asked. "What's he like? All tattoos and Jack Daniels and leather?"

Amanda shook her head. "He doesn't drink. He's old, too. He's practically sixty."

"So?" Leah interjected. "Keith Richards is older than that. Steve Tyler is older than that."

"Yeah, well, they're all a lot cooler than Stee Walsh ever was," Amanda groused. "I spent two days working with him on Mom's video, and two meals with him today, but he kept asking about art and my comic book and what I want to do for a living. It's like he's a guidance counselor or something." She nabbed the last chicken nugget. "Let's face it, all the Stones have these model girlfriends. Stee's making out with *Mom*."

"He used to be hot," Leah said. "My mom has a couple of his early CDs. He kind of had that manorexia look in the Seventies and it worked for him."

"Not anymore," Amanda laughed. "He looks like a potato on

popsicle sticks."

"That's a sincere disappointment," Sophie commented. Amanda added another mark in her mental tally. *Sincere* was Sophie's over-used word of the week. In the last thirty minutes alone, she had said it six times.

"I've never heard of him," Chelsea stated flatly. "What's his big hit?"

"He's got a bunch," Amanda answered. "His songs are on the radio all the time. 'Shoot Me Now,' 'No Way Girl,' 'Red Mustang' ..."

"'Run With Me'—that's one of my mom's favorites," Leah said. "He did a lot of MTV when it started, too. I saw the video with all the zombies on YouTube. Pretty trippy."

"Means nothing to me," Chelsea sniffed. "Is he any good?"

"Actually, yeah," Amanda said, surprising herself. "He did this soundtrack for this movie that nobody saw that was really good. He told me Icky Sticks is working with him now."

Sophie's face lit up. "He knows Icky personally? Can you meet him?"

The thought hadn't even occurred to her. "Maybe when I visit Stee in California."

"Hide me in your luggage then," Sophie demanded.

"How much money does he have?" Chelsea asked dreamily.

"I don't know," Amanda replied, screwing up her face. "A lot, I guess."

Chelsea continued, "Maybe he'll buy you a car."

"Chelsea, he's known my mom for two months. He's not buying me a car!"

"Elvis gave away cars, didn't he?"

"But he was stoned on painkillers and fried peanut butter sand-wiches. Jesus, Chelsea!"

"Do you like him?" Leah asked earnestly.

"I like him," Amanda admitted. "He's not slimy or anything. He means well."

"Is your mom happy?" Leah continued.

She sighed. "Yeah, it's the first time she's gone out with anybody since Dad died. She's been in a really good mood for weeks."

"That's gotta be nice," Chelsea offered.

"Are you afraid he's trying to become your dad?" Amanda knew this was a raw spot for Leah since she had gotten close to her mother's first boyfriend after her parents' divorce, and when it didn't work out, she was devastated.

"No, it's not like that."

"Do you think they'll have a kid together?"

"Chelsea, SHUT UP!" Amanda bellowed.

Sophie suddenly burst out laughing. "God, it must kill you that your mom has a boyfriend when you've never even been on a date."

"Neither have you, Soph," Amanda said defensively.

"You'll always have me, Sophie," Chelsea said melodramatically, grabbing her hand and kissing it with a loud *smack!* Sophie pulled it away and wiped it on Chelsea's t-shirt with a squeal of mock disgust.

Leah put a reassuring arm around Amanda. "Mandy, I'm happy and sorry for you. You want your mom to find someone so she won't be alone the rest of her life. And it's cool that he's rich and connected and a good guy, but it's gotta be weird to see her with someone who's not your dad. It just makes you miss him all over again, no matter what you dad did to you."

"Yeah," Amanda replied, glad someone finally found words to explain the ache she had been fighting all night. "You got that right."

———

It was the middle of the night when Stee jostled Connie awake as he moved to spoon her. She settled easily into the C of his body, and his arm came to rest around her waist, anchoring them together. He began tracing the curve of her shoulder with his lips, scattering kisses as he went.

His tenderness was overwhelming.

Her breathing became jagged and her eyes started to well up. Out of the blue, she was a hair's breadth away from sobbing.

"Why is this happening?" she whispered, taking a deep breath, trying to quell the tears.

"You thinking about Chris?" he asked gently.

"No."

Stee turned her toward him. "How long has it been since some-one's held you in your own bed, baby? How long since someone's taken care of you?"

She buried her face in his chest, and her cup, already filled to the brim, overflowed.

chapter 18

Stee cast a worried eye toward the scene in the Sun studio lounge to gauge the River Runners' first impression of Icky Sticks. He couldn't help but overhear as he introduced himself to Larry and Caldwell. The guy only spoke in exclamation points.

"I am like the fucking biggest River Runners fan *ever!* Never in a million fucking *eons* did I think I'd be called up to the *majors!* Johnny and Newt are pissing their *pants* with envy right now! Being here is the *shit*, I'm telling you! I can't thank you *enough* for this opportunity to sit *in* with you guys!"

Caldwell pressed his lips together to keep a straight face. Larry listened intently as he backed up, turning his head slightly sideways so he could cast his dental student's academic eye on that magnificent set of teeth. Stee nervously stroked his lip with his thumb and turned to his guitarist.

"What's the verdict?"

"He's awfully cute," Chad affirmed.

Stee sized up the new recruit: the Oscar the Grouch t-shirt and shredded black 501s roped with bike chains; the spiraling Maori tattoos encasing both arms; the jet-black fauxhawk and studded earlobes; the mushroom pallor and flabby midsection; those unfathomable teeth. "He doesn't strike me as your type, brother."

"Not cute in that way. More like, cute in a Raggedy Icky way."

"How old is this kid?"

Chad thought for a moment. "Let's see ... *Read MN Weep* was out in '91, and he was probably in his early twenties then ... forty-one? Forty-two?"

Stee groaned. "If that's how old kids are today, I'm a fucking fossil." He roamed over to place a paternal hand on the drummer's shoulder. "You ready to give it a go, Icky?"

"Please, call me Mel," the drummer replied eagerly. "I'd rather be myself in the studio." Stee arched an eyebrow but nodded.

"Okay, Mel, let's get to work."

The musicians filed in, suited up and checked the charts on their music stands, readying to barrel through "Matchbox." In the booth was T Bone Burnett, as tall and courtly as Jon had been round and relaxed. He leaned into the microphone.

"Gentlemen, whenever you're ready. We'll record just for chuckles, but this time through, just get a feel for it."

Stee balled his chewing gum up in its wrapper and adjusted his microphone. He looked over his shoulder at the drum set. Mel was adjusting the height of his stool and testing the sound of each drum in turn. Stee shivered for a second.

Bobby's not coming back.

Not this time.

Stee turned toward his music stand. The lyrics were written in 24-point type, with the chord changes clearly marked so he could keep his bifocals in his pocket. He said a small prayer of thanks to Angie for preserving this one small piece of his pride. He coughed to clear the gunk off his vocal cords and, after checking in with each man in turn, Stee counted off.

The rockabilly intro kicked him into the first verse. Stee looked over his shoulder to check on the new recruit. Mel's head was bouncing along to the rhythm and he was keeping the beats crisp and clean, helping the piano and guitar lines stay on the rails.

As they made the turn into the instrumental break, there was space for a drum fill. Mel rounded out the phrase without busting a hole in the drumheads. He'd clearly done his homework on the song. He was having a blast, too, sporting a face-splitting grin and swinging his head back and forth.

They gunned through to the finish, with Mel punching the last chords with a satisfying cymbal crash. The band held off for a couple of seconds until the engineer gave them the all clear. Then, as a unit, they turned to the drummer and applauded. Mel pumped his fists into the air in delight and bellowed, "That was going to the fucking *moon.* That was Neil *Armstrong* shit! Thank you *so* much!"

Stee liked this guy, and as much as he hated to admit it, it wasn't simply because he was gracious.

It's because he's a much better drummer than Bobby.

From the beginning, Bobby played to serve his ego rather than the music, and Stee would accommodate him. During more than one tour, once Bobby ducked offstage after a sound check, Stee would surreptitiously give the signal, and the engineers would pull the sound levels down in the house but raise them for the drum monitor so Bobby would think he was playing louder than he really was. As Bobby's drug problem ran amok, they'd do take after take in the studio just to get the basic rhythms right and would sometimes have to paste together his harmony vocal track syllable by syllable.

It wore them all down. Stee even decided to record *Wild Women and Perfect Gentlemen* solo simply so he could use a session man for percussion and avoid dealing with Bobby's mess.

This guy is so much better than Bobby ever was.

Stee's stomach sank. It was clear as day. He had floated Bobby too long out of loyalty and a sense of early debts not completely repaid, and here was the proof: one rehearsal with a superb drummer was enough to lift the energy in the studio all the way up to 11. The other members of the band were retracing their steps through the song, picking through what went well, slapping the new guy on the shoulder, finding out about his history. Even Caldwell was smiling.

While Bobby had been good, Mel was great ... and grateful ... and he wasn't high, drunk or belligerent. Stee sighed.

They aren't just impressed; they're relieved.

———

Sprawled on his bed, staring at his laptop balanced on his stomach, Leonard listened idly to the bootleg of the River Runners' '97 Hollywood Bowl concert. He didn't really like this recording much. It featured a lot of tracks from *Wild Women and Perfect Gentlemen,* not his favorite album in the first place. Plus, the performances were rote and at times he could barely hear the music over the boozy adulation of the crowd.

He needed the background noise, though. Rifling through Connie Rafferty's online credit card bills and phone records was tedious to the point of madness.

With Stee still incommunicado, undoubtedly swamped with recording sessions, Leonard refocused on demonstrating the worth of ISPeye. He was determined to find incontrovertible proof that his program was just as effective in constructing someone's personality and buying habits as trolling through financial records and online communications. To do so, he just had to compare the ISPeye results to the data from real-life experiences.

All afternoon, he'd mined the guinea pig's online records to validate what her music library told him: she was a tightly wound career woman who had loosened up markedly under the influence of the SWATRR catalogue ... and maybe snagged a Southern California boyfriend in the process.

Didn't see that coming.

It would explain the evidence he'd unearthed from combing through her online life. For one thing, she had been in constant contact with someone at a private Los Angeles phone number which, even with his diagnostic software, Leonard had not been able to trace to an owner. Also, she had overnighted a large quantity of bagels and a turkey club sandwich from some weird Richmond chain restaurant to a generic P.O. box in Malibu.

Most damning, though, was the fact that she'd bought a lot of clothes lately: jeans that were supposed to make her look less like a mom; high heels; even satiny underthings.

He sniffed in disgust.

Trollop.

This all tracked with her Busker library exploding over recent weeks. Once she had swallowed the entire SWATRR catalogue, she moved on to their musical antecedents and progeny. It fit that she had come under the influence of someone with great musical taste and massive resources ... and a hankering for hanky-panky, hence the fancy underwear.

He slapped his forehead. That was marketing gold right there:

Listening to Stee Walsh can get you laid.

Shocked by the brilliance of his discovery, he glanced over to his Wall of Fame, the coffee stirrer at the center. He was seriously considering getting a spotlight installed.

He smirked.

I better email Stee. He'll get a good laugh out of this.

chapter 19

On this fine summer morning following his requisite laps in the pool, Stee couldn't have been more pleased to find Connie settled in at his kitchen counter drinking his coffee, completely at home in his house. The back and forth every other weekend meant they no longer had to ask permission to grab a glass out of the cupboard or a snack out of the fridge. Their familiarity was delicious.

She sat at the counter, her chin resting on her left hand, her right holding a paperback. A sliver of her lower back was showing above her jeans. His fingers glossed up and under her t-shirt as he looked over her shoulder.

"Whatcha reading?"

"*Outliers.* It actually made me think of you."

"Do tell," he said as he encroached on her bra clasp but turned back.

"Gladwell posits—"

"He *posits,* does he?"

"Yes, he does. He *posits* that someone can only be a genius of his craft if he's put in at least 10,000 hours of practice and labor, starting at a very young age. The Beatles did it when they went to Germany, and you and the River Runners did it when you were in high school and on the college and bar circuit, so," she continued, a little huskier than before, "it's no wonder you're a genius."

"Hm," he huffed near her ear. "I'm assuming you're talking about my musical skill right now, not my other talents." He tugged her bra strap with a satisfying snap.

"Maybe both," she replied, turning slowly around to face him. "Too bad I didn't get started earlier. I could have put in my 10,000 hours and been a genius, too."

He trapped her against the counter. "You're a quick study."

Things got hot, and mighty uncomfortable jammed against that counter, in a hurry. When he released her, blissful frustration lined her face.

"You have to go work out those last two songs, don't you?"

"That's what Dan the Man says. Homework's due."

"Do you mind if I listen to you play for a little while?"

"Not at all."

Connie followed him down to his office and straddled the wooden chair across from him, resting her chin on her hands. He had his Gibson Country Western on his lap, his left foot propped on a dilapidated orange crate. Once he plugged a microphone into his recorder, Stee strummed a meandering 4/4 and Connie closed her eyes.

He liked to let his hands wander to see what would come out, clearing his head and encouraging other musical thoughts to come by for a visit. Right now, he was in a warm mood, the body of the big guitar full to the brim with chords. She sighed and opened her eyes.

Stee caught her expression and smiled. "Looks like you just had a nice daydream." He began to pick up the tempo, the strings sounding like rain falling into a lake, steady and insistent.

"You working on something in particular?"

"Nah, although there's a phrase that is beginning to stick with me." He stilled the strings and then played four bars. "Sometimes I worry that I'm just ripping somebody off because I've gotten to know so many tunes. Does this sound like McGuinn to you?"

"Not really."

"How about Neil Young?"

"Don't know. You haven't given me any of his music."

"Look him up on your own."

She rolled her eyes and he turned back to his guitar, his long fingers flowing back and forth over the neck, his pick ringing the notes in quick succession. He nodded his head slightly as the melody intensified. He was in the room with her and he was somewhere else, his molecules vibrating with the strings.

"How do you find it, Stee? How does the music come to you?"

He didn't look up, still strumming. "It depends. Sometimes it's a sound I can't shake. Other times I have words that make their own music. Sometimes I can even hear it in the change in tone as someone speaks. I don't know why I hear it; I'm just glad I still do."

The tune had gotten lighter and more intricate, like lace. "That's lovely, Stee."

"Thanks." When he looked up, her hazel eyes were fixed on him. He mellowed the timbre of the song, making it smooth as caramel. She nodded her approval.

"Did you want to play lead guitar? You could, you know. You're really good."

"Once Chad came along, I was happy to cede the throne. I didn't want to get in his way. I knew he'd do nothing but make me better if he was out front. Besides, it gave me the flexibility to write more material."

She closed her eyes again to fully absorb the sound. "Everything you play sounds new and familiar at the same time. That's a gift."

"I'm grateful. I was given talent, anger and opportunity, pretty much in that order, not to mention bandmates who could have played with anyone in the world but decided to stick it out with me. Then there's you, baby."

She lazily opened one eye. "You're gonna make me blush."

"Good."

Her languid good humor made Stee feel utterly wonderful. He was therefore inspired to sing the first thing that came into his head.

I love you so much, my nose sweats.

She snorted. "Your nose sweats? How romantic."

His silly little ditty continued, backed up by a hillbilly guitar riff:

I love you so much, my momma frets.

I love you so much, my heart shakes.

I love you so much, my earlobe aches.

I love you so much, I wheeze and cough.

I've loved you so much, my dick fell off.

Belly laughing, Connie basked in his giddy affection. Joy thrummed in his chest as he heard her quote the one lyric he never tired of hearing:

"I love you, too."

Glorious.

"Come on tour with me."

She gave him a startled smile. "What?"

"We start after the holidays once everybody's got their Squeeze-boxes on permanent Stee Walsh shuffle. We're set to do thirty dates in the U.S. and sixteen in Europe with a break in April. I want you to be with me." He brightened. "You could shoot the tour. You could do a documentary!"

"Stee," she said with fond incredulity, "how would Amanda fit into the picture?"

"What do you mean?"

"She starts her senior year in a few weeks. She can't go with us and I don't want to leave her on her own for six months, especially when she's finishing up high school."

"Couldn't you bring her along and get a tutor?"

"No!"

"Shit, it's just high school."

"Stee, she's not skipping her senior year to go on the road. That's final."

"Okay, okay, okay." He frowned, crestfallen that his brilliant, romantic notion had been shot down so fast. "What about going to some key dates around her schedule? Would that work better?"

"Let me think about it."

Placing his guitar on the stand, he dragged his chair over to her and swung it around so he could look her in the eye. "Don't you want to do a full-length documentary of one of the brightest lights of American rock history?"

"Why, is Billy Joel touring?" She giggled as he sneered at her.

"I've never done a documentary before. You'd be getting a scoop.

It'll put you and Key Light Videos on the map. It'll be good for your business." He took her hand and kissed it. "Of course, we'd have a lot of time for pleasure, too."

She acquiesced to his considerable charm for a few minutes but didn't give him a yay or nay about the touring idea. Seeing success ahead, Stee figured he'd ask her again later, after he'd finished convincing her in the master bedroom down the hall.

———

The morning drawled on. As he coasted in and out of post-coital fog, Stee marveled how satisfying this was, pleasing Connie. It was clear she was really happy and he had made her so. That was new for him. The umpteen zillion women in his life all had been tasked with making *him* happy without much in return. This felt a hell of a lot better.

She was content, stroking his small patch of chest hair that was more silver than copper these days. It was intimate and soothing.

"Whatcha thinking about, Con?"

"I'm sorry I took you away from your writing."

"Do I look upset?"

"Whenever I come over, we tend to distract one another."

"This somehow is a problem?" He propped himself on his elbows. "Honey, we barely get any time together, especially if Amanda's visiting, too, and I miss you so much. We end up having a lot of catching up to do, which I'm happy to do. And, since you haven't come out to your friends and neighbors that I'm your boyfriend, I have to sneak in and out of your house when I come to Richmond and we never go out in the daylight. I feel like your mistress."

"I was trying to spare you. There aren't that many world-famous people holing up in Henrico County."

"I think Jimmy Dean lives out there somewhere."

"Okay, I'll grant you that you don't have anything on the king of breakfast sausage ..."

"He sang 'Big Bad John' ..."

"Duly noted ..."

"Was in a couple of Bond films ... wish *I* could be in a Bond film ..."

"Remember Blarney Goldstone's? I don't want you to have a bunch of yahoos hound you for your autograph."

"Baby, the only way that'll happen is if they get to know me. Once I'm a familiar presence, I'll be boring enough to fade into the background."

"If you say so, but I don't think you'll ever be boring." She sat with her arms ringing her knees. "What kind of life do you imagine we could have together, you know, when the animal attraction cools off?"

"Maybe it won't cool off," he replied confidently, even as he knew he was just whistling in the dark. It was taking him for-fucking-*ever* these days, and the mere thought of Viagra made him feel bluer than the little pill itself. While Connie, patient and ardent as she was, could coax him along for now, he had to accept the dreadful possibility that he might not always be able to come when called—and at some point, he might not even care.

She didn't seem worried. "From your lips to God's ear," she said, amused, "but I think we're at the point where we need to meet each other's relatives, hear the family history—see what we might be in for."

He looked away for a moment. "Getting to know my family, that's a big step. You ready for that?"

Connie nodded. "You've already met my daughter. Could I meet yours?"

He readjusted the sheets. "I can ask them, but I'm afraid they won't do it."

"Why?" The way she said it, he could tell she was searching her soul for what she could have done to offend Maude and Candace, without ever having crossed paths with them.

"The reason has nothing to do with you, Con," he assured her with a twinge of embarrassment. "I brought a few too many girls over to meet them in the past, and they were none too pleased with Kayla, either. Since they've had kids, I can visit solo, but they've made it pretty clear they aren't interested in meeting my next girlfriend."

She pressed her lips together. "Because I'm 1,001."

"No, because I'm a fuckup of a father." He sat up and wrapped his arms around her. "Maybe we should start with a more receptive audience when we're back in Virginia."

————

"Uncle Stee!!!"

"Gertie, my Gertie, all kissy and flirty," he chuckled as she sat up in bed and threw her arms around his neck. He could tell she had been waiting up for him even though her light had been off. She still had her pink-rimmed glasses on, though they were cockeyed, with the earpiece piercing her left ponytail. Smooching her loudly, he collected her on his lap, smoothing the sleeves of her Sleeping Beauty nightgown.

"Are you staying, Uncle Stee?"

"Yes, I am. Granddaddy Duane said I could visit you all for a few days. I have a few surprises for you."

"You brought me presents?" she asked, wide-eyed. "Granddaddy told me not to ask for anything and you brought me something anyway? It's magic!"

"Sure is," he smiled. "Now where did I put them?" He patted his pockets theatrically. "I can't find 'em." He looked deep in Gertie's ear and then up her nose, and she dissolved into a fit of giggles.

Stee held up a finger. "Aha! I remember now. The presents are so special, I had to have two helpers to bring them in. Oh, helpers!" Gertie craned her neck to see down the hall until a pair of ladies carrying wrapped packages appeared.

"Gertie, this is my girlfriend Connie and her daughter Amanda. They're visiting, too."

"I'm so pleased to meet you," Connie said. "Your uncle told me lots about you."

"Me, too," added Amanda.

"Your hair's pink," Gertie blurted.

"Yes," Amanda nodded.

Gertie scrunched up her eyes. "It didn't grow that way, right?"

"No," Amanda shook her head.

"I knew it," Gertie said with certainty. "Only ponies have pink hair."

Connie handed the little girl the first package. "Here you go, sweetie." The wrapping paper was on the floor in a flash.

"It's chapter books!" Gertie exclaimed, with the same level of awe as if she had been given a pink-haired pony.

"These were some of Amanda's favorites, so something tells me you'll like them, too."

She examined the front cover. "What's its name?"

"*Ramona the Pest.*"

"What's a pest?"

"It's someone who is always bugging you, getting in your business. Someone with issues."

Gertie nodded. "That boy Bowen in my class—he has issues," she replied gravely.

"Well, Bowen is a pest then."

"Got it," she affirmed. Amanda handed her the other present, which was a bracelet-making kit.

"I thought we could make these together while I'm visiting," Amanda said.

"You can use the pink beads," Gertie offered.

"Why don't you two get a little more acquainted, girl to girl?" Stee said, slipping Gertie off his lap and going to the doorway where Connie stood watching the scene.

"She's seven?" she whispered. "She's such a little thing."

"Yeah," Stee confirmed, speaking low. "She's small for her age and she's a little delayed because her mom was on heroin when she was pregnant."

"Where's her mom now?"

"She overdosed when Gertie was a few months old."

Connie processed this and took Stee's hand. "She's really sweet," she offered as the girl introduced Amanda to each of the stuffed animals on her bed.

"She's a trip," Stee said affectionately. "She says whatever's on her mind. Good thing she's cute because she doesn't have any tact."

"So, she's a normal seven-year-old," Connie confirmed.

"Pretty much. She had a hard couple of years—Duane and Gina thought they might lose her when she was a baby—but her health issues leveled off and she's in first grade and doing great."

Connie gave his hand a squeeze. "She loves you a lot."

"The feeling's mutual."

Gertie broke off her conversation with Amanda to look at Connie. "Who are you again?"

"I'm Connie."

"Why are you here?"

"She's my girlfriend, Gertie," Stee explained. Connie felt her heart *ping!* as he said that one word with complete ease: *girlfriend*.

"Girlfriend?" she replied, puzzled.

"That's right. Do you know what a girlfriend is, hon?"

"The same thing as boyfriend but with a girl?"

Stee snickered. "Even better."

"Bowen's my boyfriend," Gertie stated.

"No wonder he's a pest," Amanda muttered.

Duane called up the hall, "Gertie, you go to sleep now. You can talk to them in the morning."

"You heard Granddaddy Duane; lights out." Stee gently slipped her glasses off and set them on her bedside table, which was covered in layers of hair ribbons, broken crayons, and Happy Meal toys. "We'll see you tomorrow."

She kissed him goodnight and insisted on hugging and kissing Connie and Amanda as well. Amanda looked pleasantly dumbfounded by the attention, which made her mother smile.

Gina was cutting slices of a Sara Lee pound cake and pouring decaf into a set of daisy-motif mugs when they settled in for dessert in the den. The house was the type Connie had envied when she was growing up in her tiny ranch house: a two-story Colonial with a den, a living room and a basement family room; an eat-in kitchen; central air. Connie had seen evidence of Gina's patchwork taste at the farmhouse, and here in her home, it was in full flower: thirty-plus years of calico, lace and needlework, wedged in between Duane's hunting trophies and Southern artifacts, with a couple of Stee's gold records thrown in for good measure. Mounds of toys and Disney DVDs reinforced the cluttered comfort they had built for themselves during an extended lifetime of parenting.

Most of the conversation was basic getting-acquainted talk. Connie made a mental note to thank Amanda later for being so patient with the adults. She remembered her own interminable visits with ancient relatives and had hoped she'd never have to put her own daughter through the same slog, but here they were, and Amanda was coping politely and without complaint.

As the hour got late, Stee cast a meaningful glance to Connie and then looked to his sister-in-law. "Gina, could you help Connie and Amanda get settled in? I need to talk with Duane about something." Connie dutifully followed her hostess down the hall toting her bag, wondering what in the world this was about. Not long after Gina had handed out the towels and Amanda was granted a reprieve from adult company to do her own thing in the basement, Connie made her way back to the den.

The atmosphere was markedly tense. Connie noticed that there was a folded piece of paper on the coffee table that hadn't been there previously. The men looked at her with tight expressions. She halted.

"Sorry. Am I interrupting something?"

"No, Con," Stee said tersely. "We don't have anything else to say about this."

Duane folded his arms. "No, I got plenty more to say, Stee, but I don't want to upset our guest on her first night here."

"Never stopped you before," Stee retorted.

"Stee, you're the one who brought this up," Duane shot back. "You bring this song here and shove it in my face, saying that you're giving me a 'heads-up' but it's going on the album no matter what I think. So why bother showing it to me?"

Like many a good Southern girl before her, Connie was trained to avoid conflict whenever possible and to get the hell out of the room when an argument was brewing. Any whiff of a disagreement, whether it was about politics, religion, family or football, sent her straight to the kitchen to do dishes or fold napkins or fill saltshakers—anything.

"Let me leave you two to work this out," she stammered. Before she could even turn around, Duane was pushing the paper into her hands.

"Have you seen these lyrics, Connie?" he demanded.

"No." During the recording sessions, she had only heard three of the songs, knowing that Stee would share the rest in good time. He had his superstitions and his ingrained habits with the band, and she didn't expect him to switch them all around just because they were close.

"Well, read this and tell me what you think. Go ahead." Connie glanced at Stee, who looked equal parts defiant and defenseless in the presence of his big brother's anger.

"Stee, do you want me to read this?" she asked, knowing that she was essentially asking if he wanted her to step into the middle. He nodded, turning away with a wave of his hand as if he couldn't stop what had already been started.

She turned to the song, titled "Cold Comfort."

I won't say, "I forgive you"
That's too much to ask
After the hell you put me through
That's just too great a task.
I won't say, "Just forget it"
Some wounds cut too deep.
I fought hard to escape you.
I'm not sorry you can't sleep.
Let's get just one thing straight:
Some things I won't let slide
Neither could you—a family trait
Ain't that a kick in the side?
I've had joy you'll never witness
Found peace you'll never find

In your fight for forgiveness
You've lost more than your mind.
So keep your damn self-pity
Your ignorance—no bliss.
This is the last you'll hear from me
I got no time for this.

The bitter fury of his the lyrics surprised her. Up to now, she hadn't seen Stee truly angry. She wondered where this came from, if this was directed at some lover or an ex-wife—someone who had his trust once and betrayed him.

"Well?" Duane fumed over her shoulder. "What if that was your father he was talking about? What would you say?"

She reread the words again, now in context, and shivered.

What kind of a monster was your father, Stee? What did he do to you?

"Back off, Duane," Stee warned. His gallantry only made her nervous. She didn't want to be party to what was clearly an ancient argument ... and she didn't know Duane well enough to know if he had a temper and if he could control it.

Or if Stee could control his, for that matter.

"Duane, Stee, my opinion is meaningless," she said as diplomatically as possible. "I don't know the history here. I can't judge."

"Our father was an abusive bastard," Stee stated flatly. "He thought I was gay because I loved music so much, and he tried to beat it out of me. He hit me so many times I can't remember a week when he didn't."

"That's the way things were back then," Duane countered. "Parents used to hit their kids to keep them in line."

"Did they break ribs, Duane? Did they give their kids concussions?"

Connie put the pieces together on the fly.

Stee was physically abused by his father. Severely. Repeatedly.

My God ...

"Why are you writing this song now after all these years?" Duane stormed. "Jesus, Stee, what is this going to solve?"

"It had to come out sometime, Duane. It's part of who I am."

"What part of you is this?" he shot back, pointing to the piece of paper.

Stee was shaking, Duane was red-faced. Connie nervously checked back and forth between the two men, worried they'd come to blows. Miraculously, Stee exhaled and downshifted.

"Why are you defending him?" Stee quietly demanded. "You pulled him off of me more than once. You know how bad it was."

"He's an old, sick man now," his brother said wearily, the anger hissing out of him. "It's one problem after another: diabetes, congestive heart failure, dementia. He's harmless, pitiful even."

"I know. I've paid his nursing home bills."

"You *don't* know, Stee," Duane countered. "You haven't seen him since Momma's funeral. No friends left, only us visiting him, with him in pain most of the time. You can sit all the way out there in California and say you don't care he can't sleep. I say whatever sins he's committed against you, he's been more than punished for. You'd know that if you saw him—if you had the *guts* to see him, that is."

Stee stayed silent. Duane took the lyric sheet from Connie and handed it back to his brother. "Think about that, Stee, before you slap this song on an album. I'm going to bed. I'm done." He turned to Connie, looking at the floor in embarrassment. "In the morning, we're going to put this behind us and we'll have a real nice visit. Okay?"

Connie put her hand on his shoulder. "I have no doubt, Duane. Good night." Duane disappeared down the hall.

Connie turned to face Stee. "Do you want to talk about this?"

He was clutching the lyrics in his fist, looking equal measures exhausted and ashamed. "Not much more to say."

"This isn't what you usually write. It's really angry and personal. You sure you want this on the album?"

"Maybe it's what I have to do."

"I'm not so sure," she said.

He looked at her, his brow in knots. "Connie, I'm going to go lie down."

Her throat tightened. "Do you want me to sleep with Amanda?"

"No," he said quickly. "I most certainly don't. Just give me a few minutes alone, all right?"

Stee shuffled down to their guest room. Connie's mind raced.

Why does he do this, haul me away from home into unfamiliar territory without telling me what the hell he's getting me into?

What does he want me to fix now?

Once Stee closed the door, Gina came out of her room and waddled down the hall toward her, upholstered in a quilted floral bathrobe. "Connie, you need anything?"

She cleared her throat and forced a smile. "No, thank you."

Gina shook her head. "Sorry that Duane was his usual idiot self on your first night here. He doesn't know there's a time and place for everything."

"Not a problem," she replied as pleasantly as she could.

"It's a problem in my book," Gina said with a frown. "These Walsh men have one thing in common: they think it's someone else's job to clean up their mess. I'm out here apologizing for my husband's behavior and I don't even really know why this started in the first place."

Connie wondered whether talking about the lyrics was a good idea. She had only spent a few hours here and didn't know where the allegiances lay. Then again, she could use an insider's opinion of all this.

"Stee recorded a song for the new album about his father. It's unforgiving."

"Oh." Gina didn't look surprised; if anything, she was sympathetic. "Duane told me what it was like for Stee once he picked up a guitar and started writing songs."

"Stee said his father beat him because he thought he was gay."

"Wouldn't have been the first sensitive boy who got the hell beaten out of him. Harry's a bullheaded man, just like his sons."

Connie thought for a moment. "May I ask you a favor?"

"Of course."

"If she gets up before noon, could you please entertain Amanda for a little while tomorrow morning? I'm going to offer to take Stee to visit his father."

Gina's eyes widened. "Well, if you can get him to do that, I guess I should thank you, even though it's really something he should do on his own."

"Maybe he needs someone with him to be able to do it."

"So you're the lucky girl?"

"Looks that way."

Gina looked at her with a small measure of pity. "Listen, I've known Stee for forty-odd years, and he's got a lot of great qualities, but he's used to having other people handle the difficult parts of life so he can be an 'artist' without having to worry his little red head over the tough stuff. He's got a whole crew on his payroll to handle the business, and his band waits to do his bidding for the music part. Even if you're family and he loves you to death, Stee's not shy about sticking you with a job ... helping him manage his father, for one. One day, he's gotta start owning his own life."

Seeing Connie's expression, Gina laid a conciliatory hand on her shoulder. "Take my advice: be sure he does for you what you do for him once in a while, okay, honey?"

With that, she went back to her bedroom. Connie went to hers.

Stee was lying across the bed, still fully dressed. His eyes were closed and he pinched the bridge of his nose as if trying to relieve a wicked headache. When he heard the door latch, his eyes popped open, apprehensive and sad.

"You gotta be wondering what I got you into," he said. He sat up and swung his legs stiffly over the side of the bed.

She sat beside him. "I'd like to take you to see your father tomorrow. I get the sense that's what you wanted to do as soon as we started planning this trip. Will you go with me?"

Stee nodded. She pressed on.

"Why now, after all these years?"

He exhaled slowly. "Because you weren't with me before, and I couldn't do this without someone as grounded as you."

"What, visit your father?"

"No. Forgive him."

————

"Mr. Walsh, your son's here."

It was that nice colored lady in the pink pajamas ... that nurse ... Vera? Yes, that was what was on her nametag. She was patting his arm.

What is it, morning?

Time for those big men to drag me to the bathroom, without a piece of privacy, and hold my dick while I piss?

No, he was sitting up, the plastic armrests of the wheelchair stuck to his elbows. He was in the sunroom, the windowed place full of old people sitting around all day like sacks of laundry. He raised his head. Even with his tunnel vision, he could see the big poster on the wall:

> Today is: Saturday, July 25, 2009
> It is: Summer
> The weather today is: Hot and Sunny

"Duane here?" he asked with a crackle. His throat was dry but he couldn't make the words—*water, thirsty, drink*—stay in his head long enough to say them.

"No, Mr. Walsh. It's your other son, Stee."

Stee? Who is—oh, right.

Francine's boy.

"Stee here?"

He tried to focus on the form coming toward him. Gray t-shirt, dungarees, red beard, red hair. Old. Sad.

Walks like my brother.

"Jake?"

"No, Daddy, it's me. It's Stee."

Can't be Stee. Stee's a little boy, four, five. I'm gonna take him around town with me in the Park and Rec pickup truck this morning. He likes that.

"It's been a long time since I've seen you, Daddy."

Who is this sad old man with a beard? Where is Stee, Francine's boy, darkest blue eyes you ever saw? I have to pick him up on the way to work.

"Pretty lady there. G'mornin'."

"Good morning, Mr. Walsh. I'm Connie, Stee's friend." Not a nurse ... no pink pajamas ... snappy dresser. Sticking close to the sad man in the gray shirt. Holding his hand. Nice smile.

"Dimple just winks at you." He smiled out the right corner of his mouth.

"Always was a ladies' man," the sad redheaded man told her quiet.

"I see where you get your charm," she said quiet back to him.

The sad man and the pretty lady pulled up chairs the colors of Howard Johnson's. She took out a little cooler and opened it. She took out spoons and red bowls.

"We brought you some orange sherbet. Duane told us how much you like it, and it's so hot out today. Would you like some, Mr. Walsh?"

"Yes, please." She scooped some sherbet.

"Need some help spooning it up?" She asked friendly and matter-of-fact, not talking like a nursery school teacher like everybody else in this place.

Showing me some respect.

"Yes, please." She scooted beside him, holding the bowl near his mouth.

"It's pretty good, even though it's sugar-free."

Cold and sweet.

Dessert on the front porch.

I'll earn enough for a house with a porch someday so Francine will see I'm a big shot.

The sad man looked uneasy, like he wanted to be somewhere else. Anytime he caught the sad man looking at him, the sad man turned away.

"Stee, would you like some?"

Stee. Where is that boy? I have to take him to work with me. We'll get some barbecue for lunch. Saved up this week so I can buy him a sandwich. He likes that.

"No, thank you, Connie."

"Well, Mr. Walsh, once you've finished, I might have a bowl, too." She continued to offer him spoonfuls of sherbet. He looked up at her face, close to his.

"Nice of you to visit."

"It's no problem, Daddy."

"Not talking to you, talkin' to the lady."

The sad man sighed. The pretty lady looked over her shoulder, sly-like. "I think he's messing with you, Stee."

"Not the first time," said the sad man.

"What's your name, ma'am?"

"Connie, Mr. Walsh. I'm a friend of your son Stee."

"I have three boys, you know. There's Duane and Jake and ..."

"Uncle Jake's your brother, Daddy. It's just me and Duane; we're your sons. I'm Stee."

"Francine's boy?"

"Yes, Daddy. Francine was your wife. She was my momma."

"Right." He found that when people talked loudly about names or dates or whatever, it was best to agree with them.

Right. I have two boys. Duane and Jake.

Duane's a roughneck, can't control him. Gonna gang up on me like Jake.

Stee, train him up, make him a fighter, he'll be right by my side.

Where is that boy—red hair like that girl I'm sweet on, Francine?

Why doesn't Francine come by and see me? Where she been?

The sad man brought his chair next to the pretty lady. "Daddy, look, I haven't seen you in a long time, and you may be wondering why I show up now." The pretty lady put the bowl aside and held onto the sad man's hand again. "I spent near on fifty years hating your guts for all that passed between us, the fights and the beatings. I swore off ever coming back home because of you."

Beats the tar out of me, Jake does. Says I'm weak. Caught me singing and dancing with the radio. Fists hurt. Words hurt worse. What he called me ...

Never again. Not me, not anyone I raise will be weak.

"I don't know if you were scared of me, or scared for me. I don't know why you thought beating me was better than me being a musician. Whatever the reasons, they don't matter."

Francine and me's got a boy. Sweet kid. Dark blue eyes like you never seen.

"I just can't carry that hate anymore, Daddy. I forgive you for all that."

"What's your name?"

The sad man's eyes went wide when he said that. He answered slow. "Stee, Daddy. I'm your son, Stee."

"It's your son Stee, like in your scrapbook, Mr. Walsh." That nice colored nurse, Vera, was back. She had a big book full of old newspaper clippings and set it on the round table. She rolled him over and the pretty lady and—*Jake, that's who the sad man is, now I remember*—came over with him.

"He don't speak much, but when we bring this scrapbook out, he just lights up. On good days, he tells us about the pictures. He says, 'That's my son there.' He's awful proud of you, Mr. Walsh."

"It's Stee, ma'am. Mr. Walsh is my father." The sad man looked sadder. The pretty lady opened the book.

"What's this photo here, Mr. Walsh?" A shiny photo of a skinny man with shaggy red hair playing a big guitar slid into his hands.

I know this one.

"That's my son, Stee Walsh. He's famous. He's rich."

"You gave him the drive to succeed, that's what you told me, Mr. Walsh."

"Yes ma'am, Vera."

He pointed at the picture so the sad man could see. "That's my son, Stee Walsh. He sings on the radio."

He smiled out of the right corner of his mouth. "I'm Harry Walsh, his daddy. He wouldn't be the man he is today without me."

————

"Daniel, it's me."

"What did Stee do that he's too chicken to tell me, Angie?"

"How'd you guess?"

"You never call me otherwise, toots."

She set her jaw. "He needs to delay the album."

"Shit ..."

"By a month ..."

"Shit ... SHIT ..."

"He's gotta pull one of the songs; says it's 'no longer appropriate.' Add a couple others. Record them, mix them ..."

Daniel continued to fume and cuss for several more minutes. Angie bided her time, playing solitaire on her computer.

"You got that all out of your system?"

She heard a final, spectacular burst of cursing before Daniel concurred. "Yeah, I'll take care of it."

"Daniel?"

"What, dear?"

"I get so tired of these artsy types, I can't tell you."

chapter 20

"Hi honey, I'm home!"

Connie tucked her hotel room key in her wallet, unsurprised that no one answered. Her luggage was waiting for her, posted at the entrance like a sentry. A couple of months ago, Stee had tossed out Connie's sorry-ass Costco bags and bought her a set of European-made pieces, sturdy enough to haul across the country every couple of weeks and handsome enough not to disgrace his foyer. She laid her jacket on top of the larger suitcase and had a look around.

Stee wasn't a profligate spender but knew when it was worth dropping a few extra bucks, which explained her refined luggage sitting in the Fairmont's corner balcony suite. She went out on said balcony to take in the view and orient herself. The fog had burned off hours ago. The nonsensical skyline of new office towers, middle-aged apartment buildings, and post-quake monstrosities looked cut out of construction paper and glue-sticked to sky-blue posterboard. The air coming off the water was luscious. Her pulse slowed and her muscles relaxed with each inhale.

I've missed this so much.

She hadn't come back to San Francisco since she moved out East. Stee had press to do for the album on the West Coast and had invited her to meet him to celebrate, and help him come to grips with, his sixtieth birthday. She suspected he had another mission as well: to help her work through her issues as she had done for him, starting with visiting her former hometown.

She looked past the downtown skyline to the residential areas. Houses marched up Potrero Hill to the south. Bracing herself, she counted the two blocks over from the 18th Street exit off 280 and spotted a familiar sliver of yellow stucco: the house that she had shared with Chris, where she had raised Amanda, was where she left it. She felt nothing: no homesickness, no sense of loss. She was glad to see it still existed but it wasn't a place she wanted to return to. It wasn't home anymore. It was just a building.

"Home" wasn't an address these days. Home was wherever she could spend time with Amanda and Stee, hopefully all in the same location.

That's good to know.

Connie reentered the suite and docked her Squeezebox. Stevie Ray Vaughan chugged out of the speakers; she and Stee had been gorging on Texas blues lately, so he had loaded her up with dozens of tracks the last time she was in Malibu. A gigantic gift basket of snacks stood on the coffee table next to bottles of wine and Pellegrino, and a bowl of nectarines so vivid they seemed to glow. Angela must have requested them especially for her; Connie had mentioned once how much she liked them.

Thanks, Angie.

She selected one and bit into it, gearing up for a hike down Nob Hill for one of her favorite San Francisco pursuits: browsing Gump's. The luxe gift store was essentially a museum with price tags. She'd spent many a lunch hour when she worked in the Financial District cruising the aisles, making a mental list of the jewelry and glassware she'd buy if money was no object.

Connie stopped chewing.

Money is no object. If I like something, Stee would buy it for me. All I'd have to do is ask.

Then she shuddered.

That's just tacky, Connie.

She talked to Stee about money only once, when she was reading *Rolling Stone* a few weeks earlier and saw his name in a list of the last decade's top ten moneymaking tours. She casually asked what his cut was. He puzzled it out.

"I dunno ... what's 28 percent of 158 million?" He went back to transcribing his lyrics.

What she drew from that conversation was that he was loaded and would be loaded until the day he died even if he never played another note. He could probably eke out a decent living off his talk show salary alone. She didn't pry further; she didn't want to look like a gold digger ... or like his second wife.

Connie stared at her suitcase, hand stitched and custom dyed to match the set Stee used. Draped over it was the Armani jacket Stee bought for her on her last trip to Malibu after cajoling her into trying it on despite her insistence that it was too extravagant. Next to it was the Chanel purse he'd shipped to her after catching her complaining about her shoulder bag from Target falling apart. When she'd called to thank him, and remind him that he didn't need to buy her affection, for God's sake, he'd brushed it off.

"Shit, I'd better be nice to you every way I can," he'd told her. "With all you do for me, buying you a purse every now and then barely covers it."

As much as she believed Stee took genuine delight in being big-hearted and wouldn't do this if she didn't make him happy, sometimes she felt trapped by his generosity. It bothered her that she had no way to reciprocate on the same scale. Sitting here, in this classy hotel in this expensive city, eating a perfect nectarine, the imbalance was all too apparent.

She took another bite. Catching a drop of juice before it dribbled down her chin, she noticed a blaze of orange on the bed pillow. A single rose, in Stee's signature color, waited for her there with a note:

> The masseuse will be here any minute.
> Take a shower and relax and enjoy.
> Love,
> S

Nice touch.

She followed the instructions and a little later, the masseuse tapped on the door. For the next thirty minutes, the woman kneaded the recycled airplane air out of her muscles. For her part, Connie tried not to drool through the headrest onto the floor while face down on the massage table.

The masseuse's hands lifted, and Connie drifted off for a few moments until she was told, "You can turn over now." She dreamily flipped onto her back.

"Happy birthday, Stee."

He was at her side, smirking in a Fairmont bathrobe. "Sorry, the masseuse had another gig and had to leave early."

She reached up and stroked his cheek. "I guess you'll have to do." She sat up and pointed to the foyer. "I brought you something. Look in my purse." She watched as he took out the package, which she'd wrapped in sheet music and tied up with orange ribbons festooned with a rainbow assortment of guitar picks.

He grinned. "This is too pretty to open. I'm gonna put this next to the Grammy."

"Which one?"

"The first one."

"No, no, you should open it, although I don't know if you'll want to put this in your trophy case."

He sat on the edge of the bed near the massage table and carefully unwrapped the gift. When he saw what it was, his mouth dropped open.

"Oh, my."

It was a set of five silver picture frames the size of his palm, hinged together. He unfolded them to see a series of intricate pen-and-ink drawings.

"Did you do these?"

She nodded, wrapping herself in the sheet to sit at his side. "I made them after that first weekend you came to Richmond."

"When I told you I loved you for the first time?"

"That's right. See that scar on the right thumb there? These are pictures of you."

She'd summed up all of what she loved about Stee Walsh in five small frames tightly focused on just his hands: strumming a guitar, writing lyrics, cracking peanuts, cupping water from his swimming pool, and finally, holding her hands in his.

He stayed silent long enough for Connie to feel self-conscious. "I thought you could take them with you when we can't be together so you know I'm thinking about you. I know it's not much, but—"

"It's beautiful," he said, choked up but smiling. "It's everything I could have wanted. Just like you."

His kiss put an end to her worries.

———————

Oh my God, there he is, THERE HE IS!

An unexpected gift landed in Leonard's RSS feed that morning: a new interview with Stee Walsh in the SWATTRBlog, including a photo of the Great One looking leonine and ...

Happy?

What's wrong with him?

Mystified, he began to read.

> The Right Time for the Right Place:
> Veteran rocker Stee Walsh returns to his roots for latest album
> Stee Walsh is smiling ear to ear—and that's a major achievement.
> The typically taciturn rocker, who turned 60 this weekend, has been hard at work wrapping *Unexpected Places*, his fifteenth album and the first volume of new work in five years. The writing came hard and most of the songs didn't come together until the final weeks before entering the studio with legendary producer Jon Jonegon last spring.
> "I felt tapped out," Walsh admits, sipping Pellegrino in the corner booth of the XYZ Lounge

on a sunny Friday afternoon. "I had visited and revisited the same territory and wanted to do something new without losing our signature sound. Thing was, I had to go back through my own history to do that." So he returned to his home state of Virginia for the first time in 30 years.

In 1979, Walsh famously swore off ever returning when his then-label Sapphire Records slapped him with a lawsuit after a performance at the Hampton Coliseum for encouraging fans to use their own equipment to record the concert. (The case eventually went to the U.S. Supreme Court and was decided in Walsh's favor, enabling artists to set the terms for fan bootlegs henceforward.) He now admits that, lawsuit or no, once his mother died, Virginia was a cold and empty place.

"Francine Walsh was a sweet soul," he recalls. "As soon as I touched a guitar, she was there supporting me. She took me and the Insiders [Walsh's first band] all over the state for gigs, always standing in the back of the venue, cheering us on. She even scraped up the money for me to get out to California. Once she died I had no reason to come back, until now."

Walsh returned to his mother's family farm in central Virginia to "poke around and see what came out of the ground." Fertile ground indeed: he and River Runners guitarist Chad Haines churned out three new songs in two days before Walsh returned to begin recording in Malibu.

He credits spending quality time with family and friends outside the music industry with sparking the songs.

Leonard sucked in a breath.

He's talking about me—he's talking about meeting me! *I must have helped him break his writer's block. I had no idea …*

He read on, full of wonder.

Knocking around the family homestead also gave him the headspace to contemplate being an older man in a young man's game, a perspective that threads through many of his new songs. "No one singing in rock today is willing to admit that we're in the last years of our lives and how we're damn lucky to be able to say that, given how many casualties there are in this business."

One of those casualties was his long-time friend and founding member of the River Runners, drummer Bobby Brewer. Two days before he was slated for studio sessions, Brewer was found dead of a heart attack after years of drug addiction.

"Losing Bobby, well … I miss him terribly," Walsh admits before drifting into his own thoughts for a moment. "He and I were a lot alike, and we were walking the same self-destructive path for a lot of years. I found a way off that path; he didn't."

Given Jonegon's limited availability to record, there was little time to mourn; the band had to report to the studio as scheduled. "It was probably the best thing we could do as a band," Walsh concedes. "The work always united us and it helped pulled us through a crisis."

Still, it's been a rough few months. "I'm still working through the grief. It blindsides me when I least expect it. I'm glad for the people who love me and support me through all this."

Leonard reread the final sentence as his heart swelled.

Thanks for the shout-out, Stee. I'm here for you, man. Take as long as you need to get back to me.

Touched, he picked up reading where he left off.

> Pynchon drummer Icky Sticks was brought in to take over for Brewer. A longtime fan, Sticks was ecstatic to work with some of his heroes, tweeting from the studio, "SWATRR is f***ing elemental. Awed to be part of their next big bang." With rumors of a River Runners tour shaping up for spring 2010, Sticks is in discussions about tagging along while Pynchon is on a break.
>
> *Unexpected Places* will take its place among the rest of the River Runners catalogue to be sold as part of a limited-edition Stee Walsh Squeezebox, available November 3, after a month's delay to retool the album, dropping one song and adding three final tracks.
>
> The Squeezebox project has also allowed Walsh to cement his reputation as a rock video pioneer. The device will hold all of Walsh's videos from MTV's golden era as well as a new piece created for the title track at his family farm, directed by former San Franciscan Connie Rafferty, who also hails from Walsh's Richmond birthplace.

Leonard looked up, confounded.

Connie Rafferty doing a SWATRR *video?*

What the frak?

> "Connie and I are on the same wavelength," he says. "She 'sees' music like I 'hear' video—we're well matched."

Armpits dampening, he raced through the next paragraphs.

> Notoriously private, Walsh put his personal life
> under wraps following an acrimonious divorce from
> his first wife in 1992, after which he entered rehab;
> he has remained sober since. His second marriage
> lasted a little over a year.
>
> When pressed about whether a current romance
> was the catalyst for his recent work, he gazes
> contentedly out the window. "Let's just say I greet
> each day thanking God for the incredible woman in
> my life who takes me for who I am and makes my
> music possible."

Woman? Who, the guinea pig?

His stomach clenched.

Oh, Stee …

It made a sick sort of sense. Having a girlfriend would better explain why Stee had failed to reply to months of Leonard's faithful correspondence. It solved all the mysteries of Connie's online life, too—the phone calls to California, the uptick in quality music downloads, the underthings—

BORF!

Leonard clapped his hands over his mouth until the urge to spew had passed. He cleared his palate with the dregs of a Red Bull and grimaced. There had to be some mistake. Stee Walsh respected his longtime fans and would never shelve that for sex with a … *newbie.*

More like an oldbie. She's Paleolithic.

As much as it pained him, there was only one way to find out without tipping him off.

Good thing I installed ISPeye on his account when I did.

He tapped his computer and opened a couple of windows and soon, the Busker library of Stee Walsh unfolded on the screen.

Damn ... 242,831 songs and counting.

A couple of clicks later, Leonard had sorted Stee's library by date to see what had been added since their initial fateful meeting. Sitting in the midst of it all was a playlist, dated April 25, named "Come Out, Virginia."

It was from the guinea pig and it was full of nothing but ...

BILLY JOEL?!?!?!?

He checked the download date on Stee's files, and then he toggled over to Connie's library. She had sent them to Stee via Busker as a gift, which he accepted.

This can't be ... he hates Billy Joel with a passion.

Frantically, Leonard cut over to the BetaComp sales files and searched for the account transfer. In seconds, he found the transaction. She had sent it with a note.

> Stee, I loved these songs without reservation back when they came out. When other kids sang them and I joined in, I became a part of something bigger than myself.
> Without Billy Joel, I might not have learned how to appreciate rock music at all or connect with your work as I do now. Maybe he's worth another listen.
> See you at the shoot,
> Connie

Leonard's mind darted between the data points, trying to make sense of the full picture. He scurried back to Stee's Busker library, and his blood ran cold when he found the smoking gun. The Last Played dates in his library confirmed that Stee Walsh had indeed been boning up on the work of the man he once described as "the only living songwriter who writes like he's been dead for forty years."

If things weren't bad enough, there was also a reply message to Connie that nearly burned holes in his retinas:

Hot funk, cool punk, I believe it's old junk
It's still not my cup of tea
But if he was your gateway to real rock and roll, I'll
give him a listen—maybe even send him a bouquet.
See you soon, baby.
Stee

Leonard's breathing became quick and shallow. He frantically reread the blog entry and reexamined the photo accompanying it. Stee was signing autographs and sharing a laugh with Connie Rafferty, who was touching his arm and looking him straight in the eye.

She's his ... oh, no.

She's his Ono.

Yet instead of collapsing into a miserable, mordant lump, Leonard had an epiphany.

Someone's got to bring him back to his senses and break the spell.

And that someone is me.

chapter 21

"Stee, you're a childish son of a bitch."

Daniel was swayed back in his black leather Scandinavian reclining office chair, cradling a tumbler of really, really good Scotch. If the glass had been empty, he probably would have chucked it at his client's head.

"Sorry you think so." Stee was hunched forward in a matching chair, his face propped up on his fists, eyes cut to the side like an eight-year-old who just got benched during a Little League game.

"Well, 'scuse me for calling in some favors to get you into the Kennedy Center Honors lineup," Daniel said drily. "I just figured you might want to get your name out there during the Christmas shopping season. Those Squeezeboxes aren't going to sell themselves." He savored another sip of Scotch, thanking *his* Higher Power that he didn't have a substance abuse problem severe enough to require him to give this up.

Stee stared at Daniel and sucked his teeth. The manager tutted his disgust.

"Jesus, Stee, could you at least be happy for Bruce? He's getting a Kennedy Center Honor. They only give that to American icons. You know what it means for him?"

"That he's an American icon and I'm not?"

"You're spoiled, you know that?"

Stee lumbered to his feet and went to the window. Daniel had commandeered the penthouse office in the tallest building in Century City to be able to look down on all the lawyers in the other offices. The view was distractingly impressive. Stee stared as far out into the horizon as the smog would allow.

"I'm never going to be considered one of the greats, am I?"

"You outearn most of the greats, so how bad can you be?"

Stee came back to the recliner. "Did Jann Wenner call you about getting me onto the bill for the Rock and Roll Hall of Fame anniversary concerts next month, the Madison Square Garden gigs?"

Daniel eyed him warily. "Not everyone could be asked, Stee. There are just too many of you. I mean, they didn't book McCartney or Townshend and Daltrey either—and those boys have a Kennedy Center medal already, since you care about that so much."

"Is Neil doing it?"

"I think he's got a family thing. Bob declined, if that makes you feel any better."

Stee rolled his eyes. "Who did they get?"

Daniel shrugged. "Usual suspects. Bruce and Bono, CSN, Billy Joel."

Stee let out a strangled cry. "*Billy Joel?* Billy Joel got the gig and I didn't?"

"Well, he got inducted two years before you did."

Stee stretched the recliner as far as it would go and groaned. Daniel could barely make out what he was saying; it sounded like, "Connie's never gonna let me hear the end of that."

Daniel frowned. "I bring you in to say you have another chance to perform for the President on international TV while giving your good buddy Springsteen a big sloppy kiss for good measure, yet here you are, talking some nonsense about not being an icon."

"Yeah, yeah, I know," Stee said absently. "I'm a childish son of a bitch. You're absolutely right there."

"Stee, you and I both know you aren't. So what is this about then?"

"I've just been thinking about my legacy lately ... what my place in music history is exactly ... what people'll say about me once I'm gone."

"Because of Bobby?"

"Partly." Stee sat up, the recliner returning to its vertical position once more. "I gotta get my knee operated on," he said solemnly. "I can't wait any longer; it's killing me. The surgery is scheduled a week from Thursday. I don't want to stay on painkillers any longer than I have to, so it's going to be brutal."

Daniel's brow furrowed. "How long are you going to be out of commission?"

"A minimum of eight weeks."

His manager whistled softly. "The Squeezebox launch is in November. You're cutting it close. We were hoping to shoot the ad in a couple of weeks. Can you guarantee you can do the shoot first week of October?"

"Yeah, if I live through surgery in the first place," Stee muttered.

"What's that supposed to mean?"

"Well, there could be complications ..."

"You think you're gonna die from *knee surgery?*" Daniel snickered. "How the hell did you get that in your head?"

Stee scowled. "I'm right to be worried. The site could get infected. My heart might not be able to handle the stress after all the shit I pumped through it in the Eighties. What if I get addicted to drugs again?"

As hard as it was, Daniel made an honest effort to back off from the mockery and take his client seriously. "Stee, my 80-year-old mother had both hips done four months ago and she's back on the golf course. This kind of surgery is no big deal. You'll be able to kick Billy Joel square in the piano bench in a couple of months."

"Tell that to Joe Perry now that he's gotten over the infection he got during his surgery."

Daniel's patience was wearing thin. "Stee, I'm not sure what started this pity parade, but it's gotta move down the street."

Stee's eyes hollowed. "I don't wanna die in a hospital."

"You're not gonna die. Jesus Christ! This is a routine procedure."

"It could be some fluke, a drug mix-up or an aneurysm they didn't know I had."

"That's it, Stee. No more watching medical shows on television, you hear me?"

"Famous people are cursed. We die too young, unexpectedly, in the hospital."

The weird conversation just did another backflip. "What on God's green earth are you talking about?"

"Michael Jackson."

"*Michael Jackson?*" Daniel shrieked. "Why? You been hitting the propofol lately?"

Finally, it all made sense. "This isn't really about Michael or Joe Perry or being famous, is it? You're just scared of hospitals, aren't you?"

Stee stared at his shoe. Daniel pressed on.

"What are you afraid for? You were okay during your nasal reconstruction."

"I was so loaded back then they could have used a hammer and tongs and I wouldn't have noticed."

"Shit, you're a hell of a lot more rational now. Why all the nerves?"

"Doctors didn't do my mother any favors."

"That was thirty years ago and she had a terminal disease. You don't. You'll be back home in a couple of weeks, Angie will haul your bony butt back and forth to physical therapy, and you'll be doing jumping jacks by the time Bruce and Patti take their seats next to Barack and Michelle. Suck it up."

Daniel drained the last of his Scotch. "Or just think of it this way: if you die, I guarantee every one of your obituaries will start with the words 'American icon.' You win either way."

"Hello, this is Connie Rafferty. Uh, is this Terri?"

"I can't believe you've forgotten me already. It's only been a couple of months."

Connie was tidying up for Stee's next visit when the *Psycho* theme blasted out of her phone. The last person on earth she'd expected to hear from was the executive recruiter she'd dodged twice before.

"I just figured you'd given up on me."

"I give everyone three chances. This is your third. So, you still looking for gainful employment?"

"Actually, I'm all set. Thanks."

There was a second of silence on the phone. "You're all set? What are you set doing?"

"I have a client who's got me booked through most of next year."

"Is one of your brides doing a reality show or something?"

Here Connie halted. She hadn't told anyone what she and Stee had agreed to a few days before, and the details hadn't been worked out. Still, it would be sweet to do a little bragging.

"No, I'm doing a documentary."

"Well, well, finally using your MFA, are you?" Terri replied with an edgy sweetness.

"Looks like it."

"What's the topic?"

"Rock and roll."

"That's a little broad, isn't it?"

"I'll be following a band on tour in the U.S. and Europe through next summer."

"Which band?"

"Stee Walsh and the River Runners." Connie said this as flatly as possible, mimicking Stee's technique for minimizing the hubbub when his name came up.

"Steve Walsh?" Terri asked with a hint of distaste. "Why him? Why not someone really famous like Jon Bon Jovi?"

Connie cringed. "*Stee*, not Steve. His older brother Duane couldn't pronounce the vee sound as a kid, so when baby Steven was born, he called him Stee and the name stuck."

"How do you know his brother's name and all that?"

"I've worked with Stee for a while. I've gotten to know him pretty well."

"Really now?"

"I already worked with him to create a video for his upcoming album. It'll be on his signature Squeezebox in November."

There was a pause. "So you've risen above the corporate world and directed a real video, getting up close and personal with Stee Walsh. You've really moved up and out."

"I don't know about that," Connie replied, trying not to sound smug.

"Was that why you canceled out of two interviews I set up for you?"

"Well, the first time, I was working on the video. The second time, Stee's drummer died and I flew out to California for the funeral."

"That's the lifestyle, I guess: too many drugs and too little restraint. Years of that can be deadly."

"For some." Terri's tone was nothing but polite, which was making Connie uneasy. "Thank you so much for your work on my behalf. You've given me a lot of professional perspective, which I've appreciated, so if—"

"Stee had a pretty nasty cocaine problem, if I remember right. Cocaine and alcohol."

"That's in the past," Connie blurted.

"And he's gotta be close to seventy now."

"He's sixty."

"Oh wow, fifteen years older than you," Terri said pleasantly. "Even so, I hope he doesn't have a heart condition or a bad liver after all the coke and booze he used to do. Making long-term plans with a ticking time bomb is kind of risky."

While Terri tutted, the full import hit Connie like a crowbar.

I can't live through another death. I just can't.

"Why did you gasp? Nobody gasps any more. Hell's bells, you're in love with him, aren't you?"

"It's none of your business." Angry at herself for getting rattled, Connie decided she was going to stand her ground rather than hang up.

"Well, kiss your video career good-bye then."

"What on earth do you mean? He's launching my video career."

"Hate to break it to you, but it's not 'your' career anymore. If you're a famous guy's girlfriend, no one will take you seriously because they'll assume you got the job because you're boinking the star. You won't have your own identity until," Terri stopped to snort, "you break up. Then you won't have any identity at all. Take my advice: you'd be better off taking that insurance job in Arlington."

"I'm hanging up now." Still Terri plowed on.

"I'm only telling you what you've been telling yourself but were afraid to believe. You like being with a rock star? Connie, you *are* a rock star in the corporate world. You are amazing at what you do. With your resume and your references, you could be a VP at a Fortune 100 company. Why you quit Tripton Reid to strike out on your own baffles me."

"I was laid off," she stuttered.

"No, you quit, you little fibber," Terri needled. "I chatted up your old boss, who wanted to keep you on. You were marked to survive the layoff, but you opted to take a package and launch Key Light Videos instead. You told him your husband's death taught you that you shouldn't live in a man's shadow anymore. Then you moved back to Richmond and, after only a year of struggling on your own, whoopsie daisy! You start living in a man's shadow again. What's your career going to be now: Stee Walsh's girlfriend?"

Connie clicked off her phone and threw it as hard as she could onto her bed.

"Hey, Con, got a sec?"

"Sure, Stee." She shouldered the phone as she folded laundry. She needed something practical to do. Connie had been worked up in knots since she hung up on Terri that morning. She could rationalize all she wanted to that Terri was a bitter, unfulfilled career woman who was taking all her frustrations out on Connie out of jealousy over her good fortune. Thing was, Scary Terri had named pretty much every anxiety Connie had about her future with Stee: the age difference, his potential health problems, the lack of independence, the fact that her identity would be forever attached to his.

"I, uh, need to talk to you about something. Something serious."

Her own troubles evaporated. "What's the matter, Stee?"

"Well, uh, it's, well ..." he stammered.

"What's wrong?"

"I need surgery on my knee. I go to UCLA Medical Center a week from Thursday."

She exhaled, relieved. "Well, it's about time, Stee. You've been in pain forever."

He plowed on, sounding more and more like Lurch from *The Addams Family*. "I'm going to have major surgery, Connie, and they'll have to manage my pain meds carefully."

Connie was puzzled. "Then you'll feel a lot better. Is that a bad thing?"

He huffed. "They're gonna cut me open."

"That's what surgery is."

"Well, something could happen. I could wake up during the procedure."

"Stee, it's not the Civil War. You're not going to be given a swig of whiskey and a stick to bite down on. You'll be fine."

There was a moment of peeved silence. "Obviously I got you on a bad day."

"No shit."

"What is it?" he asked, now sounding concerned.

"I just had a really awful conversation with that executive recruiter I told you about and I'm still upset," she answered, her voice beginning to shake.

"Oh, honey, that's terrible." He pronounced it *turrible* like her dad used to, which was comforting somehow. "What'd that witch say now?"

"She doesn't think my doing a video with you was the best move for my future career prospects."

"Not a fan, huh?"

"I'm not sure what she thinks of you, but she thinks I'm a fool to turn my back on the corporate world." She deliberated whether to tell him more about why but he spoke first.

"Do you regret doing the video?"

"Absolutely not."

"Do you regret meeting me?" He was dead serious.

"Not for one second," came the instant reply.

He stayed silent, but she could swear she could hear his neurons firing. "Stee?"

"Move in with me."

"Stee, no."

"Hear me out, Connie. Stay with me out at in Malibu. You can figure out your next move and you can see me through the surgery."

"Uh ..."

He picked up steam, his enthusiasm practically squirting through the earpiece. "Wait, wait, it won't just be following me around so's I don't trip on my walker. I can introduce you to some of the folks I know in Hollywood. They can get you started. That would be great!"

"Stop, stop, stop!"

"What, baby?"

"I'm not moving to California next week," she said sharply.

"Why not?" His voice pulled up short. "I just want to help your career."

"That's the problem. If you keep helping me, it won't be *my* career, now will it?"

Terri's sneering assumption that Connie would be known as "Stee Walsh's girlfriend" and nothing else was burning hot in her ears. The last thing she wanted was for that woman to be right.

"Message received." He sounded chastened. "Could you please come out here, even just for the day I'm in the hospital? I'm going to be on my own otherwise."

"What about Angie?"

"She's got some thing and can't make it."

"Can't one of your daughters be there?"

"I don't have that kind of relationship with them."

Terri's insinuations about his age and his health being a future burden were looming large. Connie suddenly imagined herself at 65 with an 80-year-old Stee hobbled and housebound demanding that she be at his beck and call, her independence a distant memory.

Dammit ... if I love him this shouldn't matter. But of course it does.

"Connie, please come. I'm scared to death and it would be so much better if I could see your face and know you'll be there when I wake up. Please."

"Why are you so scared, Stee?" There was urgency in his voice she hadn't heard since he called to tell her Bobby had died.

"Rock stars are cursed. We always die in hospitals."

"Rock stars die other places, too."

"Strangely, that does not make me feel better."

"Stee, you will be fine."

"If you're there, I will be."

He wasn't sounding demanding or needy anymore. He was reverting to being charming, which he knew would murder her resolve.

Despite her better instincts, she capitulated a little.

"Stee, I'm not saying yes; I'm not saying no. Give me the weekend to sort through Amanda's schedule and then I'll let you know, okay?"

She could hear the sly smile creeping into his voice. "A maybe is as good as a yes with you, sugar."

"Don't push it right now, okay?"

"Okay." His relief gave away to concern. "Connie, that woman is an idiot. Your career is going just great. You're really good at what you do. I believe in you and your work."

His sincerity was a true comfort. "Thanks, Stee. I love you."

"And how I love you, baby," he purred before hanging up. Her laundry folded in tidy piles on her bed, she set her phone down next to her laptop. She nudged the keyboard and clicked the Busker icon. She wanted a little more comfort.

Let's start with a little Elvis Costello ... Wait, where is that album Stee gave me? Where'd it go?

The library screen appeared but it was nearly empty, save for the Billy Joel tracks she'd sent to Stee weeks ago. She clicked up and down the scroll bar, minimized the screen and opened it again, her panic rising.

Where are my songs? Where are my 8,058 songs???

She restarted her computer and an unopened email message popped into view.

> Dear Busker Customer:
>
> Our team is proud to announce the launch of new quality standards as part of our Terms of Use agreement. In the interest of maintaining a user's authentic musical taste, the system will now automatically delete any songs deemed too good for the particular user.
>
> We hope you'll understand we took these measures to ensure the integrity of the music we sell and protect the artists we support.
>
> Hugs and kisses from BetaComp Customer Service

chapter 22

"All I have to do is hit this button?"

Stee handed Connie the remote, pointing at "Play" and nodding expectantly. As soon as she did so, her house rang with the opening riff of the Kinks' "You Really Got Me."

Her mouth dropped open. "Wow."

"That's the beauty of SkyBusker, baby." Stee beamed. "Now you've got access to my entire music library, in any room, and it's all controlled by that little box there," he said, pointing toward a shelf above her television.

She walked from room to room, muttering in amazement. "Wow, wow, wow ... and now I don't have to worry about someone draining my library?"

"Nope."

"Did Angie get anywhere with BetaComp about figuring out who could have hacked my system?"

"Nothing yet." He joined her in the living room. "My SkyBusker back at the house is hardwired. It was one of the first ones Beta-Comp ever made. I had to put holes in the walls on all three stories and thread the cables and stereo wire from room to room. Never had to upgrade it, though. The system's indestructible."

She returned and gave him a squeeze. "Thank you."

"It'll be like I'm here even when I'm not," he said, proud of himself for making her so happy.

"Mom, the door."

Connie pulled back from Stee's embrace for a moment to yell over her shoulder. "Oh, for God's sake, Amanda, just once, could you please answer it on your own?"

Her daughter stalked away. "But you'd die of shock." A moment later, she called back down the hall. "Stee, it's for you."

Connie looked confused. "How can that be? Who knows you're here?"

Stee was puzzled, too. "Who is it?"

"Some guy. He asked for you."

"What does he look like?"

"Sweaty."

Stee stepped past Amanda and came to the door. Once he saw who was on the front steps, dominoes of dread fell one by one in his brain.

Leonard ...

That guy from BetaComp who sends me hundreds of emails that go directly to my spam folder ...

The one who told me about Connie ... and got her information illegally ...

That guy's now on Connie's doorstep.

Fuck me slowly.

What with the album, the romance, and a heavy dose of distraction mixed with a little wishful thinking, Stee had completely forgotten about Leonard. He was like a Frankenfan who had broken loose from the lab, gripping the railing of Connie's front steps, his chest heaving.

"Oh my God, how can you stand the humidity? I just got off the bus a couple of blocks from here and I'm ready to die. It's like the Amazon."

"Leonard, you have to leave. You shouldn't be here."

He pushed his glasses up his nose and fixed Stee with a suspicious stare. "You shouldn't be here either, Stee. Why on earth *would* you be here?"

Stee checked over his shoulder and came out on the stoop. "That's none of your business."

"Oh, yes it is. I deserve to know why you haven't gotten back to me all these months after we met at BetaComp."

"Stee, is there a problem?" Connie asked through the screen door.

"See if you can find Roland, please," he replied quickly, hoping to God she hadn't overheard any of their conversation. Once she left, Stee turned back to his unwanted guest. "Security is on its way. It would be better if you just go."

Leonard was frowning. "That's the guinea pig, isn't it?"

"Don't be rude."

"God, she's as old as my mother."

"Ten minutes," Connie said through the screen, adding pointedly, "Need any other help?"

He quickly weighed his options. Leonard might be deluded but he didn't strike him as dangerous. No telling where this conversation was going, but if the cops showed up the press would soon follow, which wouldn't play out well. And Connie could not learn about his history with Leonard ever, especially through a police report. He'd need to handle this until the big, bald cavalry came to the rescue.

"No, we're good. I'll be in in a minute." Stee watched her until she was well away from the door, and then he pointed a finger in Leonard's direction. "You're trespassing and you've flown 3,000 miles to do it. That's stalking."

Leonard threw up his hands. "You weren't answering my messages, Stee, and once I found out it was because of that ... *woman* ... what else was I supposed to do? I mean, I had already spent all that time analyzing her music acquisitions through ISPeye for you."

"Analyzing what ... through what?"

"Oh my God, ISPeye! The online personality predictor I created based on musical taste. What I demoed for you at BetaComp." Exasperation turned to hurt on a dime. "Don't you remember?"

"Yes, okay, I remember ISPeye," Stee admitted.

"I had spent weeks putting together a comprehensive report to show how your music impacted a fan's behavior to help you shape your new album. I compared her music acquisitions to her other online activity and—"

"Online activity?"

"You know, email and banking, online purchases and all that."

Stee's stomach dropped to his shoes. "Banking?"

"I had a great story to tell—solid proof of ISPeye's accuracy in predicting how musical taste defines a person and even changes their life for the better—but it turns out *you* were the one giving her Buddy Holly and Bob Dylan and all that music. You tainted the research and skewed my results! Stee, how could you do this to me?"

"I never asked to be involved in any of this."

"You said you wanted to see what else the data tells you. You told me to send you emails through your website. You said, 'I'm intrigued.' Those were your exact words. I wouldn't forget them."

Stee felt a drop of guilt mixed with his unease. "Look, maybe I said all that, but at no time did I tell you to break into anyone's email or bank accounts. I wouldn't have. That's illegal and invasive and kind of scary."

Leonard looked horrified. "I'm scaring you?"

"How'd you feel if some stranger appeared on your girlfriend's doorstep and confessed to hacking her bank account?"

Nostrils flared, he seemed nauseated by the term. "Stee, she's not right for you."

"I'm not going to discuss her with you."

"She's a poser, Stee. She doesn't know music. She's never seen you in concert. What kind of a fan is she?"

"I'm not dating her because she's a fan," he replied sharply. "I'm dating her because I like her. I admire her work. I feel good being around her. Can you dig?"

Leonard was unconvinced. "Other than your stuff, the only music she'd ever bought was Billy Joel."

He shrugged. "It's a free country."

Leonard turned away with an irritated huff. "Stee, when musicians fall in love their music turns to shit. Especially at your age, no offense."

"I don't care."

"How can you say that?"

Worried that Roland might be stuck in traffic, Stee knew he'd have to distract Leonard for the foreseeable future. Keeping his distance on the stairs but looking him in the eye, he said, "Let me set you straight, and pay attention because this is the last conversation you and I will ever have, you understand? Leonard, you get me? This is the last time we are ever going to talk without lawyers present."

He nodded mechanically.

Stee took a deep breath. "Ever since high school, my work and my personal life were the same thing. Anybody else would think that's great because I was making so much money and playing with my idols and being famous. But I never felt like I had anyone in my corner. I got estranged from my folks, I wrecked one marriage and I should never have done the other. My kids don't know me, my best friends are people on my payroll, and there's a greater chance I'll die alone every damn day I'm on this planet. So after nearly sixty years of getting this wrong, it finally dawned on me that no one was there for me because I hadn't ever been there for them. I'm ready to do this right. I aim to be there for the woman who loves me—and thank God she's willing to let me try. That might make us both really happy. And if you don't like the music that comes as a result of that, then just don't buy the album."

Leonard sighed, visibly defeated, his eyes wet. "I really blew it, didn't I?"

"Yeah, you did. You're going to have to own up to what you've done or I'll have to do it for you."

"All I wanted was to prove to you how much your music means to people ... means to me."

"Maybe you need to think about whether that's really enough to build a life around."

Roland rolled into the driveway and exited the black SUV quickly and purposefully.

"Mr. Walsh, what's the situation?"

"Roland, make sure Leonard gets back to San Francisco as quickly as possible."

"Yes, sir."

Leonard looked upward at the imposing man in wraparound shades and slumped down the stairs toward the Land Rover, muttering, "Love is so not cool."

Once the SUV pulled out of his line of sight, Stee exhaled and went back inside.

Connie was pale, her arms folded tightly as she stood near enough to the front door to have overheard every word. "Who was that?"

Stee closed the door and locked it. "That was Leonard, this kid I met at BetaComp. He's the one who ran your sales report before I first met you. He showed me you had bought my catalogue one song at a time."

"And now he's a stalker?" she asked, her agitation rising. "This guy could have had a gun. He could have hurt you! He could have hurt Amanda when she answered the door! Why didn't you tell me to call the police?"

"I figured I could handle this until Roland came. And I did." He tried to wave her off with a smile. "No harm done."

"He hacked into my computer and apparently you told him that was okay. That sounds pretty harmful."

"No, that's not what I said—what I meant, anyway. I couldn't figure out why you'd buy one of my songs each day for so many months, so I told him to let me know what else he found out about you." He smiled, recalling the wonder of that first glimpse of her. "You buying a song a day intrigued me. *You* intrigued me."

She stared at him. "Go on."

"I never thought he'd do anything hurtful. I mean, he gave me his word he wouldn't break into my computer."

"You didn't tell him to stop? You didn't tell BetaComp security? You did nothing?" Connie threw her hands in the air in disbelief. "It's like you gave him the keys to my life and told him to take anything he wanted as long as he promised not to touch your stuff."

"I'm sorry," he said in a very small voice. "By now, though, don't the ends justify the means?"

"You don't get it, do you?"

He stayed silent; she barreled on. "Since clearly you don't care how violated and terrified I feel about all this, think about what this can do to *you*. When BetaComp finds out you knew an employee was infecting customer computers with spyware and you didn't report it, do you think they're going to want your name on their Squeezebox? Do you think they'll want to sell your catalogue at all? This little stunt could cost you your career. Think about that." She stalked away from him. "Call Marcos while I call the cops."

"Wait, not the cops. They'll file a report, then the press will be here and it'll be chaos. Let me talk to Marcos first."

"Make it quick."

Following a long talk with Marcos, during which his lawyer found unique curse words in both English and Spanish to describe the situation his client had gotten into, Stee found Connie at her kitchen table. "What did Marcos say?"

"The cops would be useless in a case like this. Since I know who this guy is and he didn't do anything threatening, they wouldn't have any reason to even question him. Marcos will get a security detail out here to watch the house, though, and he'll work with Daniel to figure out how to bring this up with BetaComp." Stee hung his head. Just moments ago they had been sharing an uneventful evening in the suburbs, eating homemade spaghetti and meatballs with Amanda.

Way to go, Stee.

He put a tentative hand on her shoulder. "I can't begin to apologize to you, Con. I am so sorry."

She didn't move. "I'm not in a forgiving mood."

"I was stupid and careless," he conceded, pulling his hand away.

She was looking at him strangely, as if her eyes were suddenly devoid of hope.

Oh, Connie, no, don't, no …

"Stee, I can't do this anymore. This has to stop. I have to stop seeing you."

"What are you talking about, baby?" he asked, desperate and hollow.

Her voice was even. "Maybe it's just my luck that I met you right when you had a lot in your life to sort out: your father and Bobby and the album and your legacy. Well, I have a lot to sort out, too, like what I want to accomplish and who I am and who I can truly depend on. Now your problems are taking over my life again. I have to ask myself, what's in it for me?"

Stee's cell phone went off. He flinched but didn't move to answer. Connie stood up. "You need to take that. Then you should talk to Angie about getting a flight back out to LA tonight. You have to fix this mess you put me in, and I need my life back."

He heard the front door open and shut while the phone continued to blare the opening bars of the theme from *Jaws*. He hit the Talk button but said nothing.

"Stee, it's Marcos. Here's what I say we do but it's going to mean getting down on your knees."

Stee couldn't hear him over the sound of the pounding inside his head. His mouth went incredibly dry and he felt clammy from the inside out.

"Stee, you there?"

He put a shaky hand to his neck, feeling for his pulse. Marcos' voice began to rise.

"Stee, you okay? Answer me."

He couldn't reply, his thoughts racing.

Christ, am I having a heart attack?

He winced at his stupidity.

No, you idiot. She's kicking you out and your heart's breaking. That's all it is.

He finally spoke up. "Yeah, I'm here, Marcos, ready to grovel."

———————

Stee was even more restless in the BetaComp conference room than he had been back in April. Since leaving Virginia, he hadn't slept and could barely crawl through the daylight hours. His phone calls and emails to Connie went unanswered. His flowers and note cards went unacknowledged. The Apology Playlist he sent her via Busker ("I'm Sorry About That" by Wilson Pickett, The Beatles' "Oh! Darling" and so on) didn't earn him any access. Plus, with his knee surgery date looming, and Connie now unlikely to be there, lonely terror twisted his gut every waking moment.

He was in no shape to do what he had to do, but it had to be done.

With Daniel on one side and Marcos on the other like parents hemming in their son in the principal's office, he sat across from the BetaComp marketing and legal reps, none of whom looked very happy to see him.

"Tough crowd," he muttered to Daniel.

"Time to take your medicine, meathead," Daniel hissed back.

Marcos slipped a neatly printed sheet in front of him. Stee sheepishly took his bifocals out of his jacket pocket. He cleared his throat and took a long draught of water, then he began to read aloud.

"Ladies and gentlemen, let me start by saying I am profoundly sorry for this situation. I take full responsibility for failing to inform BetaComp about ISPeye and Leonard's misuse of your customers' data. My inaction was more than careless; it was irresponsible not to take this seriously from the start. My sincere apologies to you all, and I promise you have my full cooperation from here out."

The suits in front of him were unmoved. He continued.

"As galling as it may seem to your sense of justice, especially since I made you all wait an extra month to get the album in the first place, it makes poor business sense to stop production and marketing the Squeezebox. I'm much more valuable to you bringing in revenue than I am fighting a PR nightmare that'll tarnish your reputation as well. So, here's what I offer to do as restitution. I'll perform the contracted employee concert gratis, with my side paying for the venue and labor and all that. I can also make a sizable contribution to the charity of the organization's choice.

"I have only two requests. I ask we keep the terms of this agreement confidential and out of the hands of the press, something I don't expect you'd have a problem doing."

Stee came to the next bullet point and sighed quietly. He wet his lips, stared into the faces in front of him and continued.

"Second, Connie Rafferty was an injured party here. Please continue to promote her video as originally planned. Leonard has done enough harm to Connie ... Ms. Rafferty, and the rest of your customers, of course."

Stee took off his bifocals and placed them on the table. "Thank you for hearing me out." With that, Marcos took over. Stee sat in silence, his head slightly bowed.

He didn't tell the people in the conference room that he and Marcos had already worked out another arrangement to make things right.

Stee's royalties from *Unexpected Places* would be split into two equal parts. One half was for Amanda, earmarked for her education through law school, with the remaining funds to help her survive on a public defender's salary.

The other half was Connie's. He wouldn't have written the album without her coming into his life. The royalties were her due as his muse ... and, given the chaos he'd unleashed in her life, the money was the least he could do.

Stee was damaged goods. He knew it, the suits knew it. Unless *Unexpected Places* was a monster hit that would make the label and BetaComp forget all this mess, this could be the last album he ever did.

Think about that for a minute, Stee. What if this is the beginning of the end?

Despite what he had said to Daniel so many months before, he had never seriously considered retiring. Willie Nelson was still driving around the country in his biofuel diesel tour bus in his sunset years, so Stee had always assumed he had another couple decades of touring ahead if he wanted. But if he stopped releasing new material, he'd be at best a legacy act, and at worst, a hack coasting on his greatest hits until his last fan expired in an old folks' home somewhere.

His thoughts drifted to a week or so ago when, after promising to do Bruce's tribute at the Kennedy Center, Stee asked Connie for her take on the whole "American icon" thing. She'd patiently let him gnash his teeth about his legacy for a few minutes, and then responded with her typical good sense. "Forget about what you've done, Stee. Let's talk about what you can still do. Like, what is something you wish you could fix in the world?"

"What, like world peace?"

"Maybe something more in your wheelhouse," she'd replied a fond smile. "How about something you'd want to do for one musician to make his life easier, make his career better?"

A light began to burn away the fog of his self-pity. "I could help a singer-songwriter just coming up. Some amazing kid who doesn't have the connections or the cash to get out of whatever burg he was born in."

"What would you do?"

"I'd teach him the history to make sure he knows who he's stealing his licks from, and give him a firm basis in the craft. I'd show him how to mix a track and how to engineer an album."

"That's smart."

"I'd get him gigs as a session guy for more established acts, and I'd go on the road with him, pulling in audiences he wouldn't have otherwise."

"That would be a great tour."

"And I'd teach him how to protect himself and teach him all the traps the promoters and labels are gonna set for him."

"Good thinking."

"All that schooling will make him ready when the fame comes, so he doesn't implode after one hit single. That would be great."

"Yes, it would."

He'd pulled her toward him. "And if I needed a videographer to document all this, you know, to cement my legacy ... could you recommend someone?"

She had answered with a sly smile. "I'll see who I can find."

Jesus, I miss her.

Connie would be the woman he'd never get over, never replace, never be able to touch in a song again. His heart sank and his gut tightened.

How am I going to tour on this record? How can I sing the new stuff without bawling like a baby?

Daniel jabbed Stee in the ribs to alert him to the fact that everyone was standing up. By all the handshaking going on, a deal must have been reached. He meekly followed his attorney and manager out of the conference room, through the maze of offices and cubicles and out into the blinding sunshine.

––––––––––

Life in Richmond was at a standstill.

Upon entering the Panera Bread at the Oakglen Shopping Center, Connie scanned the premises. Recognizing no one, she took a seat in a blind corner of the shop and stared dully at the tabletop until a tray slid in front of her bearing a large coffee and a cherry Danish.

"Mom, I'm never doing this for you again. If my friends saw me at Panera ..."

"We can leave if you want."

"No," Amanda added, "I needed to get you out of the house. You're starting to become one with the furniture."

Connie picked a flake of glaze off a gloppy cherry. "This has to be a thousand calories."

"Mom, we're not here for the food. We have to talk about Stee. What exactly did he do?"

"He did something incredibly reckless and stupid."

"Yeah, he's the first guy to ever do that," Amanda answered, rolling her eyes. "Mom, Stee didn't force that Leonard to harass you. Besides, stalking happens to non-famous people, too. Like Uncle Bill says, 'Crazy always finds a way.'"

"In this case, Crazy found a way because Stee opened the door and told him to come on in."

"Okay, fine, but at least he's trying to make up for it. His lawyer got a restraining order ahead of the guy's trial, and Stee paid for that ninja bodyguard to keep tabs on the house."

"His name is Roland. If he's protecting our lives, at least learn his name."

Amanda ignored the correction. "Mom, why did you really break up?"

She sighed. "Being Stee's girlfriend was becoming a full-time job, with that insane travel schedule and all of the problems in his life that needed fixing. I need to make my own decisions and figure out what I want in my life."

"Which is Mom-speak for you running away. Again."

"I was not running away; I was sending *him* away. And what do you mean, 'again'?"

"Just like when you ran away from San Francisco after Dad died."

"How could you say that? I wanted to be closer to our family, to make a fresh start with a new business and maybe give us time and space to bond before you go to college."

"Mom, did you just hear yourself? You and Uncle Bill aren't close, and you left a big city for a small one where you know no one and the economy has tanked—and we could have bonded just fine in California." Amanda's eyes bored into her. "You were trying to get away from any memory of Dad, weren't you? You were trying to get back at him by showing him you could do everything on your own."

"I don't like your tone, Amanda."

"You didn't want me to remember him, either—you couldn't allow me to miss him!"

"Stop interrogating me!"

"Because then he'd win."

Her reaction was swift and angry. "You have no idea what you're talking about! I did this for you!"

Even though she hadn't laid a finger on her, Amanda yanked back like she'd been slapped. "Mom, I'm sorry, I'm sorry. I'm not trying to start a fight. I don't want to fight!"

Both of them took a deep breath and forced their shoulders back down. Simultaneously embarrassed, they slowly looked around their booth to see if they'd attracted any attention. Thankfully, the clientele was too engrossed in their bear claws to have noticed.

Looking at her daughter, Connie was nearly overcome by her desire to collect her onto her lap and stroke her hair. Instead she put her hands around her coffee cup and steadied herself. "It was killing me to watch you withdraw, holing up in your room, seeing his absence everywhere in the house. I wanted to take you as far away from that sadness as possible."

Amanda fiddled with a napkin. "Daddy really, really hurt you and me. It was humiliating and unfair and really, really awful. The second I start missing him, I wish he were alive so I could do something to him to hurt him back. Then all I want to do is hug him and tell him it's okay. It's horrible."

Connie put her hands over her daughter's. "You adjusted so quickly here. I thought you were getting through it and that you're doing okay."

"It happens just as bad now as it did in California, just not as often."

"But you made friends so fast."

Amanda pushed her pink streak behind her ear. "Well, I'm kind of the most exotic person at the school, which sort of worked to my advantage. Kids were curious about what it was like to be from the Big Gay Earthquake City, so they started talking to me." She leveled her gaze at her mother. "*You* haven't been doing okay. You haven't made any friends. All you do is clean house and run and complain about the crappy video jobs you get. Until you met Stee, anyway."

Connie quickly looked down at the table, her eyes prickly with tears.

"Mom, I don't understand why you sent Stee away. Yeah, he did one stupid thing, but he hasn't done anything like what Dad did."

"I don't want to stick around until he does."

"Do you think he'd cheat on us?"

It didn't escape Connie's notice that Amanda had included herself in the potential betrayal.

"No, not really. He's a man of his word. But he could get really sick or ... I mean, he's so much older than me ... there's so little time ... infidelity is the least of my worries."

"Then you should hurry up and make up with him. Jesus, Mom."

Connie took a halfhearted sip of her coffee. "I shouldn't have gotten involved with him in the first place. I could have avoided all this."

Amanda's eyes flashed. "Avoided what—fun? Lightening up? Being with a guy who's really into you and makes you laugh, this big star who doesn't mind coming to the boring old Virginia suburbs just to be with you?"

"But in the long run, I won't have anything for myself—no career, no control over my own time."

"Stee will hire you again. What's the problem?"

"That doesn't count."

"What are you talking about? That counts plenty. He could hire anyone in the world but he chose to hire you." She nabbed a hunk of cherry pastry. "And you do your best work when you're with him. What do you corporate people call that, a win-win?"

"I don't want to be that beholden to anyone."

"It's not being 'beholden' or whatever. He loves you. You love him. You help each other out." Amanda shot her mother a look. "You've been real independent here in Richmond and that just made you a miserable hermit. When you were working with Stee, you were being creative and really happy. So, what kind of independence are you looking for anyway?"

Connie popped a wad of pastry into her mouth. "Isn't it my job to give you advice?"

"You'd just tell me I should apply to art school and 'follow my dream' and all that enlightened parent stuff."

She smiled knowingly at her daughter. "I think you're just worried you wouldn't get accepted into an art school."

"No, I know I'd get in," she replied with a shrug. "I could sail through art school easy. I just don't want to do that for a living."

"You're that sure about being a public defender. At seventeen, you're that sure you want to give up cartooning?"

"Who said I was giving up cartooning? I'll keep doing it for me. I don't want to have to worry about making money at it. Once I do that, it's all co-opted and warped. I'd rather make a living doing something really hard and worthwhile and socially relevant. Stick it to The Man and all that." She arched her eyebrow. "I should shut up. You're an artist with a rich rock star patron now."

"I'm no artist, sweetie. An aspiring documentarian, maybe."

"Maybe you don't have to aspire anymore, Mom. You can just do it and not worry if it makes a dime at the box office. You can document Stee's European tour. That would be perfect."

Connie's jaw clenched, wondering if Stee had been cultivating her daughter as an ally on the sly. "You have to drop this romantic notion that Stee is going to solve all my problems. He's one of the most superstitious, needy people I've ever met. He wants *me* around to solve *his* problems."

"Well, that's love, isn't it? Being the solution to each other's problems?"

Amanda asked this without sarcasm, and the expression on her face told Connie she needed confirmation that she was right: that love, in spite of all the uncertainty and fear and past mistakes, would always be the right risk to take.

"Yeah, that's love." Looking at her daughter, she realized she had a stake in all this, too.

"How do you feel about Stee, honey?"

Amanda smiled warily, looking away. "Well, he's no Icky Sticks." She shrugged. "He's a good guy, Mom. I like him. He's fun. And you're more fun to be around when he's around."

Connie's phone rang. It had been so long since she'd heard that particular ringtone, it startled her. "I need to answer this."

Connie covered her free ear to better listen to the other end of the conversation. Conscious of the fact that Amanda was actively eavesdropping, she kept her responses short.

"Yes, I know it's tomorrow. UCLA Medical Center. I can't …

"No, he didn't play me the whole album. Why?

"What do you mean, *my* song?

"Not fiction? He said, 'Tell her this one's not fiction'?

"In case he dies on the table? God, what a baby!

"Okay, I'll listen to it, I promise. Just for you, though.

"Sure, I'll call you afterward. Good-bye, Angela." She hung up, sorting through what she just heard. "I guess we have to go home."

Amanda pointed at the remains of the pastry. "Do you want to toss this?"

Connie shoved the rest in her mouth, licking the glaze off her fingers. "Nope. Life's too short."

———————

"Your full name, please?"

"Steven Harold Walsh."

A nurse in dark blue scrubs, a surgical cap and paper booties held his wrist with two fingers, peering at his wristband through her wire-rimmed glasses. "What's your date of birth?"

"August 1, 1949," he said testily. "Can't you see that printed on my little plastic bracelet?"

"It's protocol, Mr. Walsh. We have to make sure you are really you." Without his contact lenses, he squinted to read her ID badge, which was encrusted with angel pins and bone-shaped stickers. Her name was Jenny, CRNA. Despite the lightness of her tone, he was half ready to leap off the gurney and stagger down the hallway to freedom as soon as she turned her back.

"Any drug allergies?"

"I'm allergic to all the fun ones ... tequila, cocaine ..."

"Shoot, then I'll have to switch out the Jose Cuervo in your IV bag," Jenny continued, double-checking the tubes running into the needle in his arm. "What procedure are we doing today?"

His breathing picked up speed. "Don't you know?"

"Each of the staff has to do this pop quiz with you, Mr. Walsh, even the surgeon. Protocol, remember?"

He licked his lips. "Total knee joint replacement on my left side."

"Very good, you get an A," she said, smiling. She checked the monitor and wrote some notes in a huge binder. "Your heart rate's a little elevated. Nervous?"

His eyes went wide. "Should I be?"

"Trust me, you're in good hands. I don't work with idiots. Standing rule." She picked up a syringe and filled it from a small bottle of clear fluid. "This should help take the edge off. Just give it a couple of minutes." Jenny put her hand on his shoulder. "Mr. Walsh, do you have anyone with you today, any family?"

"My assistant dropped me off," he replied quietly. "She said there was something she had to take care of, so she left."

Jenny pushed down the plunger and the sedative emptied into the IV port. "The surgeon will visit you soon. The next time I see you, you'll feel a lot more relaxed. You'll probably be giggling like a little girl."

"Swell," he mumbled.

Jenny took her binder and left. Stee closed his eyes. He wasn't feeling any calmer and was desperate to focus on something, *anything*, other than being alone in a surgical holding area on a gurney, wearing a ridiculous hospital gown and bright yellow nubby socks, clutching the sheet and blanket for dear life, waiting for something inevitably awful to happen.

A bubble of air in the IV tube ...

A short in the monitors that sends a shock to my heart ...

An extra zero on my chart multiplying my drug dose by a factor of ten ...

"Hey, you."

If he hadn't believed in a Higher Power before, Stee saw the proof of His existence as Connie came to his side. She smelled wonderful. She looked wonderful. She was nothing but wonderful.

"Sorry I'm late," she said, kissing him gently. "Roland's got nothing on the security they have at the information desk. Angie had a hell of time convincing them to let me come back here."

"You're what Angie had to take care of?"

She nodded. "You'll appreciate this: when they asked me what my relationship is to you, I told them 'companion, true.'"

His stomach dipped. "You heard the song?"

"Angie sent it to me." She caressed his cheek. "It's not fiction?"

"Never was, baby. Never will be."

"She told me she had strict orders to send it to me only upon the event of your death." She raised an eyebrow. "I guess she's flaunting your authority."

"If I live through this, she's fired," he said, tears beginning to cloud his eyes. He took her hand. "I'm so scared, Connie."

She smoothed his hair. "Everything will be all right, love. You'll come out of this okay. I'll be here when you wake up."

Either the sedative had kicked in, or Connie, her love assured, had taken away all his anxiety.

It's Connie. No contest.

He over-smiled, his lips peeling back from his teeth, which strangely felt a lot larger than usual. "Please say you forgive me, baby."

She arched an eyebrow. "If I don't forgive you, you have to keep making up to me. I kind of like that prospect."

"Move in with me," he continued, the sedative saturating his brain and the beaming grin still plastered across his face.

"We can talk about long-term plans later: you, me and Amanda."

"You'll be a big star video big shot big director." The words burst on his lips, like bubbles popping. As he became engrossed in saying the letter "b" over and over, some sluggish part of his brain recognized this feeling; he used to know it quite well.

Holy shit, I'm high.

He grabbed at her hand. "I'm on drugs, Connie—that's bad ... buh, buh, buh bad." He wanted to be serious, but it came out like George Thorogood. He tittered.

"It's okay," Connie assured him. "You aren't going to get addicted; it's just the anesthesia. You'll—"

He looked dreamily at her and another rush of good feeling coursed through his system. "You care, beautiful, love you, love, luh, luh, luh."

Connie laughed, covering her eyes. "Hoo, are you baked."

He clutched her hand, flying high and happy. "Me ... marry ..."

"No, *me* Mary," said a woman in surgical scrubs who had materialized at the opposite side of the gurney. At this point, Stee's reading ability was rather impaired; he barely made out that Mary Hodges was an MD. "I'm your surgeon, Mr. Walsh, remember? Jenny asked me to check in with you to make sure the sedative was working."

"Trust me, it's working," Connie said wryly.

Dr. Hodges looked at Stee's wristband. "Can you give me your name?"

"Steven Harold Walsh," he sniggered. "I get 'em all in there?"

"You sure did, Mr. Walsh." Dr. Hodges cut a look to Connie. "Yep, that sedative's doing its job."

He pointed to the doctor and grinned. "Hey, what's your favorite Stee Walsh song?"

Dr. Hodges thought for a second. "I just heard an advance single from your new album on the radio this morning—'Unexpected Places,' right? It's really pretty."

"Pretty? You hear that, Stee—it's pretty!" Connie nudged him but he said nothing. He was too busy giggling like a little girl.

"Fifteen minutes, Mr. Joel."

"How's the crowd?"

"Stoked."

"Better than when the Knicks play here?"

"Yeah, they all know *you* can play well." The stage manager placed a massive vase bulging with flowers on the dressing room counter. "You've got a delivery."

He cocked his head. "Holy shit—did I die or something? Must be from Elton." He took the card off the vase, found a pen and slid it under the flap of the envelope to tear it open. He read the card:

Billy,

All the best to you and the rest of the Rock and Roll Hall of Famers playing tonight.

Your music has made a huge impact on my life in ways you'll never know.

Have a great show.

Stee Walsh

The singer sat back.

Will wonders never cease ...

chapter 23

"That's our call. Got everything, baby?"

"Yep. Next stop, Berlin."

Connie and Stee had to arrive in each city ahead of the rest of the band to meet with the local promoter and scope out the venue with the video crew. They'd get a day or two to themselves to take in the local sights, give Stee time to swim and rehearse and Connie time to edit the previous day's footage and post a teaser clip to Stee's website before sound check.

Stee paused to let Connie enter the gateway first. They held hands until they got to the door of the plane. After conferring with the lead flight attendant to stow his Gibson Country Western in the front closet, he joined her a couple rows further down. He settled next to the window and lowered the shade halfway; she stuffed the seat pocket with a full complement of magazines and crossword puzzles and nudged her laptop case under the seat. She offered him a protein bar, which he gratefully accepted, before borrowing one of his pens to do the Sunday crossword puzzle. He glanced at the grid.

"Need any help?"

"How about you take a crack at 53-Down?" He took out his bifocals for a better look.

53—Rocker ___ Walsh.

"Please tell me there are four letters, not three. Joe doesn't need any more publicity."

She nodded enthusiastically, filling in the boxes in block letters.

"You're a clue in the *New York Times* crossword, Stee! You have nothing else to strive for; you have officially achieved everything."

He took her left hand in his and kissed it, just on the other side of the sizeable diamond ring he'd bestowed there once his knee was healed enough for him to kneel on. "That's right."

"Sweet-talker," she muttered before she kissed him, good and proper.

The flight attendant walked by, offering Perrier. Stee passed a glass to Connie and raised his own.

"Ready for the ride?"

Connie clinked his glass. "Wherever it goes, Stee. Wherever it goes."

acknowledgements

This is my first novel. The fact that it exists at all continues to surprise and delight me because I had no expectation that a few scattered thoughts in a journal would evolve into a full-fledged story. It did so because so many people have been encouraging, supportive, patient and generous enough to see this through.

The Bloomfield Township (Michigan) Library not only has impeccable decor and plenty of writers' workspace replete with lamplight and power outlets but also an exhaustively extensive music collection: rock, blues, soul, country, pop, soundtracks—you name it, they have it. What a gift to our community that library is, inspiring readers and writers every day.

My dear friend, and exceptional novelist, Sheri Holman read the first draft and was generous with her support, clarity and honesty. I can never thank her enough for pushing me to keep going and connecting me to her publishing and literary agency contacts. She has been a realist but also a source of hope and inspiration, and I cannot thank her enough.

I thank those publishing and literary agency contacts who took the time to give me specific feedback and cared enough about good writing to encourage my work, even if they couldn't represent my book (yet).

I only spoke to creative coach Tatyana Mishel once, yet that conversation continues to direct my creative life. She is a key reason this book has seen the light of day. What a sparkling presence in the universe! I also owe a debt—and a shiny red apple—to Peggy Manchester. Her job as a health and wellness coach took an unexpected turn when I asked her to help me with my writing more than my running. She has been an incredibly supportive, practical guide to finding the joy and creating opportunities for more flow moments. Thank you so much.

The Troy Writers Group accepted me into their fold when I had utterly no idea what to do next. Their perspectives and advice have been so helpful and their unstinting support means more to me than they may realize. Bob Brown, Karen Hildebrandt, Pam Houghton, Alex Morgan and Deb Pecis, many thanks.

Several friends and one nephew agreed to be my beta readers for the bargain-basement price of a bag of homemade biscotti. Thank you, Pam Houghton, Nancy Goldman, Philip Sherman and Michael Nosanchuk, for investing your time, offering your opinions and sharing your faith in its possibilities.

The Story Cartel, created by writing blogger and author Joe Bunting, has been an incredible resource for me, both in terms of giving me lessons in the building blocks of fiction and by creating a group of people who can share the experience of turning words into stories into books into careers. Thank you, Joe and the dozens of Cartelistas, for providing help along the journey.

Christopher Imlay created a knockout of a book cover, opening my eyes to the power of the right visual image to express literary ideas. Thanks for being so good at your job and fun to work with to boot.

Gail Nelson has been my fine friend for an incredibly long time and has seen practically every iteration of these characters through to the final version you've read here. She pored over every line, not just as an exceptional copy editor but also as someone who loves to read and is no slouch as a writer herself. Thank you for staying with me throughout this process for so long and for rooting for Stee, Connie and me the entire time.

My family has been bewildered, nonplussed, excited, irritated yet still incredibly supportive throughout the many hours I've holed up somewhere away from them to write this "thing." They have been my inspiration for finishing what I've started and for continuing to strive to be better. Davis, Hunter, James and especially my loyal, deep-souled and large-hearted wife Dani, I love and thank you all.

Made in the USA
Charleston, SC
26 August 2016